Praise for
SUSAN McBRIDE's
DEBUTANTE DROPOUT MYSTERIES

"Kick off your Manolos and skip the cocktail hour
to curl up with Andy Kendricks,
her socialite mother, and her blue blood buddies."
Nancy Martin

"Ms. McBride knows her territory.
She has put together a funny, eccentric bunch
of characters who bound around town
with perfect manicures, big hair,
and lots of social savvy. . . . Hilarious."
Dallas Morning News

"[A] delicious romp."
Tess Gerritsen

"As alluring as an Escada evening dress and
as tempting as a slice of death-by-chocolate cake."
Publishers Weekly

"A wonderful new series. . . .
Andy Kendricks's [next] effort
can't come soon enough."
January magazine

"Susan McBride . . . will keep you laughing
long after you close the covers."
Katie MacAlister

Books by Susan McBride

NIGHT OF THE LIVING DEB
THE LONE STAR LONELY HEARTS CLUB
THE GOOD GIRL'S GUIDE TO MURDER
BLUE BLOOD

Night of the Living Deb

SUSAN McBRIDE

Night of the Living Deb

A DEBUTANTE DROPOUT MYSTERY

AVON BOOKS
An Imprint of HarperCollinsPublishers

AVON BOOKS
An Imprint of HarperCollins*Publishers*
10 East 53rd Street
New York, New York 10022-5299

Copyright © 2007 by Susan McBride
Excerpts copyright © 2004, 2005, 2006 by Susan McBride
ISBN-13: 978-0-7394-7757-1

"I don't want anyone's life on my hands."
Night of the Living Dead, 1968

Acknowledgments

Sometimes being a writer is just too much fun, particularly when you're doing research that involves a friend driving you around Dallas to bars and a strip club. *Muchas gracias* to Dan Hale, who did exactly that. Any errors are due to literary license, not to a bad guide.

Thanks to Allison Price for lending me her name, occupation, and hair color for Allie Price—okay, and for precipitating that incident at the Chippendales' show at Harrah's, which we'll also call "research."

My undying gratitude to Ed Spitznagel for allowing me to steal a hilarious haiku he wrote and for putting up with my crazy brain and nutty schedule. I love you!

I'm a fortunate girl to have such an incredible support system, including my editor, Sarah Durand; Danielle Bartlett, ace publicist; Jeremy Cesarec; and the other folks at Avon who work so hard to make my books look great. I couldn't have better cheerleaders than Andrea Cirillo and Kelly Harms at Jane Rotrosen. Y'all rock! And, last but not least, much love to my family and friends, without whom I would be orphaned and friendless. You mean the world to me!

Night of
the Living
Deb

Prologue

Circular pleats of red velvet draped the ceiling above Brian Malone's head, a dimly lit chandelier dripping down from the center. If nothing else about The Men's Club had cried "bordello" but that, it would've been plenty.

There were tacky touches wherever he looked, if he needed reminders that he was in a strip joint.

He didn't.

Barmaids in red corsets, short black skirts, and high black boots served overpriced drinks. Bored-looking women in G-strings writhed on nearby laps, swiveling club chairs making for easy access. Green and blue laser lights flashed with Jedi intensity as deafening music pounded the air with a throbbing bass.

Like, there wasn't enough throbbing going on as it was.

The place could call itself "a gentleman's club," but it was a strip joint, plain and simple, despite the upscale clientele of horny, mostly white-collar males. When he'd pulled up to the waiting valet in his Acura coupe, it had been the lesser in a line of luxury automobiles disgorging Rolex-wearing passengers to the curb beneath a well-lit porte cochere. More Mercedes and Jags than you could shake a stick at, so to speak.

It was his buddy's idea to come here, a final request before he was due to get hitched in a few weeks, a destination wedding in Tuscany just for the bride and groom and their immediate families.

The Men's Club wasn't Brian's first choice as a site for celebration. He would've been happy as a clam sucking on the long neck of a Shiners at any number of local bars with ESPN on the tube and the noise of folks shooting pool. But Matty wanted a lap dance as a final adios to bachelorhood, and a lap dance he would get.

Brian had been to this establishment on Dallas's northwest side a couple times before, once for business when a client of the firm wanted to checked out the "local action" before he caught a flight out of nearby Love Field, and again when he'd been dating Allie Price and she'd been curious to see what was inside the pink stucco walls, behind the front windows filled with peekaboo lingerie.

He didn't plan on becoming a regular.

There was an air of desperation hanging overhead as surely as the red velvet pleats in the ceiling. Not a feeling he ever wanted under his own skin.

Another hour and then we're outta here, he decided as he polished off a third Peroni, adding to the vague fog that lapped at his gray cells. Three was his limit for tonight—he

was the designated driver on this little R-rated field trip—
so the bar was as good as closed for him.

A slender brunette in stilettos and little else strutted past
him and straddled the lap of a wild-eyed dude at the next
table, a couple pals cheering them on, and he shifted in
his own chair, embarrassed at the, ah, public display. But
then, he knew that's what this place was for: getting an
eyeful. Look, don't touch.

Right.

He wondered if Hugh Hefner ever got tired of living the
cheesy life, but figured, Naw, the dude probably bled
Velveeta.

"Hey, Bri, check out that babe's rack. You think they're
real?"

He shifted his gaze to the woman gyrating on the small
stage. She ignored the shiny pole that Demi Moore had so
energetically flung herself around in *Striptease,* doing a
truly uninspired bump and grind to AC/DC's "Who Made
Who." He'd noticed how few of the dancers ever used the
thing, except for balance.

So much for choreography.

The "babe's rack" looked anything but real to him. As
big as ripe cantaloupes, they barely moved as she shimmied, so roundly perfect and pert that they were almost
comical. Like a cartoon. Or Pamela Anderson.

"Not even close to real," he weighed in.

Matty Karas, the groom-to-be, bobbed his head. "Sili-
cone?"

"Saline, I'd wager."

"Fewer lawsuits?"

"Yep."

Their firm regularly defended Big D surgeons who'd done botched boob jobs, but that didn't mean he was an expert in augmentation. He only knew what he liked, and it wasn't the kind of uniformity he saw parading around him beneath the red velvet and crystal chandelier. It was actually kind of frightening, as if The Men's Club had sent all its "ladies" to have their chests bumped up to DD cups by a doc on the payroll of Frederick's of Hollywood.

Stepford Strippers.

Spooky.

He didn't even like breasts that looked like cantaloupes, not really; though he had a certain appreciation for those that did, sort of in the vein of admiring the curves on a shiny new Porsche Carrera.

Bigger wasn't necessarily better.

It was a personal preference, nothing more, nothing less. The girl he was crazy about was hardly built like a brick house, something she'd even apologized for in the beginning, as if it would bother him. He told her "good things come in small packages," and he meant it.

Natural was okay by him. Whatever God gave a woman was perfectly fine, especially if brains and a sense of humor were part of the deal, both of which his girl had in spades.

Despite the noise and lights and naked women, he smiled to himself, thinking of Andy and what she was doing tonight, wondering if she was having as bad a time as he was, and wishing they were together right this minute. He knew exactly what she'd say, if she were here, amidst the drunks and the bimbos. . . .

"My *gawd*, buddy, check out the lap action over there!"

No, that wasn't it.

"Hey, earth to Malone." Matty elbowed him cleanly in the ribs. "You're treating me to a private session, right?"

He'd paid for the beer and the twenty bucks' cover charge collected by the hostess at the podium in the foyer, so it only seemed fitting.

"Yeah, buddy, anytime you're ready," Brian told him, leaning over to clap him on the shoulder, thinking as soon as Matty was done in the back room, they could get the hell out of there, and he could go back to Andy's place.

Quiet, that's what he craved, and to hold her in his arms, breathe in the clean smell of her, as opposed to the stench of sweat and cigar smoke.

"Believe me, I'm ready," his pal said, a hardly sober smile plastered across his flushed face.

"Okay, just give me a minute." Brian pushed out of his club chair and stood.

Which is when he looked across the room and saw her, and for a moment he couldn't move. He squinted behind his wire-rims, doubting himself for an instant because seeing her here seemed so out of context. But it was no mistake. It was who he thought it was, all right.

So what the hell was going on?

His eyes doubtless burning a hole through her back, the blonde turned, and their gazes locked. Before he'd even moved a foot in her direction, she took off, hurrying toward the doors to the left of the stage.

Brian went after her.

"Yeah, buddy, great eye . . . bring her on back pronto, I'm good to go!" Matty called out, but it barely registered, not with the music in his ears and the strobe lights in his eyes, and his pulse thumping loudly in his veins.

He kept moving, weaving between the tables, past corset-wearing waitresses and men in swivel chairs with breasts pressed to their faces.

He hurried past the stage and opened the door through which she'd disappeared a moment before.

And down the rabbit hole he went.

Chapter 1

 "Lordy, Lordy, come to mama, sweet cheeks! Rub a little sweat on me! Shake that bonbon till you break it!"

I cringed at the screaming woman who stood but a foot to my right inside the packed hotel ballroom. Colored spotlights danced across the faces fixed ahead at the stage a dozen rows in front of me, where well-oiled male dancers gyrated and ripped off what little clothing they had on to start with. It was the first time I'd ever seen men in uniform with tear-away pants and jackets. Did any branch of the military actually wear G-strings? It was certainly one way to inspire shock and awe.

"Hey, sweet meat, over here! Gimme some lovin'!"

For Pete's sake.

The woman howled like a twelve-year-old at a Backstreet Boys concert, and she was old enough to be somebody's mother. No, more like somebody's grandmother,

I decided, taking in the white hair upswept in the bouffant 'do and the cavernous lines that pleated her face (not to mention the Stride Rite tennis shoes).

I thought of my own mother, the ultradignified Cissy Blevins Kendricks, society maven extraordinaire, and knew she'd rather be caught dead than attend a Chippendales' show, waving dollar bills in the air to entice scantily clad male strippers over for a quick round of dirty dancing.

Though I'd pay through the nose to see something like that.

Heck, I'd *kill* to see it.

Since I, Andrea Blevins Kendricks, fruit of said dignified mother's loins, stood amongst the crazed crowd viewing the, um, scenery, I guess that made me something less than stand-up. Though I was here under duress, let me make that very clear.

As Enrique Iglesias crooned, "Let me be your hero, bay-bee," the assorted buffed bods trickled from the stage and into the throngs of berserk females, pausing only to bump and grind for tips.

"Bring it home to mama, sweet cheeks!" the liquored-up woman beside me hollered louder than Minnie Pearl yodeling "Howww-deeee!" at the Grand Ol' Opry.

I wanted to tell her to give it a rest.

But it was too late.

Sweet Cheeks was heading our way.

The sight put dear old Granny in a tizzy, and she gasped, "Oh, dear Lord, oh, dear, Lord," again and again, as if a witness to the Second Coming.

I considered sticking my fingers in my ears, until I felt a nudge, as the blonde on my left leaned over to yell, "Gird your loins, Chippie Virgin, 'cuz this one's on me."

If I hadn't already been gritting my teeth—I was dooming myself to porcelain veneers someday, wasn't I?—I would've started then.

"Thanks, but no thanks, Allie," I got out, loud enough to be heard above the music, only Allie wasn't paying the least attention. "Are you listening to me?" I tried again, but the witch (with a capital *B*) in the size two Seven jeans merely raised her arm higher and wagged more bills than poor old Grandma was offering.

Damn her for being so aggressive.

She was bound and determined to embarrass me.

I sunk down into the metal folding chair, hoping I'd disappear and wishing I'd refused Brian's suggestion that I go out with Allie tonight, help Allie show Eleanor—his friend Matty's fiancée—a fun night on the town, because Eleanor had only just moved to Dallas from Pittsburgh and didn't know anybody.

Well, anyone except Allie, apparently, who happened to be Brian's colleague at Abramawitz, Reynolds, Goldberg, and Hunt (aka ARGH), as well as his ex-girlfriend.

Not a combination I liked any better than pickles and peanut butter.

And it made me just about as nauseous.

Like a numskull, I'd let him talk me into it, mainly because Brian was out on the town himself, at a strip club "celebrating" with Matty.

What better way to even the score while he was ogling

big-breasted strippers than by ogling, well, big-breasted strippers? 'Cuz these Chippies had pecs the size of Nebraska. Not to mention other bulging parts.

"Hey, Captain G-string, over here!" Allie yelled, even getting out an ear-splitting whistle, and I shrunk lower in my seat, shooting my deadliest evil-eyed stare at Blondie and her cohort, mousy little Eleanor from Pittsburgh, who had gotten into the act, standing on her chair and gesturing like an abandoned sailor on a raft, flagging down a passing ship.

Damn them both.

Aw, hell.

I saw the rows of women parting faster than Sharon Stone's knees in *Basic Instinct,* and suddenly there he was: a spray-tanned and oiled hunk with black hair to his shoulders, wearing what could only be described as a black satin slingshot.

As if in slow-mo, I watched Allie slip a couple bucks into the strap of his thong, her mouth forming the words, *Give it to her good.*

Gulp.

Before I'd blinked, the buffed body loomed over me, dark eyes seeking mine, a slim white smile spreading across the chiseled face, and I morphed into a dishrag.

This was definitely not what I'd signed on for.

I tried to stand up, but his hand landed firmly on my breastbone and eased me back down against the metal of the chair, as Enrique's warbly croon segued into a vintage ditty by the Gap Band, "Let's whip it, baby, let's whip it right, let's whip it baby, whip it all night."

Subtle.

He squatted in front of me, grabbed my legs and threw them across his shoulders, so that I straddled him. A move that surely would be frowned upon by Miss Manners, since we hadn't even been properly introduced.

"Grab my head," he demanded in Brooklynese that didn't go at all with his striking Asian features.

Instead of issuing a protest, as a good twenty-first-century feminist would, I did as he asked, not sure of any way out of this except through it. And maybe I'd have a good story to tell my grandchildren someday besides. *You want to hear about the night your meemaw had a fling with a Chippendales' dancer?*

With impossible ease he lifted me, as I clung to his head and hooked my feet at the ankles, my legs around his neck. He shimmied and gyrated, oblivious to the fact that my fingers clutched his hair and the back of his skull. I was upside down, the blood rushing to my face, heating my cheeks. The world swirled around me, and I giggled hysterically, feeling like a complete idiot . . . and enjoying myself in spite of it all.

Until Allie's two bucks' worth was up, and he lowered me to the chair. Like a spineless jellyfish, I slid against the metal frame, and my dark-haired, um, friend slithered his slick body up against me so that his scent filled my nose. He finished me off with a kiss on the forehead.

Poof.

He was gone.

Slimed by his sweat, still breathing hard, I couldn't move for a full minute after.

It was Allie who finally dragged me to my feet, though my knees felt strangely wobbly.

"Girl, that was crazier than any Six Flags ride I've ever seen," said Brian's smiling ex, slinging an arm around my shoulders and giving me a squeeze.

For a fleeting instant, I almost liked her.

"Thank God they don't allow pictures," was all I could come up with, and I meant it. "That's one Kodak moment that should rest in peace."

"Ah, but that would be a tragedy, wouldn't it?"

My stomach did a fast nosedive, not liking her tone in the least. "What's that supposed to mean?"

Which is when Allie produced her cell phone, flipped it open, and stuck the tiny screen in my face. I squinted and saw a miniversion of someone who looked very much like me, dangling from the neck of a hard-bodied Chippie. I was moving—*he* was moving—it was a video, for crud's sake.

"Oh, no," I breathed.

"Oh, yes." Allie grinned broadly. "Can't wait to see Brian's face when I download this baby and shoot him a copy."

"You wouldn't."

"Of course I would."

"But—"

She cut me off before I could come up with another lame appeal.

"Sweetie, I'm a defense attorney. I eat nails for breakfast. This"—she tapped her cell—"is too delicious for words."

Then I remembered why I didn't like her.

It was simple, really.

Allie Price was a Grade-A bitch.

Chapter 2

 It was just past midnight when I got back to my condo in North Dallas, far away from shrieking women, blinding lasers, and gyrating Chippies; not to mention the bride-to-be from Pittsburgh who'd had one too many vodkatinis and who, I sorely hoped, would puke all over the hand-stitched leather interior of Allie Price's brand-new BMW Roadster.

I pulled my Jeep Wrangler into an open slot in front of my building, half expecting to spot Brian's red Acura, to catch him sprawled on my porch steps, working off a beer buzz and waiting for me to get home.

But no such luck.

He'd said not to expect him tonight unless he called first; that he'd probably head back to his apartment after he dropped off Matty. He didn't like waking me with knocks on the door after midnight (which also woke up nosy neighbors), and we hadn't yet reached the "exchanging keys" point—my call, as I'd been independent for far too long and fiercely protected my privacy. Still, I'd assured him that he was more than welcome to come by at any time, so long as I was awake enough to hear him rapping.

The fact was that I missed him.

I hadn't gotten to see Malone very much lately. He'd been working so hard on some big case or another. I could never keep track, and he didn't go into detail about them besides, or maybe it was that I didn't ask. He probably spent more time with that damn Allie than with me, though I tried not to think about it like that.

Maybe I didn't feel all warm and fuzzy toward his ex-girlfriend, but I'd gotten over being jealous of her months ago. Okay, weeks. Um, days?

All right, I was still working on it.

One thing I did know and appreciate was that he wasn't anywhere near her at the moment. They couldn't have had their heads bent over papers full of legalese back at the firm, because I'd been with Allie watching half-naked men dance for our viewing pleasure; because of her, I smelled like cheap cologne and sweaty Chippendale.

As sure as shooting, I'd pay for it, too.

I thought of my legs wrapped around that black-haired Chippie's neck and imagined Brian viewing it on his PC at the law firm on Monday morning while he dribbled hot coffee on his tie.

Oy.

With a sigh, I stabbed my key in the lock (wishing it were Allie's black heart), telling myself I didn't care if Brian saw the minivideo on Blondie's cell phone. He knew where I'd gone. Heck, he'd practically insisted. So what if things had gotten a tad crazy? Wasn't that what was supposed to happen on a girls' night out?

Besides, he couldn't get on my case when he'd spent the evening at a strip club doing the "boys will be boys" thing, could he?

All's fair in love and bachelor parties, right?

I tossed my purse and keys onto the kitchen table, thought about getting something to eat, but nixed the idea. It was nearly morning—well, technically it *was* morning—and I was out of Häagen-Dazs besides.

So I went into the bathroom to wash my face and brush my teeth, before donning a worn pair of flannel pajamas. I plugged in my cell to charge it then cut the lights, lit a caramel-vanilla candle, curled up in a corner of the sofa and dared to check my landline for messages.

As I suspected, I had awaiting me a prolonged monologue from Cissy aka Her Highness of Highland Park née Mother Superior Attitude:

"Andrea, darlin', please, don't forget about brunch tomorrow. Stephen and I have a reservation at the Mansion, and we're expectin' you and Mr. Malone to join us. I've got a few ideas for your birthday dinner, which I know you asked me not to do, but you're my only child so forgive me if I want to throw you a little party at my house. I thought we'd have salmon, perhaps, with spinach orzo and a nice chocolate soufflé for dessert. . . ."

Salmon?

Mother knows I detest any food that's remotely fishy, except when it comes in shells. I do love crab cakes.

As for dessert, I rolled my eyes at the idea of anything

but layer cake for my birthday. Chocolate with butter-cream frosting, like I'd had when I was a kid. How could you put over thirty candles in a soufflé? Wouldn't they sink?

"... *I thought I'd take you shopping at Stanley Korshak for a special outfit, because I know what's in your closet....*"

Oh, boy, Stanley Korshak at the Crescent, where Mother made sure they had my measurements on file in the bridal salon, "just in case."

"*I'll expect a ring before ten, so I know if you're both coming, or if it'll just be you—*"

I hit Delete, knowing it was too late to call her back now, telling myself to remember to phone in the morning by the anointed time or I'd never hear the last of it.

Yawning, I leaned deeper into the sofa cushions, wishing that I had a good excuse for skipping brunch, as I'd rather stay burrowed beneath the covers and sleep in tomorrow after spending tonight with Allie and the Chippies. I wagered Brian would be keen on sleeping off his evening, too.

Besides, the Mansion on Turtle Creek was Mother's turf, not mine. A five-star hotel and restaurant where shirts and shoes (and coats and ties) were required, preferably couture and not off the rack. Though they did have moan-worthy pancakes with banana topping, and I tried to focus on that.

As long as I was done by noon, so I could spend the rest of Sunday alone with Brian as opposed to playing "double date" with Cissy and her new boyfriend.

Oh, no, *she* didn't call him her boyfriend, but I did.

Behind her back.

His name was Stephen Howard, and he was a former IRS agent with a military background. Admittedly, a stand-up guy, though it was hard to imagine my mother with anyone but Daddy. My father had died a dozen years ago, right before I was set to debut (and had bailed, to Cissy's everlasting chagrin). Mother's loyalty to my daddy might give her pause about what to call her new relationship. But Stephen was her beau, just the same. Sent her flowers, took her out to dinner, escorted her to the symphony; even coughed up big bucks for tickets to ritzy charity functions.

If anyone asked me—and they didn't—I'd say the man was smitten.

Cissy enjoyed his company, I knew that much. Beyond that, I wasn't sure where my mother stood, and I wasn't any more certain I wanted to know. As an only child and a daddy's girl, it was difficult to imagine my sixty-year-old, Chanel-wearing mummy had a love life.

Sometimes it was best to be left in the dark.

As I was—literally—that very moment.

My eyes soaked in the dim of the room, so soothing after the assault of laser lights. My ears enjoyed the solitude, too.

I watched the candlelight flicker, casting pale shadows on the walls of my tiny living room. I tipped my head so my gaze fell upon an oil painting I'd hung on the wall above the fireplace, one I'd finished not long ago and had framed. The brilliant slashes of color appeared darker in the absence of a bright light, but I smiled as I studied it through the flickering flame. I thought about an offer made by a friend who had opened a gallery in a newly gentrified area of Oak Cliff, and I considered saying yes, as I'd always wanted to see one of my works on display. Though I wasn't inclined to sell.

I spent so much time on the computer these days, designing Web sites for foundling or struggling humanitarian organizations that often couldn't foot my bill. That's when my trust fund came in handy, so I could survive and make time for the thing I loved most: my art.

I had experimented over the years, trying to find my own voice, my unique style with pen and ink, and finally brush and canvas.

Resting my chin on my knees, I stared at the abstract some more, at the way the heavy strokes of gold seemed to dance in the wavering candlelight, at how deep the blue seemed, how truly crimson the red. When Brian had asked what I would call the painting, as wild as it was, I laughed and said, *"Andy's Brain."*

"I like it," he'd told me, and I couldn't tell if he was teasing or not.

I pulled the throw from the sofa arm and drew it over me, feeling an ache for him and deciding I'd try to stay awake for a while more, see if he called. Closing my eyes, I pictured the boyish face I knew so well, the bright blue eyes behind the wire-rims, the tousled hair that tempted a thorough brushing; though I liked the unruly way it fell onto his brow. It was the only thing about Brian that *was* unruly.

He was so clean-cut, such a straight-arrow, not the kind of guy I was normally attracted to, which, in the past, had translated into mostly unemployed artists-cum-bartenders. Definitely not lawyers who went to work in suits, collected regular paychecks, and paid their own rent.

So, in an odd way, Brian Malone was a breath of fresh air.

He reminded me so much of my father, the calm he wore like a mantle, the sense that everything would be all right. He had the confident demeanor of a Boy Scout who knew how to start a fire with a stick and wore a face of calm even when trouble simmered below the surface.

The only way I could sense something was wrong was when he started to stammer the least little bit. That spoke volumes.

I was still learning to pick up signals from him.

Malone could be hard to read at times. He didn't feel the need to talk unless he had something to say. He was a great listener, balanced out my tendency toward yakking with a quiet reserve. But there were moments when I sensed he was holding back from me, keeping things bottled up rather than opening up. Maybe that was a common genetic deficiency in all men—at least, the straight ones—still, it bothered me, like he didn't trust me enough to share.

He never spoke of his job much, except to sporadically complain about the hours, or the drudge-work dumped upon him as a junior associate. Once in a blue moon, he'd spill a few details about a case. In the beginning, I'd asked more questions, out of curiosity if nothing else; but I'd stopped doing that, as I didn't want to pry. If he needed to communicate, I figured that was up to him, right?

It was a tug of war between a Left Brain (him) and a Right Brain (me).

The rational vs. the temperamental.

Analytical vs. emotional.

Honestly, when I mulled over how diametrically opposite we were, it seemed amazing that we'd come together
at all, and we wouldn't have, strangely enough, had Cissy
not interfered. Though, lately, she'd been downplaying
Brian's and my relationship, not sure she liked the idea
that her unmarried daughter had a boyfriend who stayed
overnight without the sanctity of marriage to bind him to
me, to ensure he came home at night (like a wedding ring
had that much power). Unfortunately, Mother got regular
reports on the subject from Penny George, my nosy neighbor and member of Cissy's Bible study group at Highland
Park Presbyterian.

Was there a place in Heaven reserved for tattletales? I
wondered.

Compared to Brian's reserve, I was an open book. I
wore my heart on my sleeve. Said what was on my mind
without a pesky internal censor. Whatever Malone didn't
know about me—like my past relationships, which were
part of my "don't ask, don't tell" policy—wasn't worth
knowing.

My life in a nutshell: prep school grad, debutante
dropout, art school not Ivy League, jeans not couture,
paint over pearls.

My mother would doubtless describe me as a stubborn
girl who tended to color outside the lines and who'd always picked up strays (animals and people).

And she'd be right, too.

I saw a slogan on a T-shirt when I was at Tom Thumb
several weeks back: WELL-BEHAVED WOMEN DON'T MAKE
HISTORY. Something I'd adopted as my personal motto,
despite being a lifelong student of the Dalai Cissy and her

mantra of "good girls don't," not to mention having graduated the Little Miss Manners classes she'd insisted I attend when I was in kindergarten.

In my mind, misbehaving sounded perfectly suitable for someone who'd worn camouflage pants (courtesy of Goodwill) and pink high-tops to a debutante tea.

Not that I needed a slogan as an excuse to be who I was, which had always seemed the antithesis of what my mother had wanted, i.e., a miniclone of herself: Hockaday and SMU alumna with an impeccable nose for designer labels, the sense to marry well and marry young, and an eye toward philanthropy.

I had failed on all counts but the first. The Hockaday School was also my alma mater, though I was hardly their poster child.

A prissy little debutante, I wasn't. But I was a pretty good daughter, not perfect by far, but my heart was in the right place. Those weren't mutually exclusive, or so I thought, although Cissy might have a different take entirely, as was often the case.

Despite being flip sides of the same genetic coin, I loved my mother very much, and I understood that she loved me. We just had a wee bit of trouble showing it sometimes. But that was another familial trait we shared: lack of gushiness.

After being with Brian for four months, I still couldn't get out those three magic words, had I wanted to. I'm not sure I was ready for that yet. Maybe I just hoped he'd say them first, so I wouldn't have to deal with a crushing response, like, "That's nice." Which would surely kill me.

What I did know was that I trusted him.

What I was less certain of was if he trusted me.

Did he feel as sure about me as I'd begun to feel about him? That, perhaps, I was Ms. Right, and I belonged with him?

Dang it.

Where was he?

What was he doing right this minute? Did he have a stripper in his lap? I sure as shooting hoped he didn't have one with her legs wrapped around his neck.

Oh, boy.

I was too tired to be asking myself such heavy questions. I could hardly keep my eyes open, and I knew I should blow out the candle and hit the sack.

But my limbs were too heavy to move. Getting swung around by that Chippie must've worn me out. Let that be a lesson. Never dangle from the neck of a male stripper unless you've had your Wheaties.

I could only summon enough energy to lean toward the coffee table and blow out the candle before I fell limply back onto the couch.

I curled up beneath the throw and listened as my breathing turned slow and steady, the darkness creeping softly into my head, turning off my dimmer switch.

Chapter 3

Tweet.

Tweeeeet.

My eyes flew open, and I found myself bound mummy-style in the crocheted throw. I wiggled and kicked to unwind my body from the yarn cocoon as the telephone rang again, sounding way too much like a demented bird. Couldn't anyone invent a soothing tone for landlines, more akin to waves lapping on a beach than a cockatoo gone berserk?

Tweeeeet!

I snatched up the handset and uttered a groggy, "Hello?"

"Andrea! Where in God's name have you been?" The flutter of hope that it was Malone fast died when I heard my mother's drawl, and not the honey and molasses voice either. The impatient tone. Her version of Scarlett O'Hara pissed off.

"I left you several messages," she went on, "which you

never returned. Didn't I train you better than that?"

"Well-behaved women rarely make history," I murmured.

I don't think she saw the same merit in those words that I did.

"Well, ill-behaved daughters tend to get written out of their mothers' wills. So you'd better shape up."

"Leave it all to the Humane Society," I told her and yawned, wondering what time it was and realizing I'd slept with my contacts in. The plastic had stuck to my corneas, so I blinked double-time to loosen them up.

"Well, if you're going to be like that, maybe I'll just split everything between the NRA and the Young Republicans," she drawled, clearly trying to torment me.

"What time is it?" I asked to change the subject, and because I couldn't make out the clock on the mantel and didn't want to get up to look. The phone cord didn't stretch that far. Darned landlines.

"It's eight-thirty, darling, so rise and shine. You'll need to shower and dress before you join Stephen and me for brunch."

"Would you mind too much if I passed?" I attempted, futile though it was.

"Don't be silly. We need to talk about your birthday party. Besides, it's my treat, so you can have whatever you please."

On cue, my stomach growled, and I realized I had nothing more appealing than Pop-Tarts for breakfast. And they weren't even the iced kind. Poo.

Buck up, Kendricks, I urged myself. *It's only brunch.*

"You sound tired, darling. Didn't you sleep well?"

"I had a late night," I told her, though I didn't explain where I was and whose shoulders I'd been slung around. "If I go, I can't stay long, okay?"

I planned on spending most of the day with Brian. Well, as soon as he regained consciousness, whenever that would be. He'd been so wrapped up in work lately that I'd hardly seen him. I explained this to Mother, praying it might get me a reprieve; but no such luck.

"Mr. Malone is invited to come, of course."

I figured he'd rather be dipped in a vat of boiling tar.

Okay, I'm exaggerating, but I was sure he'd rather sleep in than endure a prissy brunch with Her Highness of Highland Park the morning after his boys' night out. "That's sweet of you, Mother, but I'd wager he's not fit for linen napkins and mimosas, not after the bachelor party."

"Bachelor party?" I envisioned her perfectly arched blond brows lifting. "For whom? Anyone I know?"

"Not really a party." I scrambled to fix any damage caused by my loose lips. "Just him and a pal from the firm. Someone junior. I'm sure you've never met him."

Though she might have. ARGH handled my mother's legal affairs, had worked out the sale of Daddy's drug company to a pharmaceutical giant, on whose board Cissy sat to keep an eye on things. Mother was quite chummy with J. D. Abramawitz—old Abe—one of the founding fathers, and stayed current on all the ARGH gossip.

"So Mr. Malone isn't . . . with you?" she asked, like I hadn't seen that one coming from fifty yards back.

I sat up straighter, rubbing my forehead. "No, Mother, he didn't stay here last night. I haven't heard from him since before he went out."

"Well, then don't bother him, darling. Let him sleep as late as he wants, and you can join us for brunch. There's something Stephen and I want to tell you besides, and it would be best if you were alone."

Okay, that stopped me in my tracks.

Something to tell me? Best if I was alone?

My heart caught in my throat, jumping to a hefty conclusion that shook me to my daddy's girl core. "Please, don't tell me you two have gone and done anything rash?" Like getting hitched, I nearly asked, but Cissy too quickly jumped in.

"I'll see you at ten, sweet pea, and, please, don't wear a ratty T-shirt or jeans with holes in them. Kiss kiss," she cooed, before I heard that telltale sound of her hanging up.

I sat stunned, phone still clutched to my ear, the dial tone humming tunelessly until I set the handset back in its cradle and stared into space, numbed by what I imagined.

Had Stephen proposed to my mother?

They'd only been dating for a month. But then, they were both in their sixties. Maybe they figured they didn't have a moment to lose.

No matter that I liked the guy, in what little time I'd spent around him, the mere idea of Cissy remarried to anyone unsettled me. She'd been alone the past twelve years, and I'd grown accustomed to that, after finally digesting my father's death (yeah, I'm slow with closure).

Stop it, Andy, I told myself.

Maybe it was something else entirely.

Like Stephen had agreed to co-chair the Boot Scoot to Stamp-Out Hunger Hoedown this year. A former IRS agent might know a few tactics to pry money out of tight-fisted blue bloods.

Which meant I had to go to brunch, didn't it? There was no skipping out if I wanted to find out Mother's secret.

Rats.

Foiled again.

Amazing how Cissy could get me to do what she wanted with barely a twist of my arm. She was a master in the art of coercion.

With a groan, I dragged myself from the sofa and to the shower.

It was nine-thirty before I had my hair dried, minimal makeup applied, and my nicest pair of khaki pants on, topped by a long-sleeved cotton sweater since it was supposed to be downright chilly this fine fall day.

Lower seventies were forecast.

Brrrr.

I wondered if the ladies at the Mansion would bring their fur out of storage so they wouldn't freeze to death.

Before I left the house, I called Malone's apartment, let the phone ring six times before his voice mail clicked on.

"Hey, it's me," I said. "You're incredibly lucky that I'm so generous and letting you sleep, instead of forcing you to join me at the Brunch from Hell with Mother and her boyfriend. I should be back by noon, and I want to hear how things went. So give me a buzz then, if you're up, or I'll call and wake you."

Just for sport, I tried his cell, too, which clicked over to his messages immediately.

Interesting.

That meant he had that phone turned off, pretty atypical for him, as he was always worried about his boss being able to reach him 24/7. Still, it could just be that he wanted to get some shut-eye after partying with Matty.

Good for him.

If I'd been smart enough not to answer the phone this morning, I wouldn't have to trek down south to brunch with Mummy Dearest.

I left a brief "Call me" note on his cell for good measure, then locked up the condo and prepared to head down to Highland Park and its posh environs, or "Cissy Land," as I liked to call it. It was like a very upscale Survivor Island, where the motto was "Out-Shop, Out-Bitch, Out-Class."

Not surprisingly, I had been booted off the island long ago, after I'd decided not to go through with my coming-out, about as severe an infraction as existed, second only to marrying down or attending Texas A&M.

I started the Jeep, cranked up Def Leppard's "Rock of Ages," and said a little prayer along the lines of, "May the Force be with me."

When I pulled up at the Mansion on Turtle Creek and turned over my keys for the valet to park, it was ten o'clock on the nose.

At least I wasn't late. The less ammo I gave my mother to use against me (even at a future date), the better.

Despite its snooty clientele, I did love the Mansion's gorgeous architecture and design. Its Old World ambiance made me feel like I was walking into another century: cathedral doors, stained glass, molded ceilings, carved columns, and plenty of antiques.

As an artist, such things of beauty lifted my spirits.

Mother had apparently reserved one of the private rooms situated off the main dining area, and I followed the maitre d' past tables filled with big-haired blondes adorned with loads of diamonds and older men who paid a pretty penny for their trophy wives' upkeep. It felt like the gentle clinking of silver on china and the hum of conversation paused as I walked past; but it was probably just my imagination.

I put on my big-girl smile as coiffed heads turned to give me the once-over—resulting in a host of disapproving frowns, and I wasn't even wearing my ripped denim—though I didn't let them get to me. Still, I considered what a release it would be to stick out my tongue or blow them a raspberry.

But I refrained, for Cissy's sake.

These were her people, after all. I surely wouldn't want her embarrassing me in front of my friends (although she had done that plenty of times in the past, come to think of it).

"Rise above, pumpkin," as my daddy liked to say. Though there were times when it would sure feel good to get down in the sandbox and play dirty.

I didn't need that kind of karma.

Not with my stomach already knotted up, worried about what Mother had to say. I squared my shoulders at the first breath of Cissy's familiar Joy perfume, preparing myself for the worst before I entered the room where my mother and Stephen waited.

Or Mother, anyway.

"Good morning, sunshine," she said, glancing up as I

approached. Her chin-length blond bob shined gold beneath the fixtures. The rose of her Chanel suit matched the blush on her face. Whatever was up, she looked happy.

"Morning." I went to her side and bent down to air-kiss her cheeks.

I took the seat beside her, unfurling the napkin in my lap. I hadn't yet seen hide nor hair of Stephen Howard, though the chair across from my mother's was slightly pushed back, the napkin a bit rumpled, as if someone had been there and gone already.

"He's getting some air," my mother explained, following my eyes and sensing the direction of my thoughts. "He wanted to give us a moment alone."

Jesus Crust, as a friend's preschool-age daughter liked to say.

"This sounds serious," I got out, reaching for the goblet of ice water, taking a generous gulp, and managing to dribble some of it down my chin. I used my sleeve to wipe away the drops.

"It's not so much serious as, well, adventurous," she assured me and patted my arm.

Adventurous?

If she'd imagined that would soothe me, she was wrong.

I noticed she still wore the diamond engagement ring and wedding band Daddy had given her, smack-dab on the third finger of her left hand. So if Stephen had popped the question, perhaps Mother had declined. Could be their wild adventure amounted to little more than a trip to the theatre to see—*hush my mouth*—Tony Bennett on his "I'm Not Dead Yet" Tour!

That perked me up.

"Go on," I urged her, feeling vaguely less afraid.

"All right, Andrea, I won't keep this from you any longer, as you'll find out sooner or later." Her pale blue eyes settled firmly on mine, her smile verging on nervous. Odd, because I so rarely ever saw Cissy nervous about anything. She reached for the strand of gray Mikimoto pearls at her throat and fiddled with it. "Stephen and I will be taking a trip together," she started haltingly.

"A trip together?" Was that my voice? It sounded horrified. "What does that mean?"

"What do you think it means? Packing a suitcase, getting on a plane, and going to some prearranged destination."

Thank you, Mr. Rogers. I *knew* that. I just didn't *get* it.

"When?" I asked.

"Next weekend," she said without a pause for a breath.

I blinked at her. So much for early warning. I gulped, wet my lips and croaked out, "Where will you stay?"

"Oh, it's all on the up and up," she rushed to say with a flutter of eyelashes. Then she set about rearranging her silverware, no longer looking at me. "We'll have separate bedrooms, of course, though it appears we'll share a large suite. Stephen got an upgrade at the hotel. Isn't that wonderful?"

Sharing a suite? How was that wonderful?

That meant bedrooms accessible through connecting doors. Confines too close for comfort.

My comfort.

"Mother, don't you think that's moving a little too fast—"

"Listen to me, sweetie," she cut me off, surely knowing where I was going with this. "It's perfectly innocent."

"Flitting off with a stranger to a hotel suite is innocent?"

"He's hardly a stranger, darling. He practically saved my neck, if you've forgotten."

Okay, so maybe Stephen had helped out when Mother had gotten herself into trouble at an old folks' home—I mean, retirement village—but it wasn't like he'd given her the breath of life or anything.

Still, did that qualify him as a proper suitemate for Cissy? A woman who revered Amy Vanderbilt and Emily Post, the Patron Saints of the Properly Behaved?

"I don't know about this," I murmured. My cheeks felt warm, I was so uncomfortable with the whole idea of my mother gallivanting off with this man I hardly knew. Hell, a man *she* hardly knew! She'd always made it clear how she'd dated my daddy for a full year before they'd become engaged, and it was another year still before they'd married (and clinched the deal, if you get my drift, which is why I was forever getting the "milk for free" lecture with regard to Brian Malone). Yet she planned to share a suite with this fellow she'd met a month ago under rather strange circumstances (don't ask).

"It's Stephen's annual reunion with some of his buddies from the Navy," Cissy spelled out for me, her drawl sweet but firm. "He wants them to meet me, and me to meet them."

"Can't they come to Dallas?"

"No, darlin', they congregate elsewhere."

I drew in a deep breath and let it out before I asked, "So,

where exactly is this reunion going to be held? Please, tell me it's at least on this continent."

If she answered, "Paris," I'd have to nip this puppy in the bud.

"I won't even need a passport," she quipped, and her blue eyes fairly crackled. "We're booked at the Bellagio," she said in a conspiratorial whisper.

"Isn't that in . . . ?"

"Vegas," she popped off before I could finish.

Las Vegas? Aka Sin City, Glitter Gulch, the Strip?

Where what happened there stayed there? Where a dude dressed like Elvis married people at one of the many quickie wedding chapels? Where my mother could overindulge in champagne and awaken with a tattoo on her fanny that declared, "Navy Seals Do It Better." Egads!

"You're shacking up with this guy in Vegas?" I blurted out, loudly, and suddenly I realized why she'd reserved a private room at the restaurant. Otherwise everyone brunching at the Mansion this morning would have witnessed my meltdown.

I could picture the headlines in the *Park Cities Press*: DEBUTANTE DROPOUT DETONATES! (See the Society page for details.)

"My gosh, Mother, Vegas is so . . . *tacky*. I can't believe you'd want to spend time there," I threw at her. "Besides, what would Daddy think?" I added for good measure, no matter that it was hitting below her fashionably slim crocodile belt. I didn't care.

"Andy, I'd expected more from you, I really did." She sniffed, pale eyes clouding. Her rosy-cheeked exuberance of moments before disappeared as fast as the sun behind a storm cloud. She gently shook her head, dropping her hands into her lap. "Your father has been gone for years and years, and he wouldn't want me to be lonely, not when there's a fine man like Stephen to keep me company and make me smile."

How was I supposed to respond to that?

She wasn't finished. "I honestly imagined you'd be happy for me. Aren't you always the one who says life is too short not to take chances?"

"But I meant . . ." The protest died on the vine. Because I'd meant *me,* not her.

Well, crap.

Trapped by my own words.

There was nothing more I hated than Mother being right.

Maybe it was appropriate that it was brunchtime, since I clearly had egg on my face. It was as if I were possessed, not my usual nonconformist self. I was acting like all those tight-assed, judgmental, disapproving heiresses I'd gone to prep school with and had sworn I would never resemble.

And just last night I'd had my legs wrapped around the neck of a male stripper.

Holy cow, I was a hypocrite.

I had no cause telling my mother what to do any more than she was justified in directing my behavior.

We were both grown-ups (one of us more grown-up than the other).

And I'd always hated when she judged me, or acted like the decisions I made were less than wise.

It was like *Freaky Friday,* where the mother and daughter switched bodies, and I didn't like it one bit.

I sighed, tucking loose hair behind my ears and biting back any further argument. "I'm sorry, Mother," I murmured. "Of course, you should go with Stephen to Vegas, if that's what you want. You're old enough to make your own decisions."

"My, how big of you," she said dryly and shot me a look that made me feel like a knock-kneed twelve-year-old who'd burped in front of company.

I raised my chin, an idea taking form in my head. "However you want to conduct your private affairs is up to you. Just as my relationship with Malone is no business of yours."

Her finely plucked brows arched. "Is that so?"

"Yes, it's so." My realization that her burgeoning, um, friendship with Stephen had leveled the playing field had me feeling suddenly brave. "So no more digs about loose cows and free milk, and call off that nosy Penny George, too. Stay out of my business, and I'll stay out of yours. *Capisce?*"

"I'm not sure what you're talking about, Andrea. Penny George is in my Bible study class, that's all. She doesn't spy for me."

Liar, Liar, Chanel tweed on fire.

"Is it a deal, Mother, or not?" I asked and extended my right hand to prove I meant business.

Mother warily eyed my proffered palm as if it were slathered in grease. "Oh, for heaven's sake, if it'll make you happy." She wrinkled her nose. "I still don't quite understand this need for a moratorium on motherly advice, but I'll do my best," she said and started to lift her hand from her lap just as Stephen strode through the doorway.

He was a tall man, slim with faded ginger-colored hair

and a smattering of freckles on sun-weathered skin. Mother visibly perked up at the sight of him. Had to give her credit. He had a Robert Redford outdoorsy edge to him, not the polished metrosexual appearance of so many Dallas men. Nope, no ambiguity there.

"Everything okay in here, or do I need body armor to safely enter?" he remarked, and went over to Cissy, giving her shoulder a gentle squeeze and exchanging a warm glance before he settled into his chair.

I scrunched up my face in the semblance of a smile. "Did they teach you bad jokes in the Navy or the IRS?"

"Who was joking?"

Ho ho.

My mother had hooked herself a regular comedian.

"Oh, Stephen, no body armor's necessary, truly," my mother assured him, and her hand settled into her lap. "Andrea's *thrilled* with our plans," she drawled in gross exaggeration. She focused her steady blue gaze directly on me, vaguely challenging. "Aren't you, sweet pea?"

"I'm positively giddy," I said and gave Cissy the evil eye in return, not particularly pleased that our deal had gone unsealed. Which meant Penny George was still on nosy duty, and Mother could harp on the fact that Malone hadn't yet coughed up an engagement ring despite the intimate state of our relationship. Yet I apparently had no power to dissuade her from taking a trip with this man who was not her husband.

It wasn't fair.

"So where's Brian?" Stephen asked, filling in the pregnant pause. He turned to me. "Is he on the golf course? Beautiful day for a round."

I started to respond, but Mother beat me to it. "Apparently, Mr. Malone went to a bachelor party last night and is sleeping off the ill effects somewhere other than Andy's apartment."

Geez, she made it sound as though Brian were snoring on a park bench, an old newspaper draped over his body for warmth; a regular alcoholic recovering from a recent bender, not a mild-mannered lawyer out for a simple night of fun.

"A bachelor party, eh? I've been to a few of those in my lifetime. Can't blame him for skipping out on us. He's probably got one heck of a headache this morning." Stephen sent a wink my way.

"It wasn't a party exactly, and Brian isn't much of a drinker," I began, instinctively wanting to defend my boyfriend, but Malone *had* gone to The Men's Club with Matty to kiss his friend's bachelor days good-bye, and I had no doubt he'd put down a beer or two . . . or three. So I pressed my lips together and let it go.

I stared at the condensation on my water glass, contemplating going home to my Pop-Tarts, because I wasn't having any more fun than I'd imagined.

"How about we eat, hmm?" my mother said, like food was some kind of peace offering. "Then we'll discuss my plans for your birthday."

"So long as they don't include salmon or chocolate soufflés," I told her, and not just to be contrary.

For nearly a full minute, Cissy and I locked gazes, neither willing to budge and look away first.

Stephen cleared his throat and nudged my hand, causing me to glance over and ending the starefest. "Hey, Andy, those flapjacks with banana topping calling your name like they're calling mine?"

Oh, they were calling all right.

Mummy wins again! I envisioned those buttermilk boys chortling. *Looks like you got the short end of the stick, or is that* stack?

Damn them.

Nothing I hated more than smart-ass pancakes.

Chapter 4

 I felt grumpy and defeated as I retrieved my Jeep from the valet and steered that sucker away from the driveway at the Mansion.

I checked my cell for messages as soon as I escaped the Brunch from Hell—leaving Mother and Stephen exchanging moony eyes over decaf—but my voice-mail box showed zip.

Why hadn't Brian called back yet?

It was already noon. Was he in some kind of post-stripper-induced coma?

I dialed his landline from my cell en route to safety (i.e., my condo), only to get his voice mail again.

What was up with that?

It unbalanced me, not being able to reach him when I needed to. I wanted someone who'd sympathize when I ranted about Cissy's menu choices for my birthday dinner (shouldn't she at least serve food I *liked*?) and how she was running off to Vegas with an ex-IRS agent, when I heartily disapproved.

Since Brian wasn't picking up his phone, preventing me from letting off steam, I felt all bottled up and tense. I had an ache in my chest, drumming at my temples, and my skin was crawling like I was getting a virus but it wasn't full-blown yet.

Wherefore art thou, Malone? I thought, not happy in the least that he was hiding out from the world. Sheesh, hiding out from me.

Just to make myself feel better, I started going through all the horrible, dreadful explanations of why Malone couldn't pick up the phone on his end. I devised a simple multiple choice test, like so:

(a) A thief had broken into his apartment, tied him up and gagged him.
(b) He was lying unconscious in a ditch.
(c) He was dead.
(d) He'd drunkenly gone home with a stripper, only to wake up with her panties wrapped around his head, and he was too embarrassed to talk to me.

I shuddered at the last one, figuring it had better be one of the other three or I would personally put Malone in a coma and/or kill him with my bare hands, and no jury in the State of Texas with even one sympathetic woman seated on it would ever convict me.

Lucky for me, I knew that murder wouldn't be necessary.

My boyfriend was no slime ball.

Brian Malone was a good guy, reared by parents who were still alive and happily married and who lived in St. Louis, smack-dab in the honest-to-God Heartland. (Though that was pretty much all I knew about them.) He had an undergrad degree from Washington University and a J.D. from Harvard, and did pro bono legal work for Operation Kindness, a humane animal rescue organization and one of my pet nonprofits (no pun intended).

All right, so he was the second worst kind of lawyer—a defense attorney—not far behind the bottom-feeding ambulance chasers, but he was hardly shady or sleazy.

He was honest to a fault.

I'd never seen him be less than straightforward.

So for now I'd go with gagged, unconscious, or dead.

Never panties on the head.

No way.

That settled, I arrived at my place within about twenty minutes, my stomach filled to the brim with banana-topped pancakes, and I changed into an old pair of jeans and T-shirt. If Malone wasn't around to otherwise occupy my time, I would do something else I loved, because I had to stop dwelling on things that made me go "Ick."

Like my mother and Stephen flying off to Vegas together next weekend.

Something I still wasn't feeling any too open-minded about.

I put on some music, a set of *Best of Mozart* CDs rather than my usual playlist of anything Def Leppard, and I sat at my easel, dabbing a plastic palette with generous blobs from my assorted tubes of acrylic.

As the warm midday light filtered in, I let my mind drift

to somewhere else completely. Then I picked up a clean brush and began to have at it.

For some reason, I saw bold streaks of black, grays, and reds in my mind's eye, a veritable vortex of them, and I used heavy brushstrokes, sweeping and swirling, something fierce and tangible directing each motion.

I got so immersed in the act of creating that I lost track of time, only vaguely noticing the change of light, the warming of the tiny living room as the sun rose, shifting as the hours of afternoon slipped past.

The phone shrieked, and I came off the stool with a start, nearly sending a wide stroke of bloodred sailing across waves of gray.

Geez, Louise.

My heart pounded as I set down brush and palette, rubbed my hands on my jeans, and raced to grab up the handset.

The clock on the mantel showed three-thirty.

A good three hours since I'd left the Mansion.

"Brian?" I said instinctively, thinking it was about time.

"What, you can't find him either?" a self-satisfied voice remarked on the other end. "Because I've been trying all day and getting nada."

Crap.

It was my dear pal Allie.

Brunch with Mother and then *this.*

Had I broken a mirror recently? Was I doomed to seven years of bad juju?

Fitting that Mozart's "Requiem" played at precisely that moment. Funeral music seemed the appropriate ambiance for a conversation with Allie the Impaler.

"Did you want something?" I asked her, perching on the arm of my sofa, a gentle pounding taking shape behind my eyes. I wondered if a preventive Excedrin was in order.

"Well, if Brian's not there, then where is he?" she demanded. "Don't tell me you lost him already, Kendricks. It took me six months to drive him off and y'all have only been dating for, what, three?"

"Four," I snipped.

"Whatever."

If there was a way to send an electric shock through the phone line, I would've done it just to hear the woman scream.

"He's not lost, Allie. He's a grown man with free will, you know. I'm not his mother or his keeper." Well, I wasn't. I rubbed my forehead. "He's probably at his place, recovering from his trip to Stripper Land with Matty."

"Nope, not so," Allie insisted. "I dropped by his apartment a few minutes ago, and I didn't see his Acura in the lot. His Sunday *New York Times* was still on the mat, so I knocked till my knuckles bled. The woman next door even poked her head out, said I could stop the racket because he wasn't there. Not that I didn't want to take her word for it, but I let myself in and poked around, and she was right."

The pancakes turned in my belly.

"You have a key?" I asked—more like gasped—not sure whether I was more upset about that or the fact that Brian wasn't home.

Allie laughed, and not in a good way. "My God, Kendricks, he keeps a spare over the door frame in that little spot where he peeled out a hunk of wood putty."

"Oh, yeah, that key," I said, though I had no idea what she was talking about. Malone had never informed me about the hidey-hole to which Allie was obviously privy.

"His bed wasn't slept in, so I don't think he ever went back to his place," she continued in her self-assured manner. "So you don't know where he is? He's got some papers from the file of a big-time case we're working on, and I want to get cracking, even if he's slacking off. Only I couldn't find the documents or his briefcase. You think he has it all with him?"

"Shackled to his wrist, no doubt," I said, because Malone didn't go anywhere without his attaché. Well, except the shower and bed. "Maybe he's at Matty's," I suggested, only to be shot down again.

"Nope, not there either. I checked in with Eleanor this morning, and she said Matty had to take a cab home from The Men's Club. Brian apparently left him there, high and dry. Well, high, anyway."

"That's not possible," I said, because it couldn't be.

Brian wouldn't have taken Matty out on the town only to leave him stranded at the strip joint. That wasn't his style.

"Hey, Kendricks, I'm just telling you what Eleanor said. I figured Brian was with you, since I can't track him down anywhere. But you're obviously clueless, too. I'll drop by the office later and see if he's there. We've got so much work to do on the Oleksiy case, and Abramawitz has been breathing down our necks about every little detail, since he trusted us to be part of the defense team in such a high-profile trial."

Did ARGH handle any other cases than high-profile? I

nearly commented. I figured media attractiveness was one of the requirements for taking on a client. That and the client's ability to plunk down a huge honking retainer check.

Allie continued to rattle on: "There were a couple new prosecution witnesses we're supposed to vet, though Brian supposedly got a head start on Friday. We were going to meet today, so he could fill me in." She made a noise of impatience. "Would you ask him to call me if you hear from him first?"

"Yeah, sure," I murmured.

But I'd stopped listening to her.

Pretty soon she got the picture, said, "Good-bye," and hung up.

I barely noticed she wasn't on the other end.

My brain got stuck a ways back on some things she'd said, namely that Malone had left Matty stranded at The Men's Club. His car wasn't at his apartment, his Sunday *Times* still lay on his mat, and his bed had not been slept in. He wasn't answering his cell or his landline. And, according to Allie, he wasn't at Matty's.

Where the heck was he?

If he'd had to take off for parts unknown, at a moment's notice (which had about a snowball's chance in hell of happening, as he was disinclined toward spontaneity and more inclined toward overplanning), then why hadn't he touched base with anyone?

With me, in particular?

I pushed the Reset button on the handset and returned it to its cradle. That flulike sense of unease washed through me again. This time I didn't brush it off.

Sinking down on the sofa, I rubbed paint-smeared hands on paint-smeared jeans, going over the whole situation—if it was a situation—and trying not to get crazy until I had a good reason to be.

Something was funky.

Brian wasn't the kind of person who took off without a word to anyone. He was the kind who'd do the opposite, call ahead, make a reservation, plot an "impromptu" trip to death, not the reverse. He didn't do the unexpected, didn't let people down or leave them guessing.

So maybe Malone was in trouble. That's the only answer that made sense.

I just didn't know what sort of trouble he might be in.

Damn, why didn't he call me, like a good boyfriend?

I picked up the phone again and punched in Brian's numbers for the third time that day. Six rings on the landline, then I got his voice mail. I left yet another message. Then I dialed his cell, which instantly clicked to his mailbox.

"For Pete's sake, where are you?" I said, unable to hide rising panic in my voice. "Please, please, call as soon as you get this. Apparently, Allie's been looking for you, and now I'm worried, too."

I'd give him a few hours to call back. If he didn't, I'd find Matty in the phone book and give him a buzz so we could have ourselves a little chat. The dude was obviously confused. He'd probably had way too much to drink last night, and maybe Malone had gone over his limit and ended up taking a taxi instead of driving under the influence. Perhaps he'd assumed Matty had called himself a cab as well.

That would explain Brian's car being absent from his parking lot.

It wouldn't explain why he was avoiding me, if that's what he was doing. And I was beginning to wonder if that's what it was.

I put the image of him awakening in the bed of a stripper with her panties around his head out of my mind.

Maybe he just needed some time to himself. Could be that his friend's impending marriage had struck a chord in him, made him introspective about losing so many single pals to holy matrimony the past few years. But if he needed space, he could've told me. It might've stung a bit, but I would've let him have it.

I'd never known Brian to act cowardly, even though I realized he didn't like confrontations in his personal life, as opposed to the courtroom. Still, he should be able to talk to me.

I was his one and only, wasn't I?

I mean, it wasn't like we'd had any real conversation about our status, the whole "being exclusive" deal. We just *were*. I knew he wasn't seeing anyone else. When would he have the time between hanging out at my condo and working on that Oleksiy case, or whatever Allie had called it?

Working on that case with Allie, I repeated silently and found myself tensing.

How many guys had to deal with a former lover every day on the job? Except Hugh Hefner, but his, er, office took "sleeping with the boss" to an extreme.

I wonder how Brian put up with it, being stuck on a legal team with a woman he'd broken up with, who was everything I wasn't: a few inches taller, several sizes smaller, naturally blond (so she claimed), not a zit or freckle in sight, able to wear four-inch heels without toppling over, and self-assured to the point of arrogance.

Okay, so maybe I could see why Brian had been attracted to her, but she seemed awfully high maintenance to me, so demanding and pushy.

It's a wonder she and Malone had lasted six months before he'd thrown in the towel (he said it was mutual, but Allie had implied she'd driven him away, which was entirely plausible, from my viewpoint anyway).

I might've thought, *Ah, must've been the sex,* but I didn't want to go there, even briefly. That was like imagining my mother and Stephen Howard . . . gaaah.

Squishing my eyes closed, I shook that thought from my head, like a dog shakes off water.

Yuck.

Back to Allie and Malone. I didn't know much—and didn't care to ask—beyond the fact that they'd started seeing each other soon after he'd moved here, two fledgling attorneys who'd bonded over late nights, long hours, and lack of sleep.

I figured I'd chalk it up to bad judgment and loneliness. Knowing Allie as I did—which translated to "not at all"— I'd venture to guess that she'd instigated their romantic relationship. Brian had such a shy streak, so it was hard to imagine him pursuing the Blond Bitch from Hell. Odd to consider the same man who'd been attracted to that harridan now kept company with me.

Was I more his type? Or was she?

Enough already.

I could work myself into a tizzy, worrying about where Brian was and dwelling on his old affair with Allie.

But it was a lovely, lazy Sunday, and I didn't want to waste it.

So I closed my eyes, visualized calm as the sweet sounds of "Eine Kleine Nachtmusik" swelled joyfully in my ears. I pushed all the tension aside, stretching my arms overhead to loosen my shoulders. With a sigh, I went back to my easel, feeling lighter than just a few moments before.

For a long, long while, I simply sat and scrutinized the canvas, getting an emotional read on what I'd done so far and where I was going with it. Finally, feeling focused, I used a small rag to wipe my brush, took a deep breath, picked up where I'd left off, and let the rest of the world disappear again.

Soon I was deeply in the zone, working in an altered state, apart from the here and now, from the ticking clock, from anything real.

I just painted.

Minutes spun into hours, though I wasn't cognizant of how much time had passed, not until the phone rang again, the high-pitched twitter erupting from across the living room, snapping my peace clean in two, like a bad omen.

Chapter 5

Tweeeeet!

The obnoxious noise made minced meat of my concentration, and I winced as it pulled me out of my trance, as I'd been deep into adding texture to streaks of silver paint by dabbing the thick bands of color with crinkled foil. I briefly considered ignoring the call until I realized it could be Brian.

So I dropped what I was doing, raced across the room and breathlessly answered, "Malone?" as I picked it up.

"Lord Almighty, Kendricks, you mean you still don't know where he is?"

Well, shit on a stick.

It was Allie again.

I glanced at the clock, surprised at how late it was; but I'd been so absorbed in my painting I hadn't noticed the light weakening beyond the slanted window blinds.

It was already a quarter past six.

"Has he made like ET and phoned home yet?" she demanded, then rushed on before I could get a word in. "'Cause hell if I can find him. Went to the office, and he was nowhere in sight, and he hadn't been in unless he snuck past the front desk. I asked Security to check the names logged in since midnight, and Bri's not on there anywhere. I've paged him, like, three times, and he hasn't answered one. Even called a few of the guys from the firm that he pals around with, though they haven't seen him since Friday. So what's the deal, Andy? Has he gone AWOL, or is he just being a prick?"

I bristled. Malone was never that. Not to me or anyone else, unless he had a split personality that I'd never glimpsed.

If she hadn't gotten me worrying all over again with her comments about Malone not being at the office and not returning the papers to the file, I would've hung up on her, then and there.

The witch.

"Listen, Allie, if you couldn't find him at his apartment or ARGH, and he isn't with his friends, then something's odd and you know it. Brian doesn't blow people off, or pull a diva and disappear"—which I'm sure Ms. Seven Jeans had done a time or two herself—"so he's either with another friend and his cell's not working or something's happened to him, and we need to find out which it is."

She sounded only vaguely less snarky as she answered, "You're right, I'm sorry. It's not like him. He's Mr. Dependable. Captain Clockwork. Sir Stick in the Mud. If he's not dodging the both of us then he's probably lying in a ditch somewhere or bound and gagged—"

"Stop it. That's not funny."

If she'd stood in front of me, I would've slapped her. I'd already ventured down that road myself, but I was joking. This felt suddenly serious.

"I didn't mean—"

"Shut up, Allie."

"But I—"

"Just shut up," I snapped then added instinctively, "Please."

Thankfully, she did.

My mind raced ahead, needing to figure out a plan, something to grab onto so we wouldn't go round in circles again.

Be calm, I told himself. *Think, don't panic.*

But a very panicky chorus of "What to do, what to do?" tick-tocked in my brain, keeping time with the beat of my heart as it slapped against my ribs.

I quickly made a mental list that began with calling Matty to see if he'd heard from Malone since last night.

"What's Matty and Eleanor's number?" I asked the incredibly still-silent Allie as I stretched the phone cord as far as it would go; luckily, far enough to reach my cell and detach it from where I'd plugged it in to recharge.

I could imagine Allie rolling her eyes as she recited the digits, which I dialed with my thumb, telling her to hang on as I listened to it ring.

One ringie-dingie . . . two . . . then success.

A high-pitched voice uttered, "Hello?"

"Eleanor? It's Andy Kendricks, from last night," I reminded her, in case she'd forgotten after one too many vodkatinis.

"Oh, yeah, hi, Andy, wasn't that the most fun you've ever had with your clothes on? My God, when that dancer came over and—"

"Would you put Matty on?" I had no patience for small-talk. I still had Allie on the other phone, so I was doing this two-fisted. "It's important."

"We're just about to sit down to eat—"

"It's about Brian. I can't seem to find him, and I thought if I talked to Matty, we could figure out where he is." My own voice sounded odd to my ears, anxious, bordering on tearful.

My worry must've come through loud and clear to Eleanor, because she murmured, "Just a minute," and I heard mumbled voices before a man said, "Um, Andy, you do know Brian ditched me at The Men's Club last night, so I'm not exactly high on him right now?"

"Yes, I know. Allie told me." I took a deep breath. "But he hasn't been to his apartment or the office, and I've left him tons of messages on his cell and his landline, and Allie's even paged him, but he doesn't answer, and I'm getting scared," I yammered without so much as a pause. "Please, tell me you've heard from him?" It was impossible to cross my fingers with a phone in both hands, so I did it mentally.

"No, I haven't."

Well, crud.

"I'm not surprised he's somewhere, hiding with his tail between his legs, since he took off after that woman last night and ditched me completely. I had to bribe a waitress to go backstage and look for him, which is when I heard he'd left with the chick through a back door."

"Left with a chick?" I echoed, thinking I'd heard wrong, what with my pulse pounding so loudly in my ears. "You saw him go backstage with a woman? And he took off with her?"

"Oh, hell, Andy, I don't think I should be telling you this."

I doubt I'd ever shaken with disappointment before, not so my teeth chattered, but I was doing it now. My whole body quivered, my knees fairly knocking, "For God's sake, Matty, spill, or I'll come over there right now and drag it out of you."

"All right, all right." He sighed. "But I shouldn't be the one to do this. If Brian's got something going on, he should tell you himself."

I didn't move. Didn't say a word. Just stood there, holding the phones to my ears with trembling hands, and waited.

"He was supposed to go arrange for me to have an, um, *lap dance*." He whispered the two words as if not wanting his fiancée to hear. "I thought that's what he was doing when he zeroed in on the blonde and took off after her like a rocket."

"Okay, what blonde?" I found the voice to ask. "Who was she, Matty? Did you recognize her?"

"Are you sure you want to hear—"

"What blonde, for God's sake!" I cut him off, screeching, feeling the heat in my face, not understanding any of this. Wanting just to stop everything and start the day over again. It couldn't get any worse.

Matty's voice was a sad monotone as he reeled off, "She was obviously a stripper. All she had on was a thong. She had lots of hair, kinda Farrah Fawcett retro, if you know what I mean. I didn't really see her face."

Of course, you didn't, I wanted to scream. *You were too busy eyeing her bare-naked bazoombas!*

"This may sound stupid, but they sort of stared at each other from across the room for a minute before she took off. He followed her backstage. I was pretty blitzed, but I do remember thinking he'd picked her out for me and was setting up my, er, private party." Again, he finished the sentence with a whisper. "But he never came back. I tried to go after him, but a goon from the club stopped me. So I gave the barmaid a twenty to look for him. She was back in about ten minutes. Said she saw him vamoose with the blonde through a back door. Barmaid's name was Lu, I think, but I don't know anything else except that Malone had better turn up soon 'cuz he's holding onto some important hardware for me while Eleanor and I get settled into the new place, though it's not like I trust him much at the moment. Wish I knew more, but I don't."

More?

Like what he'd said wasn't plenty.

"Do you know if he took his car?" I asked, not ready to give up.

"His car?"

"Was it left in the parking lot, by any chance?" I asked, because that in itself would be highly suspicious. Malone loved his Acura coupe, maybe more than some people. He'd never have gone anywhere without it.

"Sorry, yeah, I checked with the valet before I called a cab, figuring I could drive Brian's ride home, since his vanishing act had totally sobered me up. But the dude said a guy had picked it up and taken off."

"Maybe that guy wasn't Brian," I surmised aloud,

because I had so little to cling to, what with all of Matty's devastating statements. I'd rather buy the idea that someone had carjacked Malone's coupe than imagine he'd sailed off with a stripper to her sleazy apartment.

"Sure, Andy, maybe it wasn't Brian," Matty said, so obviously wanting to appease me that I didn't believe he meant it.

For whatever reason—however it had happened—Brian had taken off, hadn't told anyone where he was.

I felt totally abandoned, and it shook me to the core. I could hardly stay upright, my legs wobbling, but I was no weeble. So there was no guarantee that I wouldn't fall down.

"I'm sorry, Andy," Matty muttered. "I'm really sorry. I don't know what the hell he was thinking . . . or not thinking. It's just not like him. And I thought he . . . that you two . . . man, I'm as confused as you are."

My head was spinning. My stomach lurched.

Brian had left The Men's Club with a stripper? And nobody knew where he was, except maybe said stripper?

Good God.

That was my worst worst-case scenario, and this time it was no joke.

It was all I could do to keep my pancakes down.

Chapter 6

I had the sense to ask Matty to give me a call if he heard from Brian, and he assured me he would. I believed him, too. He sounded so guilty about what had happened, kept apologizing to me. Like whatever Malone had done was his fault.

Then I flipped the cell closed and set it near my purse.

"You still there?" I said into the receiver of my Princess phone as I followed its hyperextended cord back to the sofa table.

"I'm here," came Allie's voice.

So unnaturally subdued.

I realized she'd heard my end of the conversation with Matty and understood the gist of it, or at least my rattled responses. Still, glutton for punishment that I was, I repeated nearly verbatim what Malone's friend had told me—as Matty's words had been burned in my brain—all the while fighting the tremor in my voice, because I would not crack. I would not disintegrate into self-pity and tears.

It was not the Kendricks way.

If there was anything I'd inherited from Cissy, it was a spine made of rebar. My mother had strength to spare, and some of it had trickled down to me. Ironically, I wouldn't have survived dropping out of my deb ball without it. Though Mother would deny it, she'd also passed on her chutzpah, and I had enough stored up to get through any horse manure life threw my way.

Including this.

Oh, yeah, and I would get through it, no matter what, though the dreamer in me still hoped for a happy ending.

Andrea meant "courage" in Greek. My father had told me it's why he'd picked out the name for his baby girl. For eighteen years, Daddy had impressed upon me not to jump to conclusions (as Cissy was so fond of doing). "You must have the patience to wait for the truth, pumpkin. Not everything's real, just because it's right in front of you."

Sort of like the warning on side mirrors: objects may be closer than they appear. Sometimes objects weren't what they seemed at all, except in our imaginations. A blur in the flash of headlights. A dark shadow that didn't exist.

Daddy would've wanted me to give Malone the benefit of the doubt, at least until Brian could speak for himself.

I would allow him that much.

Allie seemed less willing to forgive.

"The bastard," she kept muttering. "I can't believe he'd turn into such an ass overnight. It's so out of character."

"Exactly," I agreed, because it was true. It wasn't like Brian to do any of the things he'd been accused of doing, and I was having a heck of a time believing any of it.

Something in my gut was doing the arm-flailing, robotic, "Danger, Will Robinson!" warning dance.

Every loyal ounce of me would rather believe that Malone had gotten himself into a sticky situation he couldn't get out of instead of buying that he would rather have let Matty down or betrayed me with a stripper from The Men's Club.

That whole scenario bothered me immensely. Bugged me in a way it probably shouldn't. If I were an average, everyday scorned woman, I wouldn't need any further confirmation. I'd be ready to rip Malone's head off, pluck his heart from his chest with my fingernails, and throw what remained to the sharks.

But I wasn't a normal, everyday anything.

I was me.

And I just wanted to understand this whole sordid mess, because something felt very off-kilter, and that made me afraid for him.

"You'd better believe I'm gonna give him a piece of my mind when I see him at the office tomorrow. Men!" Allie snorted, and yet I was hardly aware she was actually offering sympathy.

I was still trying to figure out how to proceed.

Trying to decide whether to crawl into bed and not emerge for a week. Run to my mother's house, go through all her Kleenex, and wallow in sappy movies on the Hallmark Channel. Head to Malone's apartment, find that key above his threshold, and tear the place apart, looking for answers (which didn't sound like such a bad idea, really).

But I was leaning toward something less destructive, and more productive.

Something that would tell me one way or another if Malone had really ditched me for a girl whose idea of formal dress was to wear high heels with her thong.

"Is there anything I can do for you? You want to have a drink?" Allie was rambling on. "Hell, lots of drinks. I'll pay, and I'll drive so you can get bombed out of your gourd. The son of a—"

"Allie, take me down there," I cut her off, knowing exactly where I had to go and what I had to do.

"Take you down where?"

"The Men's Club," I told her. "I want to talk to someone who might've seen him, try to find this barmaid named Lu and get her to cough up where her stripper pal might've gone with Brian. I have to track him down, wherever he is. I need to talk to him."

He had a lot of explaining to do.

"Talk to Malone? Are you out of your fricking mind?" she sputtered. "After he dumped you for a hootchie mama without even having the balls to explain it to you face-to-face? You should run over him in your Hummer then back up and do it again."

"I don't have a Hummer."

"Then buy one, for God's sake! It'd be worth it to smoosh him beneath those giant wheels."

Allie was obviously a woman of action. Unfortunately, she wasn't a very good listener.

I tried again. "Will you or won't you?"

"You really want to do this, Kendricks?"

"Yes." And I needed her to go with me.

It was dark outside already, and I didn't want to venture

into that neck of the woods by myself. But I would, if I had to.

I heard her sigh and knew she'd caved. "Okay, okay. I'll go. But if I see Malone, I might have to bitch slap him for doing what he did."

"We don't know that he's done anything, Allie. Not for sure."

Call me Tammy, but I planned to stand by my man until I had all the facts. So far, everything was secondhand, and that wasn't good enough, not when my heart was in the balance.

"Hello, Kendricks? Aren't you paying attention? Even if Malone can prove he was possessed in the past twenty-four hours, he snuck out of the strip joint with a tramp, bailed on Matty, neglected to buzz you and clue you in, and he left me hanging when he was supposed to confab with me over a case."

"Thanks for the Cliff's Notes version, but I've read the book."

Part of me almost wanted to hang up on Allie and do this on my own. But I believed in the buddy system, particularly when traipsing down to a strip joint in a not-so-lovely area of town was involved.

"Allie? Yes, or no?" I prodded.

After a rather lengthy and, I'm sure, purposeful pause, she gave in. "Why don't you meet me down here, in the West Village? We can have margaritas first at Taco Diner."

Um, did she think this was a party?

"Not a good idea," I said, not being a fan of drinking and driving.

"Okay, you can hold the margarita until after we hit the club and play Matlock, but I'm having one first. I'll get it in a plastic cup and wait outside, so you don't have to park or come up to my condo."

Which meant I'd play taxi driver on this trip.

"Taco Diner, right," I said then, "Oh, wait, um, Allie?"

"Yeah?"

I wasn't even sure The Men's Club was open on Sunday night, and I mentioned that to her, which nearly cost me the hearing in my right ear, since Allie's response was to laugh like a maniacal hyena.

"Are you kidding?" She chortled, snorted, then chortled again. "You're hilarious, Kendricks. You really are. Who d'you think runs the place? The Catholic Church? 'Cause there aren't a whole lot of nuns with a pole dancing habit. Get it? Nuns with a habit?"

Someone needed to tell the woman to curb her enthusiasm. Was she this obnoxious in the courtroom?

Yeesh.

I'd convict a client of hers just because she was annoying.

"I'll be there in twenty, Allie," I said, as politely as I could.

I hung up before she could offer another nun pun.

Somehow, I just wasn't in the mood.

Chapter 7

It was not much past eight o'clock, but it was fall, which meant dark.

Not that I minded driving at night, except I had astigmatism that my contacts didn't correct (the right kind of lenses made me dizzy). So the streetlights and head-lamps had extra yellow rings around them. Kind of distracting when a person needed to pay attention to the road and not to glowing aureoles floating at them from the opposite lanes.

I did love how Dallas looked after sunset, particularly as I drove south, toward Lemmon and McKinney where Allie lived. Not that I didn't like my own turf of North Dallas, in the quiet of the 'burbs, apart from trendy spots and a safe distance from my mother. But places like Turtle Creek and the Park Cities, and even downtown, were an eyeful to see, both in daylight and when dusk descended.

Malone and I had driven around Mother's neighborhood

after we'd been summoned for dinner there several weeks back. We wound along Lakeside so we could glimpse the mansion I'd always thought looked like the White House reflected in Exall Lake. A coyote had shot across the road ahead of us. Yellow-brown fur with the stub of a tail, so scrawny it looked like a stray dog in need of an Alpo fix.

Who'd have figured there was wildlife living amongst the richest of Big D's rich? The kind that nature made; not the playboys and party girls, just in case there's any confusion about what I meant.

I loved viewing the silhouette of downtown, glittery windows lit up like Christmas, the green argon lights that framed the NationsBank building and Reunion Tower with its rotating globe.

There were things I had not missed about my hometown while I'd been away in Chicago at art school—like, the insecurity of not having big enough hair, boobs, and jewels—but there was more still that I'd pined for.

My roots were solidly entrenched in the sandy dirt, buried beneath the soil several generations deep. Occasionally, I considered living elsewhere, the Pacific Northwest, maybe. Or I imagined what it might be like to shuck the real world for a while and move to Paris, go Bohemian, immerse myself in the history of the place, and paint like Van Gogh during one of his happy periods (because I'm sure he had happy periods before the whole cutting-off-his-ear thing).

But I couldn't do it.

I carried Dallas in my DNA, felt its brand on my skin as surely as if someone had taken a cattle prod with a big *D* to my butt. I was bound by kin to stay near enough to Cissy so

I would be close if she needed me. Try as I might to fight the bond between us—both the city and my mother—there it was. And it was steel.

Malone occasionally talked about going back to St. Louis, and I hoped he wouldn't. Because I'm not sure I could leave my home again, not even for love.

Or in spite of it.

As I approached the West Village, I spotted the Magnolia Theatre's red and blue neon lights, and I suddenly found myself wishing I were heading there with Brian, to sit in the back row of a cool art film, his arm around me, my head on his shoulder.

Instead, I aimed to pick up his ex-girlfriend, who'd promised to drive to a strip club with me so I could grill a barmaid named Lu about whether or not my missing beau had slipped out the back of the joint with a girl in a G-string.

Oh, boy.

I'd run that one through my mind a couple hundred times already, and it still sounded awful, any way I phrased it.

I swallowed the lump in my throat, assuring myself I'd have the situation ironed out before the night was through. Then Brian could come home, and everyone could return to their regularly scheduled lives.

Man, how I hoped that was true.

I double-parked the Jeep alongside a shiny black Escalade that easily took up two spaces in front of the Taco Diner, and I honked the horn lightly, noting Allie was right where she'd said she'd be: under the eaves, sipping from a plastic cup and chatting with a blond-haired guy in a Tommy windbreaker. (Not that she said she'd be flirting with anyone, but I wasn't surprised.)

Another toot of the horn—which sounded a shrilling duet with the horn of the Audi behind me, no doubt wanting me to move my double-parked butt pronto—and Allie finally glanced my way. I watched her palm a card off on the unsuspecting gentleman before she scurried my way, climbed up, and hopped in with a, "Whew, did you see him? Wasn't he hot?"

I doubt Mother Teresa had ever hit on anyone before one of her missions of mercy. Allie needed a little more practice apparently.

She could've used a few instructions on backseat driving, too, for as soon as we got going, she was giving me heat.

"Oh, no, don't go that way, do it this way, Kendricks," she commanded, and wagged a finger to point out her shortcuts until we were safely on Northwest Highway and heading west, toward our target.

Obviously, she knew the route by heart.

I didn't want to ask how.

She sipped her margarita and blabbed about some of the less than stellar men who'd done her wrong, obviously her attempt at a sisterhood-type bonding, but I didn't even have the generosity of spirit to feign interest. All I could think about was Brian and what was going on with him. Nothing I could come up with was anything less than anxiety-provoking on any level.

Instead, I tried to focus on the road ahead, on the surroundings and the far from picturesque scenery, though my thoughts kept skipping in.

Under the Marsh Lane overpass we went.

What was it my daddy used to say? That there's always

a light at the end of the tunnel, but sometimes it was the headlamp on a train?

To my left, a generic-looking Walgreens squatted beneath the looming presence of a Jack Daniel's billboard.

Did Brian drink too much, do something stupid that he woke up regretting? That rendered him too guilt-ridden to call me?

Planes with blinking lights multiplied against the dark blue sky as we neared Love Field.

Did he let some big ol' jet airliner carry him too far away? Did he have a blond bimbo packed in his suitcase?

Auto lots with No Credit signs abounded.

If he'd skipped out without leaving me so much as a Dear Andy note, he'd better not plan on coming back.

I caught the flickering red letters of a Family Dollar.

What's a broken heart worth these days? Did it even rate a buck?

Shabby edifices with neon advertisements for "restaurant" and "buffet," missing letters like a poor man's version of *Wheel of Fortune*, minus Vanna in sequins to jazz things up.

I'd like to solve the puzzle, Pat. The phrase is, "My boyfriend abandoned me for a stripper." I won, I won! So what's my prize? A trip for one to Loserville?

The Jeep zipped past Webb Chapel toward Harry Hines, passing countless liquor stores, gas stations, and Mexican places. A bingo parlor with a churchlike steeple flashed blue and pink neon.

What if something happened to Brian? I should be praying that he's okay, not envisioning him living out Paul Simon's "Fifty Ways to Leave Your Lover." Unless he jumped on the bus, Gus, or made a new plan, Stan. He had no key, Lee, so he could set himself free pretty damned easily.

A Jaguar dealership sat right next door to a Best Western. *Could be we were just too different to pull this off. Maybe Mother was right. What if Brian and I were avoiding discussions of, um, anything more permanent than what we had because we both realized subconsciously that artists and lawyers don't mix any better than oil and water? That we'd been doomed from the first?*

"It's there, Andy," Allie piped up from beside me, flinging a pointed finger into my peripheral vision. "Take a left about half a block."

I saw an IHOP, and farther up the road, the sign I'd been dreading and seeking. I nudged the blinker.

"Got it," I said as a left arrow click-clacked on the dash, and I turned into the driveway that took us toward a pink stucco wall with a sign that declared, THE MEN'S CLUB. A pair of ornamental lions perched on either end, intended to add a touch of class, I figured, as if that would do the trick.

Minispots illuminated the pale pink façade. Strands of tiny white lights rimmed the roof. As I pulled around to the porte cochere where valets awaited in white shirts and dark pants, Allie let out a dry laugh and remarked, "Oh, God, I still remember when Brian first brought me here. It wasn't at all what I'd expected. No, scratch that. It was pretty much just what I'd pictured, so it was kind of a letdown."

When Brian first brought her here? Malone had taken her to a strip club?

"C'mon, Kendricks, wipe the stricken look from your

face," the Blond Menace said, and lightly smacked my arm. "I asked him to do it. It wasn't his idea or anything. In fact, he tried to talk me out of it. But I just wanted to *see*. I was curious. I'm sure you know what I mean."

Um, actually, no. I didn't.

I'd lived nearly thirty-one years of my life without the desire to go inside a place where women took their clothes off for money. I didn't even want to traipse inside *this* one on this particular night, but I had no choice.

"You and I are very different, Allie," is all I said, a huge understatement.

"You think?" came her sarcastic reply, and I bit my tongue to keep from uttering another word, likely one I'd regret.

As tempting as it was, I wasn't about to play the superior game, not when she was doing me a favor by being there. Much as I hankered to pin an insult on her skinny tail, it didn't seem right.

The pimple-faced valet didn't look any too surprised to see two women in the Jeep when he opened the door for me, while I let the car idle. I'm sure he'd seen everything several times over.

"Be gentle," I said as I left the key in the ignition (minus the rest of my key ring) and scrambled down and out.

"Have a good evening, ladies," he drawled, and I expected a salacious wink but didn't get one. Neither did he comment on the dusty state of my Wrangler, despite it being outclassed by the shiny Jags, Mercedes, and Beemers waiting in line behind it.

As far as I was concerned, that valet had already earned his tip.

"C'mon, Kendricks. Let's go."

I swallowed hard, tucking my purse tightly under my arm as I followed Allie up the steps, toward the doors, trying to keep my jaw from dropping as I noted the front windows on the right-hand side were filled with naughty lingerie.

What kind of men shopped at a strip joint, for Pete's sake?

Geez, but I'd led a sheltered life.

"Yo, girl, pick up the pace," Allie called, already at the door and holding it wide. "There's nothing to be scared of, for God's sake."

Oh, really?

I wondered if Brian had felt as discombobulated when he'd walked up these stairs to enter The Men's Club with Matty, or if it had seemed more matter of fact for him, something that guys did every once in a while, sort of a rite of passage, a male-bonding thing.

No biggie.

Just dropping in for a few hours to ogle naked women they didn't know.

Andy, Andy, Andy.

I chastised myself, feeling so damned judgmental.

Honestly, was it any different than my going to the Chippendale's? Although those guys didn't do the full Monty, merely unwrapped everything *but* the package. It was a dance revue, albeit a slightly risqué one. But nobody did any lap dancing, not really.

Okay, okay, so maybe I'd even been in a vaguely compromising position with a sweat-drenched, partially clad male dancer who shall remain nameless (because I had no clue what his name was); but it wasn't the same. Was it?

Besides, I'd gone home last night. I hadn't disappeared and left behind rumors that I'd run off with a bimbo.

"Kendricks! Snap to!" Allie barked again, pulling me through the doorway with not a little force, as a pair of college-age boys made impatient noises behind us.

Could she blame me for dragging my heels?

Allie smartly held me aside and let the pair in their SMU sweatshirts pay the pretty hostess at the podium. Beyond, another pair of thick doors awaited us, and I glimpsed the lights and noise within as the back-patting buddies practically skipped their way inside.

Then it was our turn.

"How much?" I asked the overprocessed blonde in the bulging bustier.

When she told me, I balked, but Allie clapped a hand on my shoulder, reminding me to pull myself together.

Before I shelled out the cover charge for each of us, I removed a photo of Malone that I'd tucked in my bag. I passed it over to the hostess, who glanced at me like I was a stalker, or a downtrodden wife looking for a stray husband.

"You're not a cop, are you?" she asked instead, and a burly bouncer who'd been standing on the sidelines moseyed on over, like things had suddenly gotten interesting.

Allie tensed beside me and shot me a look, like, "What the hell is that about? You want to get us thrown out?"

But I didn't care.

"No." I shook my head. "I'm just trying to find my boyfriend. He was here last night with a friend, for a sort of two-man bachelor party, only he didn't make it home and no one seems to know what happened to him."

The bouncer glanced at Brian's picture, the frown on his face unchanged.

Apparently disinterested in my plight, he wandered back toward the double doors.

The hostess sighed. "Sorry." She passed the photo back. "Can't say as I remember the guy. You know how many men pass through here each night?"

I figured it likely even beat the answer to, "How many inches of makeup am I wearing?"

I didn't want to know.

"If anything comes to mind, maybe you could call me," I said and fished for a business card in my purse, which I dutifully handed her. "I have money, so I could pay for any information you recall."

"Money?" The tip of her tongue slid along her lips, and I could tell I'd pushed the "greed" button. "How much?"

"Depends on how helpful you are," I said while she stared at my card. "Anyway, spread the word around, okay? And thanks for your time," I told her, though she'd been no help at all.

"Hey, miss . . . um, hostess person." Allie shouldered her way up to the podium. "You know if Lu's working?" she asked the Guardian of the Cover Charge, something I probably should've checked on before we'd driven all the way down to this mangy spot on the map.

"Lu McCarthy?" The made-up mask of a face appeared skeptical. "You a friend of hers? Don't believe I've seen you around before."

"Yeah, we're friends," Allie said, faking it like the professional liar she was. "Though I don't come here much, sorry. Not really into eyeballing the home team."

"Ah, well, your loss." The Hostess with the Mostest grinned. "Lu's around. Her shift's till closing. Go hang by the bar and you'll find her fast enough," she offered, before she ignored us entirely and bestowed a wide grin on a tribe of already inebriated fellows noisily stumbling into the foyer.

"Hop to, Nancy Drew." Allie took my arm and tugged me toward the double doors, and I felt my heart beating hard enough to jump through my rib cage.

Only the thudding wasn't all my heart, I realized, as Allie pried open the portal to Stripper World and shoved me in.

Chapter 8

Music assailed my ears, the bass thumping palpably through the air, and I felt its pounding in my chest, keeping pace with my frantic pulse.

I stood stock-still for a long moment, drinking in the place: the blue lights punctuated by green flashes of laser; the sight of a lone female, working a boa on a brightly lit but tiny stage, completely ignoring the pole. There was a bar to my right, and a raised area to my left where people moved in shadow.

Barmaids in tiny corsets and skimpy skirts sashayed back and forth between the bar and the sea of tables, and ladies (should I call them "ladies"?) with pasties over nipples or flat-out bare-breasted, sauntered this way and that, clearly looking to make a few extra bucks by various and sundry means.

Across the room, a pale rump raised itself from a table-top, and a man pantomimed spanking. There were any number of lap dances in progress, and I found myself watching, like a rubbernecker would a car wreck.

Good God, was this really playing out right in front of my eyes?

Could it get any more surreal?

If I hadn't known better, I would've sworn I was on a movie set. Real life—*my* real life—seemed so far removed from this.

So this is what a purportedly high-class strip club looks like, I reasoned, my brain assimilating what my gaze took in, wishing I could see the fun in it; but the sole description that came to mind was, *Ick.*

No, *Double ick.*

No wonder Gloria Steinem looked so tired. If this was part of what she was fighting, she had no time to sleep.

"Hey."

I don't think I blinked until Allie toed me with a pointed pump.

"Yo, Kendricks, let's make this quick, okay? You're looking pretty green, and I don't think it's the lighting."

I did feel a bit queasy.

Normally, I'd be the one barging into a situation, using any means necessary to find the answers I was seeking.

Only something was different this time. It was as if a part of me was afraid that the answers might be ones I didn't want to hear. What if I was in denial and this was the beginning of the end for me and Brian?

I couldn't bear to consider it.

Thankfully, Allie didn't wait for me to take the initiative. Instead, she took the reins and headed straight for the bar. I tagged along behind her, not moving quite so quickly, disconcerted by my anxiety as much as by the barrage of ZZ Top's "Pearl Necklace" on my eardrums while a redhead—literally, red as the stripes on the flag—shook her booty on the stage. I wondered if her mother had a clue where she was working or what shade of Miss Clairol she was using.

By the time I caught up with her, Allie's attention had homed in on a brunette in a red bustier, approaching with a tray of empties. As the bartender had stopped ragging the bar to point a finger directly at this particular serving wench, I had a pretty good feeling it was Lu McCarthy.

My insides clenched, and I hovered at Allie's elbow, waiting as the barmaid sauntered up and plunked her tray atop the ledge.

"I'm on break, Cricket. Be back in ten," she said to the bartender, loudly enough so he could catch her words over the music.

Cricket?

The guy was as burly as a linebacker, with a shaved head and eyebrows that resembled mating caterpillars. I could even make out a tattoo, or at least the angled tips of a winged critter—I'm guessing a hawk or an eagle as opposed to Big Bird—wrapping around his thick neck.

"Hey, Lu? It is Lu, isn't it?" I heard Allie say, before I even considered opening my trap. "Any chance my friend and I can chat with you a spell? We're hoping you can help us."

The fierce-looking bartender chirped—and I mean *chirped,* which might explain the "Cricket" thing—"Girlfriend, they want to chat with you 'bout that dude you saw leave with Ms. Trash."

Ms. Trash? I mused. Man, the folks around here had weird names, but maybe that was part of the ambiance.

Lu looked blank, or else she was doing a damned fine impression of Little Orphan Annie.

"Guy looked a little like John Cusack in his *Say Anything* days, only with glasses," the bartender added to jog her memory.

I squinted, trying to picture Malone as John Cusack, or the reverse. I didn't see it. I'd always thought Brian had more of a Tom Hanks "aw shucks" quality.

"With a touch of Matt Damon from *Good Will Hunting*," Cricket added. "He had that brainy look to him."

Okay, I'd give him that.

"Oh, yeah, that dude," Lu said, apparently recovered from her brush with short-term memory loss. She turned from Cricket and gave me a chin-jerk. "So your man never made it home?"

"No," I said, squirming in my shoes. "The friend he was here with last night, Matty, said he paid you to go backstage after Malone. He told me you saw him leave with a woman."

"Yeah, with a girl who works here." Lu took a long look at me. She had a nice face with large brown eyes and short dark hair. "He really hasn't turned up since then?"

"No," I got out, my voice scratchier than a wool sweater. I was still having trouble believing this whole scenario was real, when it felt anything but.

"So he's missing, huh?" the suddenly talkative barmaid continued giving me the third degree. "Like that TV show with the FBI guys who're really hot?"

"Um, I guess, sure." Except no hot FBI guys were

involved in this hunt for Malone, just me and Allie Mc-Squeal. "He's, um, kind of been out of touch since last night," I said, and felt that lump in my throat return, though it had never really left, not since I'd talked to Matty.

Lu threw a glance at her pal Cricket before she addressed me again. "Look, hon, I don't know you, and I've got no right to tell you this, but the dude's obviously a jerk. Maybe you're better off," she said and crossed her arms over the swell of breasts that overflowed the tightly strung corset.

"Yep, he's a jerk all right," Allie repeated. "The poor girl's going out of her mind, wondering what happened to him. He hasn't even called, for crying out loud."

Thanks, Dr. Fraud, but I hadn't gone out of my mind quite yet. Still, all this drama was doing a fine job of turning my guts into a twisted mess, like funnel cakes at the Texas State Fair. All that was missing was the powdered sugar.

The brunette in the lace-up dominatrix boots glanced over at Cricket as if for reassurance. He shrugged, apparently finding the two of us plenty harmless, and Lu's face puckered, making a decision.

"Let's see if Trayla's in back," she said. "She's got half a set to make up tonight sometime, since she took off with your dude before she finished last night. She should be getting dressed"—wait, shouldn't that be "undressed"? I wanted to say, but didn't—"though I haven't seen her yet. She's kinda flaky, Trayla is, more into men with dough than the dancing. But if anyone can set you straight, it's her. Follow me, all right?"

So we did.

I had Brian's picture in my pocket, which I planned to slide under the nose of this stripper called Trayla—*what the heck kind of name was that, anyway?*—just as soon as we reached a place with better lighting than inside the club, where everything but the stage was dimly lit.

Maybe the guy who took off with G-String Girl wasn't Malone at all, and it was purely a case of mistaken identity. A lot of guys in Dallas wore button-down shirts and glasses. Preppy had never gone out of style, not here. Although, if Lu said, "Oh, sorry, I was wrong, that wasn't him," it would leave me with even more questions, wouldn't it? Namely the unresolved biggie of where on God's green earth *was* Malone?

My mother's announcement of her trip to Vegas with Stephen was unsettling enough. I definitely didn't need this on top of everything. If I got any more unwelcome surprises, I'd have to hit the Pepto hard before I went to bed.

I followed on Allie's heels behind Lu, weaving around the stage, showered in vibrant red lights as a woman peeled off a crimson-feathered brassiere and tossed it to the floor, while she worked what her mama (and, obviously, the plastic surgeon) gave her.

Lu approached what looked like a dim rectangle cut into the wall to the left of the stage, drew the portal open, and the three of us slipped inside.

As the door settled shut with a firm click, I realized the music had faded to a more bearable decibel, though I could still feel the thump of the bass through the walls. It brought back memories of the tiny apartment I'd shared with my friend Molly O'Brien in Chicago during college, when I'd learned to appreciate ear plugs and the whir of a fan when I needed peace and quiet.

Through a narrow hallway we went, doors on either side, some closed and a few cocked open wide enough that I could see girls in front of mirrors, getting dressed—or, rather, undressed—for the stage.

But Lu didn't stop until she'd reached a room at the farthest end, near a glowing EXIT sign with a fire door heading outside. I noticed a star, cut out of foil, taped to the painted metal with a giant black *T* in the center. It looked like a child had made it. Still, I was impressed the woman had her own dressing room.

"Hey, Ms. Trayla Trash, it's me. You in there?" Lu called, but didn't wait for a reply. She put a hand on the knob and pushed.

Trayla Trash? That was her name?

Are you kidding me?

Though, come to think of it, why not? I mean, what better to precede "trash" than "trayla," and it had a nice redneck ring to it.

I watched Lu go in and Allie after her, before I went inside, nearly bumping into them both as they stood still as statues.

Though I wasn't sure why.

I'd expected a mess of feather boas and sequins, itty-bitty outfits slung over a chair or an old-fashioned hinged screen, but not *this* kind of a mess.

The only chair in the room lay on its side.

A square mirror lit by round bulbs had smudges of makeup all over it. A photo with the edges curled clung to the edge of the frame. Tiny chunks of Scotch tape still glued to the glass told me there'd been more pictures once, though someone had obviously snatched them off.

Below the mirror, an enormous makeup case spilled its contents across the vanity. Tubes of lipstick, powder compacts, and tubs of eye shadow littered the ledge of Formica. Some kind of lotion with glitter gleamed in a shiny puddle.

Yuck.

On the floor beneath were several tissues smeared red with rouge. At least, it looked like rouge.

I wasn't touching those babies with a ten-foot pole, even if they were crumpled maps drawn in Revlon guiding me directly to my missing boyfriend.

"She wasn't exactly a neatnik, was she?" I remarked, for want of anything better to say. *She walks in filth,* came to mind.

Lu let out a humorless laugh. "Girl, it's looked a whole lot worse than this. Only something's different. Let me think."

She put a finger to painted lips and made a few slow turns in the tiny space, and I tried to imagine how things could look any worse.

"Ah." Lu stopped and stared at a bare nail on the wall. "What happened to her pretty picture? A rich dude she was dating gave it to her, and she was so proud of it. Showed it off to anyone who'd look. She wouldn't take it unless—" The barmaid in the bustier froze for a second, the skin beneath her overdone makeup suddenly several shades paler. "—unless she wasn't coming back," she finished in a much quieter tone.

"You think she took off and didn't plan on returning?" Allie asked, voicing my thoughts exactly.

Lu pressed glossy red fingertips to her forehead. "But when I saw her leaving last night, she only had her robe on. Why would she split without getting dressed? And without finishing her set?"

"Could she have been fired? Told to leave without packing?" Allie offered, and Lu shook her head, clearly upset.

"If she was, nobody said a word, and she was making a bundle in tips, so I know she wouldn't have quit unless something came up all sudden-like." Lu looked at me accusingly. "I'll bet it has something to do with your man. Maybe she ran off with him."

Oh, puh-leeze.

This had gone far enough.

If I had to listen to one more misstatement about my boyfriend and this "hootchie mama," as Allie had called her, I would explode like a carton of toxic yogurt.

I whipped the photo of Malone out of my back pocket and held it right in front of Lu's kohl-lined eyes.

"Is this the guy you saw going out the back door with your friend? Because, if it's not, don't be afraid to admit your error. He was wearing a pink button-down shirt and blue jeans. I can understand your making a mistake, since it was late and kinda dark and really loud."

If my heart wasn't banging in my ears before, it was now.

She chewed on her glossy lips for a minute, studying the shot I'd taken of Malone while we'd moseyed around the Botanical Gardens last weekend. It had been a gorgeous fall day, more like spring, and we'd enjoyed every minute.

Lu exhaled hard, like she was blowing out smoke, and pushed the photo back in my hands. "Yeah, that's him. I'd recognize him anywhere."

My heart did a nosedive. "You're positive?"

"Yeah, I said so, didn't I?"

"But—"

"But nothing." She narrowed her eyes on me, and I saw pity in them. "Hon, it was him. Same preppy glasses. Same button-down collar. He looked so straight, but I guess he's a bad boy at heart, huh? So many of 'em are like that."

No, I wanted to shout. *He wasn't.*

Or was he?

"Was he someone important?" she asked. "Like a politician?"

"No," I said softly. "No one important." Except to me.

I held the photo before my own eyes with a shaky hand, staring at the face I thought I knew so well, the gentle smile, the blue eyes warmly crinkled behind the thin wire-rims. It was all I could do to keep breathing.

"What else do you want, Kendricks?" Allie was quickly on me. "An affidavit? A videotape? A signed confession?"

I glared at her.

Lu murmured, "Sorry, girls, but I'm as confused as y'all," before tacking on, "Stay put, okay? Let me check with the office and see what they know."

She took off, leaving me with black-hearted Allie, who probably wouldn't know what sympathy was if it ran over her in a bulldozer.

She had a sour look on her face that I didn't like. Her slender nose wrinkled, her eyes squinted meanly.

"Spit it out, for Pete's sake, and quit looking at me like that," I demanded none too nicely; because I knew exactly what she was thinking, and I didn't want to hear it. "Don't you dare tell me you honestly believe Brian ran off with this . . . trailer trash person, or I'll have to kill you with my bare hands."

"All right, I won't say it." But she continued to stare squarely at me, forehead pleated. "No, dammit, I will. I'll say exactly what I'm thinking, because it's sounding more and more like the truth every minute."

"Stop—" I tried, but she didn't listen.

"They hooked up, Kendricks. Malone got a buzz in his britches for a hootchie mama, and he went home with her, now he's too embarrassed to show his face. What other explanation is there?"

"Stop it." Despite myself, I started trembling. This was wrong. Completely wrong and upside down. Not really happening. "I won't assume the worst before I have the chance to talk to Brian."

My daddy had always taught me to never judge too swiftly, for fear of getting things totally ass backward.

I *knew* Brian. Maybe not backward and forward, perhaps not all the littlest details or even some middling ones, but well enough to be sure he wouldn't pull a stunt like this. It didn't sound like him at all, and I was not going to buy it until he looked me in the eye and said, "Andy, I've left you for another woman."

Only then would it be true.

"Don't be a fool." Allie made a noise of disgust and toed a sequined boa lying near her sharp-toed pump. "The stripper in question has obviously flown the coop, and there's no sign of Malone, not at home, not at work, not with any of his friends. I'm piss-poor at math, but I can put two and two together."

"It's not what it seems," I resisted. "You're wrong, Allie. It doesn't add up."

"You're in denial, girl."

I fought the urge to attack.

If I hadn't hated Allie Price before, I hated her now, with a passion.

But pulling her hair out by the roots wasn't going to help.

As Allie righted the room's only chair and planted herself in it, I stepped over to the mirror and plucked the photo from the frame.

It showed a petite woman with enormous blond hair—flipped up like Farrah Fawcett, just as Matty had described—wearing the tiniest of panties and a spangled bra, posing in this very room, only there was a small framed painting hanging on the wall behind her. I could just barely make out a horse's hind end.

Must have been the "pretty picture" Lu had mentioned.

I put the photo back just as Lu reappeared. Her expression didn't reassure me any, not with her eyes all teary.

"Nobody's heard from Trayla since last night," she said and blinked back tears with tarantula lashes. "I can't believe she'd bail without telling me. Not that we were that tight, but she used to stay and have a drink with me after hours sometimes, before we closed. She had dreams, Trayla did. She wanted to be somebody. Said she had big plans for herself." Lu sniffled. "Could be her plans included your guy."

My guy?

Straight-Shooting, Straight-Laced, Full of Midwestern Sensibility Brian Malone?

Impossible.

There was a greater chance of The Men's Club turning into a nunnery.

"No," I said, because Lu was dead wrong. Any plans her stripper pal had with a man definitely didn't include Malone.

Allie laughed, and I felt relieved at first, assuming I wasn't the only one who found Lu's assertion absurd. Until she opened her pie hole and cackled, "This is priceless. Really. Brian's probably never screwed up in his life, and all of a sudden he's walking on the wild side with a woman who straddles a pole for a living."

"I'm gonna miss her," Lu babbled, off somewhere in her own little miserable world. "Betsy was a real firecracker."

"Betsy?" Allie piped up. "So her real name wasn't Trayla?"

"All the girls make up names for the stage," Lu replied.

"You know Betsy's last name?" Allie went for broke.

"No," Lu said. "Sorry. I never asked. She wasn't much for hanging out with the girls. She always had some kind of rich boyfriend who was takin' her out."

Well, that counted out Malone then, as he still had student loans to pay off, and the last time we'd gone to the movies, I'd had to pay for the tickets *and* the Junior Mints.

But it didn't explain why Brian had chased Trayla backstage and why he'd left with her, if that's what really happened.

It could've been a weird coincidence, I told myself.

One of those rare cosmic occurrences that only happened when there was a Harvest Moon.

Or not.

My teeth began to chatter.

"So no one knows where Trayla went off to?" Allie asked, because I stood there like an idiot, staring at the makeup-smeared mirror and the way it distorted my reflection.

"Nancy in the office said Trayla's home phone was disconnected and that one of the girls had heard her mention something about getting a ticket out," Lu related.

A ticket out, huh?

Hopefully, that was a solo flight and not a trip for two with my missing boyfriend.

A wave of nausea hit me, just contemplating it.

No, no, no.

This wasn't happening, not to me.

Brian would never *ever* cheat.

Would he?

I shook my head, saying, "No," repeatedly, even as a wave of dizziness swept through me, so fierce that I had to lean on Allie to stay upright.

"Kendricks, you okay?"

Her voice was garbled, thick as peanut butter.

"You're not gonna faint, are you?"

Faint? Me?

Hell, no.

I'm a Blevins Kendricks. We don't swoon.

Nope. What we have are weak stomachs.

With a gut-wrenching heave, I leaned over and puked on the vinyl flooring.

Adios, banana pancakes.

Or what was left of them anyway.

"Jesus, Kendricks! You nearly tossed your cookies on my Jimmy Choos!" Allie screeched.

I balanced hands on thighs, my legs vaguely shaking, lifting my head to mutter, "Sorry," but I didn't mean it.

I'd missed her Choos?

Damn.

This was clearly not my lucky day.

Chapter 9

Allie took the wheel on the way home. Said she didn't trust me in control of anything as deadly as an automobile when I was nearly catatonic.

She was afraid I'd drive us both into a tree, and all because I couldn't summon the energy to do more than stare blankly at her rapid-fire questions: "Are you gonna puke again? You need to lie down? Want me to call your mother? How about your therapist?"

I didn't have a therapist—surprising, huh?—nor did I have the oomph to utter anything but monosyllables; though she needn't have worried for her life.

Odd as it sounded, it wasn't her I wanted to kill, not this time.

It was Malone.

If he had truly done the terrible deeds that everyone was trying so hard to convince me he had, I figured a raking over hot coals while tarred and feathered was too good for him.

But I had to find him first.

I had to hear the words "We are through . . . over . . . done . . . kaput" from his lips before I'd wave my white flag and surrender to heartbreak.

Oh, and I would.

Find him, that is.

That Nazi Hunter dude had nothing on me. I was pushy, nosy, and I had plenty of resources, not to mention infinite vacation days.

Being that I worked for myself—thanks to the trust fund Daddy had bestowed on me from the time I was eighteen, meaning my mostly pro bono Web design work didn't have to pay all my bills (and seldom did)—I could take off as long as I needed to track down my errant boyfriend.

I'd left business cards with Lu the Busty Barmaid and the soprano-voiced bartender, along with the offer of money for information—ditto the overly made-up hostess and bouncer in the foyer—all on the off-chance Malone turned up at The Men's Club again or someone would remember something they'd forgotten to mention. (It's amazing how often cash can jog one's memory.)

Although I seriously hoped the next phone call I got was from Brian, explaining this whole mess away.

Just in case he had and I'd missed him, I checked my voice mail—cell and home—only to come up empty yet again.

Was it possible to feel so mixed up that you imploded?

If so, it surely would've happened to me right on the passenger seat of my years' old Jeep.

For cryin' out loud.

I leaned my forehead against the window, the glass cold against my skin, and I was glad for it, as hot and bothered as I was (and not in a good way). The nighttime scenery whooshed past in a blur of neon and traffic lights, and I paid attention to none of it.

My mind was back in Stripperville, as was the bulk of my brunch.

How could he? the uncertain part of me screamed, while the reasonable half calmly answered, *He didn't.*

I squeezed my eyes shut and recalled all the things Malone had said to me in recent days, how he was tired, couldn't wait to be done with this latest case so he could spend more time with me and catch up on his sleep (I wasn't sure which came first in his list of priorities, but I was hoping it was me). He'd mentioned taking me to Mother's for my birthday dinner on Wednesday, plus something about a "surprise" for the coming weekend. I usually didn't like surprises, but I'd been anxious to see what he'd cooked up.

So long as it wasn't his running off with a wench called Trayla Trash. If so, that could well be the shittiest birthday present I'd ever received from anyone, including the time in first grade when Mike Weber had given me a booger sandwich.

Yuck.

Imagining Brian canoodling with a stripper gave me a double dose of the heebie-jeebies.

It went way beyond "ick."

I shuddered, figuring that was one picture worth a thousand words . . . all of them curses. The only worse thing than imagining Brian with another woman was thinking of attending my mother's dinner without him.

Oh, Lord, why had I gone there?

My brain did a momentary freeze.

Dinner at Mother's.

Gulp.

What if I hadn't gotten this insanity straightened out by then? What if Malone didn't come back by Wednesday?

How would I explain showing up at Cissy's house sans boyfriend? Particularly if the explanation was X-rated?

I'd never hear the end of it.

"I told you so," would undoubtedly be Mother's warm-up act. I didn't even want to ponder Act Two.

I groaned loudly and dropped my head to my hands, which must've freaked out Allie, as she jumped all over me again: "Do I need to pull over? Are you gonna puke? Roll down the window and hang your head out, why don't you?"

Hang my head out the window? Did she think I was Lassie?

"I'm fine," I told her, sounding anything but.

"Listen, Kendricks," she started in, as if I needed another of her lectures, "I'm nearly as mad at the son of a bitch as you, so there's no need to mope alone. We've got loads to do on the Oleksiy case and Brian knows it, so if he really skipped out, I'll murder him for you. And I'll know by tomorrow morning, bright and early. If he's left town, he'd better have called in to work with a dandy excuse, or he'll find his ass on the street. I'll buzz you as soon as I hear something."

Great.

A morning wake-up call from the Blond Menace.

Yet another thrilling moment to look forward to.

Why didn't God just strike me down and be done with it? Why was I being tortured? Was this payback for missing so many Sundays of church? For deciding organized religion just wasn't my thing? For bailing out on my debut?

If God worked in mysterious ways, would His plan for teaching me a lesson be so elaborate as this? So gut-wrenching?

Although I had learned one thing that surprised me.

Allie Price wasn't as completely unbearable as I'd pegged her initially. In fact, she was being awfully close to nice, when she could've easily shoved the knife in good and given it a turn or two. She might've reminded me again how Malone and I hadn't even lasted as a couple as long as they had. She had ample opportunity to expound for the hundredth time on how even Boy Scouts can be pigs.

Instead, she did an amazing thing, offering to drive me home in the Jeep and take a cab from there, though I told her no, I could handle the return trip all by myself. She did a quick "how many fingers am I holding up" test, as if to check my level of alertness—if not my sobriety, though I hadn't drunk a thing—and seemed satisfied when I passed.

When she pulled the Wrangler into a parking space at the Taco Diner, she shifted the Jeep into Park, turned to me, and asked if I wanted to head in for a margarita or three. "Don't beat yourself up, girlfriend," she told me. "'Cuz when you think about it, really, how well do we know anyone? Everyone has secrets. Even Malone."

"No," I said. "Brian and I had"—why did I say that? I meant—"we have a great relationship. We talk about everything."

"Nobody talks about *everything,* Kendricks. That's just a lie we tell ourselves to keep from feeling insecure."

I had no strength to argue with her. Besides, it wasn't worth it.

"Sure you don't want to have a drink? I'll buy, and you can bitch if you need to," she suggested, but I'd had enough "bitch" for tonight.

"I want to be by myself," I told her, because it's how I felt. I needed time alone to wade in my self-pity without spectators.

"You sure you don't want company, just in case?"

Just in case *what*?

Did she think I aimed to swallow a bottle of Drano (definitely the most lethal substance I possessed) or slit my wrists with a butter knife (the sharpest object in my house, since I was afraid of pointy things, being that I was a Grade-A klutz)?

"I'm fine, Allie, really I am," I assured her, though she didn't look like she believed me. Maybe because I hadn't said, "I'm fine, bitch," which would've been more in line with our relationship, if not my rotten mood.

"You have my number, right?"

"Yeah." It was stuck on my phone after her calls earlier in the day.

"Let me know if you hear anything from the ratfink."

I didn't need to ask who she meant. "I will."

She hopped out of the Jeep, and I crawled over to the driver's side, sliding my legs beneath the steering wheel.

I shut the door, threw the car into gear, and left her standing on the curb.

If that was ill-mannered, I'm sorry. Add it to my long list of misbehavior that would've required confession if I'd been Catholic. As a bad Presbyterian, I'd probably just get my retribution at the Pearly Gates, when I realized my key didn't fit the lock and the room I'd booked was much nearer the furnace.

Oh, well.

After tossing my cookies on the floor of a stripper's dressing room, I figured I couldn't sink much lower than that.

It was funny how life's curveballs could toss etiquette out the window (sorry, Amy Vanderbilt).

My mother would be appalled were she to learn where I'd been tonight and why, which is precisely why I planned to keep mum on the subject. Though, feeling as weak as I did, I couldn't vouch for how closed-mouth I would be if Mother out-strong-armed me, like she had last Christmas when she'd bamboozled me into a stint behind the cookbook booth at the Junior League Holiday Bazaar.

Cissy was a wily one, for sure, especially if she knew I'd kept a secret from her. My mother wasn't big on secrets between us (unless they were hers).

As I drove to the condo, I did a pretty good job convincing myself this had merely been "one of those days"—although an extremely sucky one—and, by tomorrow, everything would look peachy keen. My boyfriend would return with some amazing tale of how he'd had to play hero and whisk a barely breathing Trayla Trash to the E.R. after her boa had caught fire (or something equally life or death); my world would fall back in order, and this would be one hilarious blip on my cosmic EKG.

I parked the Jeep, unlocked the door, went inside and brushed my teeth to get the rotten taste from my mouth. I checked my voice mail one last time before I peeled off my jeans and crawled in bed in T-shirt and panties.

It'd been a while since I'd said my prayers, but I said them that night.

Maybe that was what eased me into dreamland so quickly, when I'd figured I'd lie awake forever, staring at the ceiling through the dark, worrying until the dawn began to fill my room with sunlight.

I don't even remember dreaming; but I did feel the jerk as I came awake.

For a moment, I didn't move, heard only my slug-slow breaths and the noise of my heartbeat.

Then I realized what had interrupted my dozing.

The phone was ringing.

Not my cell, atop my bedside table, but the landline in the living room, though it was damned loud enough for being so far away.

Tweeet.

I would've ignored it, as worn out as I was, but something propelled me forward, the flood of hope in my chest.

I stumbled out of bed, kicking aside the covers, banging into the doorjamb as I flew as fast as my feet would carry me toward the sofa table, where I snatched the receiver off the Princess phone and gasped, "Brian?"

There was a pause that seemed eternal before I heard the familiar voice.

"Andrea?"

He sounded far off, like his cell needed charging, but it was him all right.

Hallelujah and Amen! My heart did swan dives in my chest.

"Do you know how worried I've been—" I started, but he wouldn't let me finish.

"P-Please," he stammered, and I sensed his urgency. "Don't talk, just listen."

Despite a million questions on the tip of my tongue and the equally strong impulse to ball him out, I stayed silent.

Whatever he had to say, I was all ears.

Chapter 10

 "I wanted to call s-sooner, but I couldn't get . . . I'm sorry," he said, more like a muffled murmur through the crackling line.

He faded in and out so much that I had to press the phone hard against my head so as not to miss anything. *Where was he? In a tunnel?*

"I didn't mean for this . . . it isn't what I wanted . . . things c-changed rather suddenly."

Uh, well, duh. I'd figured out that much, unless he'd meant to cause so much conflict by dumping Matty, keeping trial documents that Allie was dying to get her hands on, and breaking my heart.

What were you thinking? I wanted to cry, though I kept my lips zipped and slumped onto the sofa, weak in the knees with relief at just hearing the sound of his voice, knowing he was alive, at least, when I'd imagined the worst.

"Apologize to Cissy for me, will you? I can't attend her dinner p-party," he continued, as I strained to hear each word.

I couldn't blame him for his nervous stutter, not when he had to realize how worried sick I'd been since he'd pulled his vanishing act.

"Tell her I'll miss her famous cabbage soup. But I won't be back . . . I have to, um, go away. And don't try to find me, Andy, p-please. I need my, uh, space."

What famous cabbage soup?

Was he on crack?

I highly doubted my mother had ever cooked anything, with or without cabbages, in her entire life. In fact, I think she thought of the stove as a great big paperweight.

Had Miz Trayla Trash taken him back to her single-wide that doubled as a meth lab, and he'd inhaled too many fumes?

That would explain a lot.

"Look, Brian, I've got a few things to say myself "—I could only be quiet for so long, and I'd reached my quota. All my frustrations and fears of the past twenty-four hours bubbled to the surface, unrestrained. "I've been going crazy trying to track you down, and you know my birth-day's this week, so what do you mean you're taking off? How could you even think of bailing?"

"Andy, no—" he started, but the words were choked off, and I picked up the click of what sounded like an air conditioner turning on. But it was in the sixties, chilly for Big D. Who in his right mind would have his AC running? "It's not what you think," he finished.

"Then what is it?" I demanded.

There was a bit of a muffled noise, like he'd dropped the phone. I figured he'd lost his signal, and I nearly hung up when he came back on again.

"I have to go . . . I'm so s-sorry, babe." His voice caught so hard I knew he meant it. He sounded near to tears, or maybe it was the bad connection.

"Hey, wait a sec—"

But there was only dead air on the other end.

An earful of nothing.

"Brian?"

I stared at the phone for a minute before my instincts kicked in. I hit the redial button, but his voice mail picked up after a single ring.

Well, damn him!

He wasn't answering.

So that was it, huh?

The pulse at my temples began to throb, and my heart stung, as if I'd been target practice for the Olympic dart team.

I'd waited twenty-four long hours to hear from the guy, and it was over in a twenty-second cell phone call. Sort of a technological version of the old *wham, bam, thank you, ma'am.*

Sling a cow pie at my head and call me Bubba.

This wasn't possible.

I clutched the receiver, hand trembling, my guts gripped with confusion; blinking into the dark, disbelief sliding up my throat like acid reflux so I couldn't even let flow a string of curses. The sound I made was more like, "Uhhh."

I couldn't react. My limbs felt weighted, too heavy to do anything but sit there, zombielike, biting on my lower lip.

I'm so sorry . . . things changed . . . I need space.

Had he really said that?

Had he *meant* it the way it sounded? Why not add the tried and true—and utterly barf-inspiring—"Let's just be friends" line, too?

Or maybe I was still dreaming and had imagined the entire pathetic one-sided conversation. I clunked myself in the head with the receiver and winced at the sting of pain in my skull.

I was awake, all right.

The realization made me groan, and I dropped the handset of the phone onto the cushion beside me, burying my face in my hands.

Brian had blown me off three days before my natal celebration.

That's what this was: a cell phone dumping.

No nicer way to put it.

Happy Birthday, loser girl.

I'd been skunked.

Which meant that everyone else was right and I was wrong, didn't it? Malone had turned to the dark side virtually overnight. Four months together, and I was being tossed for a chippie who wore fringed tassels on her nipples.

Oh, wow. Was that it?

I winced as a sudden thought struck me.

The age-old "good girl vs. slut" conundrum.

Could that be the problem? Was sex at the crux of everything?

I wore big T-shirts and flannel jammie bottoms to bed. I didn't own a pair of tassels or even a push-up bra from Victoria's Secret.

Was I not woman enough for Brian? Was I too much the girl next door and not enough ho?

I knew that teenage girls were getting bikini waxes these days, paid for by their superhip mommies, so they'd be ready for bidness at the drop of a zipper. Every MTV video bordered on soft core porn, as did half the beer commercials. The world moved faster than a quickie in the broom closet; nothing was romance or even innuendo anymore. It was hooking up and one-night stands and "drunk sex," as a friend of mine called it (without apology, I might add).

Perhaps Cissy wasn't the only one who was old-fashioned in our family, at least where love was concerned. Because that's what it was about for me, the feeling close and caring, the *emotional* part, not body parts or dirty talk or trashy accoutrements.

Is that how I'd lost Brian? After one night in a strip club to celebrate Matty's upcoming wedding?

Had he felt trapped by his faithfulness, by the mere idea he might be spending the rest of his life with me, under the thumb of my overbearing mummy? By the fact that Said Mummy expected him to put a ring on my finger and purchase this cow on layaway?

Did it scare him to imagine that maybe the idea of marriage didn't sound so all-fire awful to me either? That the idea of being legally bound to one another at some point in the future wasn't Cissy's alone?

Ohmigawd.

There it was, out in the open.

I'd admitted it, if only to myself.

I wasn't falling for Malone good and hard: I'd already

hit the mat. I was sunk, a goner, snookered, down and out for the count.

All right, so maybe I'd realized it before, but I'd been too wary to even whisper how I felt to anyone. Besides, I'd figured I had plenty of time to tell Brian, when the moment was right.

The right moment.

Talk about missing the bus.

Hell, I was sucking up exhaust fumes.

I balled my hands and tapped my fists against my forehead.

How stupid was I?

I thought I was being smart, guarded even, protecting my heart as I waited for the perfect time to say something. Though what made any time "perfect"? How did we even know we'd have another tomorrow or the next day?

We didn't.

I thought Malone and I had forever.

Instead, he'd taken my vulnerable heart and stomped it with the verbal equivalent of golf cleats.

I felt like my guts were bleeding out, and I had no Band-Aids large enough to patch up all the holes.

"You sappy-ass girl," I berated myself, making a feeble attempt at laughing into the dark and empty room where the only noise was the beep-beep-beeping from the handset that I hadn't hung up until I tossed it to the floor, yanking the phone off the sofa table and sending it clattering to the floor.

Like I gave a hoot.

I shuffled into the kitchen, where *2:35* glowed in bright blue on my microwave clock. Instinctively, I went for the freezer, pulling it wide and reaching for the Haagen Daz, until I remembered I had none.

What're you doing? I asked and stopped myself.

I shut the freezer door with a smack.

Because what I needed wasn't anything edible, it was food for my sad, just-dumped, beaten-down soul.

I walked over to the stereo and fumbled in the dim, finding the CD I'd burned years ago just for such situations. I dusted off the cover, popped that baby into the player, hit the power button, and set the volume at a reasonable level, one that I could hear but wouldn't wake up my neighbors.

Disco's infamous "I Will Survive" bounced through the speakers.

Sing it, Gloria, I thought sadly as I made my way back to the sofa and curled up, dragging the throw over me and listening to my favorite "screw you jerk for leaving me" song of all time.

I closed my eyes as "The King of Wishful Thinking" came on, another quintessential post breakup song. It was all about ignoring the hole in your heart and pretending you'd be all right, even if it wasn't the truth.

How could you, Malone? How could you do this to me?

I squished my cheek into the pillow, fighting the tears as hard as I could. I was so angry, so disappointed, so utterly confused, but I'd be damned if I would cry myself out over a man. Not again. I'd done it enough through the years, and I refused to do it now, no matter how much it hurt.

Sting started to wail "King of Pain," and I jumped up from the couch and shut my CD player off.

Enough already.

Pathetic jilted chick sobbing into her pillow.

How totally cliché.

And how totally not me.

I had never been the kind of female who didn't feel complete without a man. I had a great life, loved my independence, and I was perfectly fulfilled when I was all by my lonesome. Surely, I had better things to do than act like a dopey girl who'd been wronged by her dude.

Damned straight I did.

Besides, Malone wasn't exactly beating his breast and wailing over me, was he? No, siree Bob, he was getting his kicks with a piece of Trayla Trash.

Not worth the salt of my tears.

Roughly, I wiped my eyes and slapped at the switch to turn on the lights. Then I headed over to my easel.

I initially filled my palette with black, picked up a clean brush and let her rip, sweeping boldly across the crimson and silver with angry strokes.

I didn't stop for hours, didn't rest until I was too exhausted to lift the brush to the canvas. The result was something more violent than I'd intended, rawer emotionally, but there it was, my guts laid out in acrylics.

It felt good, somehow, to have released all that pent-up angst, and I knew that I could sleep, at least. Well, it was something.

So I went to bed, making sure to turn off the cell phone on my nightstand before I slipped under the covers and closed my eyes, too tired to weep.

But not too tired to dream.

I found myself wandering around the grounds of a state

fair, brightly colored lights and overloud laughter swirling around me. I didn't see anyone, though all the rides were in motion, the Ferris wheel rotating, the Tilt-a-Whirl spinning.

I heard a voice, someone calling, "Andy, please, help me," and I tried to follow it, but I wasn't sure where it was coming from. Everything seemed to echo in my ears. The lights blurred my vision.

Out of nowhere, a figure in a red cape flew at me, hooded so I could see no face, though she proffered a black pot in which a green stew bubbled.

"Cabbage soup?" she asked in an odd sort of cackle. "Homemade cabbage soup?"

I turned and ran from her, hearing that voice, still calling my name, and I entered the House of Mirrors, where I was suddenly surrounded by infinite reflections of myself, so I hardly knew where I started and the mirrors began.

"Andy."

There it was again, only it sounded so near.

I spun around and saw him, standing smack behind me.

"Malone," I said, glancing back, over my shoulder.

But he wasn't really there. Only more mirrors, deceiving me.

"Brian, where are you?"

I ran ahead to where I thought he was, but I hit the glass. Turned around and went the other way, only to smack into another dead end.

"Tell Cissy I'm sorry to miss the party," he was saying, starting to fade, looking blurrier by the moment. "I love her cabbage soup."

He kept talking, but it turned into gibberish, words that made no sense.

I pounded the mirror with my fists, screaming his name, until the silvered walls around me shattered, raining shards of glass.

Raining.

Pitter-pat, pitter-pat.

My eyes flew open, and I blinked at the gloom, grabbing at my clock on the nightstand, which showed nearly eight-thirty. The dim outside the shutters made sense when I realized it was actually raining, water tapping on the windowsill.

Not slivers of glass.

Then I heard a louder *tap-tap*, and it wasn't my head hammering.

I sat up in bed, strained to listen.

Someone was knocking on my door.

My T-shirt and striped sweatpants rumpled, I swung my feet to the floor and padded across the carpet that stretched wall-to-wall throughout the condo. Squinting through the peephole, I sighed at the sight of my mother, standing on my doormat, shaking out a large umbrella.

What was she doing here?

Mother rarely showed up anywhere uninvited. And I definitely hadn't extended an invitation. Although she did have a sixth sense as to when I was at a low point; often the perfect time for her to twist my arm into doing something I wouldn't do if I felt stronger. Maybe she needed another warm body for a committee she'd agreed to chair to raise money for out of work oil barons.

God only knew.

With Cissy, it could be anything.

Reluctantly, I opened the door, and she looked hard at me, wearing an impatient frown.

"Do you realize your phone is off the hook?" she asked, front and center, before using her umbrella handle to push the door out of my hands, wide enough for her to enter past me. "I've been trying to call you all morning, for heaven's sake. What on earth's the matter with you? Are you sick?"

Was I sick?

Interesting question, I mused as I shut and locked the door.

Did heartsick count? Although I was officially in denial about that, being the neofeminist that I purportedly was at heart, far beneath my ever-sensitive girlie girl skin.

"I have to finalize the menu for your birthday party with the caterer by noon, since you keep changing your mind . . ."

I kept changing my mind?

". . . and I've got a million things to do before Wednesday besides, not to mention getting ready for my trip with Stephen this coming weekend. Only you seem to be avoiding the world, so Mohammad had to come to the mountain. You don't look well." Her finely plucked brows shot up. "Good God, you're bleeding!"

I had no idea what she was talking about, until I glanced down at my arms and realized I had smears of crimson on them. No one ever said that art was neat.

"It's paint," I told her. "I was up late last night. Couldn't sleep," I admitted, then bit my lip to keep from saying more. I wasn't yet ready to tell her about Malone. I didn't know if I'd ever be ready for that.

"You don't have the flu, do you?"

She held the umbrella between us, perhaps to ward

off potential germs. In her dark cape, she looked rather like Mary Poppins, if Mary had been a society dame and dressed in Chanel and pearls instead of funny outfits.

"Do I need to call Dr. Cooper?" she pressed.

When I shook my head, she lowered her weapon, which was dripping onto my carpet, as if it were sobbing in sympathy.

Seeing as how I had no umbrella stand, she simply propped the thing against the wall then proceeded to remove her driving gloves, but not her black Burberry. She had on black suede boots that should've been destroyed by the rain. But, like Cissy herself, they appeared indestructible.

"Did you hear what I said before, Andrea?" she prodded. "About trying to reach you and not getting through?"

"I heard you," I replied.

"All I got was a busy signal, so you must've knocked the receiver awry, and your cell was turned off, though I left a message . . . ah, there! I was right."

She zoomed in on my old Princess phone that I'd pulled off the sofa table, and she gracefully stooped to retrieve it and the handset, returning both to their rightful home. The moment she did, the damned thing twittered maniacally.

Mother raised her eyebrows, and I shrugged.

So she answered, with a perfectly drawled, "Andrea Kendricks's residence," as if she were my social secretary. A hilarious thought, though I didn't smile.

"Yes, all right, well, I'll see," she replied to whoever was on the other end, before she proffered the handset. "It's someone named Allison Price. She has news about Mr. Malone. Is there a problem with your beau, my dear? Is he ill? Is that why he didn't show up for brunch?"

"He's not ill, no," I said, though he could be, for all I knew. He could have some type of rare brain fever that caused him to act like a lout.

"Andrea, your eyelid is twitching. Do you need a Xanax?"

Oh, baby, a whole lot more was twitching than my eyelid.

"No Xanax"—not yet—"just the phone, Mother, please," I said, and snatched it away, spewing into the receiver, "I don't want to hear, Allie, because I don't care. He called here last night, apologizing for bugging out on me, can you believe, and told me he needed space. *Space?* For crud's sake, what kind of an excuse is that when I gave him all the space he needed? It's not like I was his keeper or anything."

Amazing how quickly I'd taken up the "Brian is a jerk" banner after Malone's terse "Dear Jane" message delivered in chicken fashion via Ma Bell. I'm surprised he didn't go all out and send an e-mail.

My mother stood at my elbow, listening ever so intently, perfectly made-up eyes going wider by the minute.

Allie tried to say something, but I beat her to it.

"You were right. He's a jerk, a clod, a caveman, and I don't care if he does go to Vegas with that dancer slash hooker, because he can rot in Hell for all I care," I went on in a rush, only to have her cut off my tirade with a shrill, "Shut up, Kendricks, and turn on your TV right this minute! Channel 8, and hurry!"

Not that I made it a point to obey the Attila the Blonde, but I was too curious not to, being as how she sounded downright frantic.

I picked up the remote, gave it a punch, and flipped to Channel 8 just in time to see my boyfriend's—um, former boyfriend's—face in a photograph with the caption WANTED FOR QUESTIONING beneath.

Geez. I mean, I was certainly pretty upset with him, but I didn't expect the police to get in on the act.

As if that weren't enough, I saw the SkyCam helicopter zeroing in on a red car that looked uncannily like Brian's. They did a quick zoom, and I stepped closer to the TV screen, noting yellow crime scene tape and orange cones boxing in the vehicle while men in dark shirts removed items from the trunk in paper bags.

What was this? A morning rerun of *CSI*?

I turned the sound up, catching a single word before the perky anchor babe veered away from the scene and to a story about food poisoning at a local cafeteria.

My head spun, as the word I heard wasn't a good one at all, considering that it was "murder."

Chapter 11

"Did you see it? Did you see it? Can you even *believe* it? It's like a soap opera minus Susan Lucci and starring Malone!" Allie screamed in my ear, and I couldn't tell if she was horrified or excited. "It's hard to even fathom that the boys in blue are on the prowl for our man Brian, who, God knows, is about as dangerous as Charlie Brown."

Brian was a wanted man.

So I'd been dating a "bad boy" after all?

Despite his always saying "please" and "thank you" and "yes, ma'am," and dressing nicely, showing up on time, and never letting a door close in my face?

Who'd have thunk it?

Allie's squawking continued: "It's been all over the airwaves this morning, and the firm's already fielded so many calls from reporters that the switchboard operator nearly had a nervous breakdown. They had to bring in temps just to handle the overload. It's worse than when Abramawitz was defending that councilman's wife who poisoned her philandering husband by putting coolant in his Gatorade."

I barely caught her every other word, as I was still digesting the fact that the police were after Brian.

How many women saw their boyfriends' faces on the morning news, noting that the police were hunting for them, unless they'd dated the Unibomber?

"Oh, boy" didn't even begin to cover it.

And what the heck did "murder" have to do with Malone? Other than my own lethal thoughts about him.

Obviously he wasn't dead if the police needed to chat with him—though if I'd gotten my hands on him last night after his "Dear Jane" call, I would've committed assault and battery, at the very least, to say nothing of homicide.

So who'd been iced? And how was Brian involved, other than the red coupe surrounded by crime scene tape zeroed in on by the news chopper looked a lot like his Acura.

Could be lack of sleep, but I suddenly felt dizzy.

If my body had an error message, it would have been blinking, "System Overload."

I hadn't read the paper lately, but I was beginning to think my horoscope must've had a big warning label that said: Danger! Cosmic Crapping Ahead!

Just wish someone had alerted me that merely breathing these days was bad for my health. I had that sinking feeling again that I should've stayed in bed, the covers pulled over my head, ignoring the world entirely. Maybe even through the week ahead, missing my birthday completely, which might not be a bad thing seeing as how I was racing past thirty at an alarming speed, obviously slated to die alone, from the looks of things.

"Kendricks, hello? Are you still there?" Allie barked.

"Metaphysically? Or literally?" I asked, because there was a difference; but she didn't seem to care.

"Well, there's more to all of this, if you'll pay attention."

My my, but she was snippy. And I was the one who'd been dumped like a pound of rotten hamburger.

"I'm all ears."

"Malone is AWOL, girl. He didn't show up at work this morning, and he didn't leave any kind of message, not even on anyone's voice mail. Old Abe isn't any too happy with him, particularly right after he put us on the Oleksiy case and we've got a preliminary hearing on that one in a matter of weeks. We just started the process of interviewing some newly added prosecution witnesses. Well, Brian did, anyway. I was busy with a depo. He set up a couple meetings for Friday afternoon, but that's all I know. Only now Malone's bailed, and no one can find the list or any notes on his interviews."

So Brian had bailed on me *and* the firm, when he and Allie were working on a big case, ticking off the Big Cheese, J. D. Abramawitz?

All right, dumping a girlfriend wasn't nice, but it wasn't career-ending.

But crapping out on a job he loved right before the start of a trial?

Uh-uh.

No way.

No how.

That was one thing I knew, deep down inside and every which way but loose, that Brian would *never* do.

Every nerve in my body tingled as my emotions flip-flopped, from wanting to kill my missing dude to "Uh-oh, something's wrong."

Well, wasn't it a woman's prerogative to change her mind (in this case, by the day, if not the hour)?

So I returned to the Land of Denial, bypassing the duty-free shop altogether and heading straight for the emotional-baggage claim.

I didn't care what all the signs pointed to . . . it didn't matter that Malone himself had called to personally punt our relationship . . . or that Barmaid Lu at The Men's Club swore she'd seen him leave with Trayla, the pole dancer who purportedly had a ticket to a new life; because something stronger needled at me, reminded me of my daddy's words about rushing to judgment.

I wouldn't do it again, not until I fully understood the breadth and scope of recent goings-on and how they concerned Malone.

"Hello, space cadet?" Allie trilled, not sounding thrilled that I kept drifting off during our conversation. "Earth to Andy Kendricks?"

"Here," I said, adding quickly, "How much trouble is he in, Allie, really? And don't sugarcoat it." Like she'd ever do that.

"You recall the hurricane that demolished New Orleans?"

Oh, man.

"That big, huh?"

"Bigger." Allie paused, but a second later blurted out, "Abramawitz called an emergency board meeting for this afternoon. I think they're planning to can Malone if he doesn't turn up and explain himself by, like, yesterday. He must be thinking with that pea brain in his pants if he'd risk his career at ARGH for hot sex with a stripper."

I did a mental delete of that last sentence, my mind so focused on everything else she'd said: the calls to the firm, the emergency board meeting, Brian losing his job. A job he loved intensely.

Oy vey.

I gnawed on my bottom lip, getting a serious knot in my belly; sure that something was controlling Malone's behavior besides his own free will.

But what?

Or who?

"I truly don't think this is about sex with a stripper, Allie," I said, though of course I didn't know what it was about, not yet. "You have to realize by now that all of this is inconsistent with who Brian is. Secondhand stories aside, he just wouldn't do any of this. His job means everything to him."

Maybe more than me, or at least as much.

"Wow, Kendricks. I'm amazed at your loyalty. You're hell-bent on defending the guy, aren't you?" She sighed, clearly reluctant to concede I might be right, that perhaps Brian wasn't at fault, just in way over his head. "Let's table the 'is Malone a liar' discussion for now, okay? I'm not sure what I think, but I'm having my doubts. Does that make you feel better?"

I said, "I'll feel better when Brian's back." And not a minute sooner.

"Let's talk about the news bite, shall we?" Allie was ever so adept at changing the subject. "Did you hear why the cops want to interview our boy Brian?"

"He's wanted for questioning." My voice sounded so croaky. "Something to do with a murder," I said, gnawing on my lip. "That looked like his car, didn't it, with all the yellow tape around it? Was something in the trunk?"

"Something?" she repeated snidely. "Oh, it was something, all right."

I figured whatever the cops wanted from Malone had to do with a murder trial he was involved with at ARGH. Nothing else seemed logical.

"Have the police talked to you?" I asked. "Does it have to do with some criminal case you guys are working on?"

"Police? Criminal case?" my mother echoed, standing at my elbow. I'd almost forgotten she was there. "What's goin' on, Andrea? Are you in trouble again?"

"No, Ms. Scatterbrain, it hasn't got a thing to do with what we're working on," Allie said in that patronizing tone she did so well. "Hello? Pollyanna! Don't you get it? Weren't you listening? Didn't you hear *why* the cops put out a BOLO on him?"

"Because of a murder," I said, not for the first time, "but I don't know whose. One of your clients?"

"What murder? Darling, please, what have I walked into here?" Cissy had removed her cape and gloves and was folding them over the sofa arm, inching near enough to give me a polite jab in the ribs. "Did you kill someone and not tell me about it?"

"No, Mother, I didn't kill anyone. Not yet." I waved her off, though she didn't go far, just across the living room to inspect my work-in-progress. I saw her cock her head, then scratch it, evidently bamboozled by my artistic genius, and I figured that should occupy her for at least a few minutes.

Back to the business at hand.

"It wasn't a client." Allie lowered her voice. "Though the victim's name should ring a bell."

"Who?" Why did I suddenly wish I'd fortified myself this morning? Like pouring vodka on my Captain Crunch, or spreading Valium on toast?

"Brace yourself," Allie warned. "I'll give you the skinny, but I guarantee it's not going to make you any happier than it did Abramawitz."

So much for the Surgeon General's warning, I thought, and girded myself.

"Here goes," she said before she started to spill, like the kid who took his finger out of the hole in the dike. The dam overfloweth.

I concentrated on Allie's voice, blinking as I took in the tale she told, and, Lord, but it was a whopper.

Brian's red Acura had turned up early that morning in a no-parking zone at Love Field. Since Security these days doesn't mess around with unattended vehicles in places where they're not supposed to be, a tow was immediately summoned, and while the car was being hooked up, the trunk sprung. Lo and behold, wrapped up in a plastic tarp tucked over the spare tire was not Malone's prized Calloway clubs, but the lifeless body of a young woman.

"A *naked* young woman," Allie clarified, in case all she'd told me thus far wasn't enough to give me a stroke.

"Naked," I murmured, unable to utter a coherent statement while my brain processed the rest.

It had to be a prank, something faked, and I remarked as much, though Allie's "very naked and very dead" assured me it was real enough.

And she wasn't done.

"My source at the DPD says the DB is a twenty-two-year-old exotic dancer well known to the flatfoots downtown. She's been arrested for solicitation a time or two, though she's always made bail," the Blond Menace informed me in her know-it-all tone. "Robby—I mean, my source—wouldn't give me her real name, but he did let it slip that she uses the nom de plume of 'Trayla Trash' when she dances. Sound familiar?"

Goose bumps rose, rashlike, over my skin.

"How?" I said.

"I was told that her head was bashed in with a golf club."

"Not a Big Bertha?"

"I don't know, Kendricks," Allie snapped. "Putter, driver, does it matter?"

If her head was smashed with Calloway clubs belonging to Brian Malone, well, yes, it did. But I didn't want to go there.

I swallowed hard, but the lump in my throat was too big to go down. Instead, I felt like I was choking as I repeated for good measure, "Trayla Trash is really dead?"

"You can rest assured she's not in Vegas with Malone."

Call me a cold fish, but somehow the idea comforted me, though I was truly sorry she was dead. Dancing half naked for men and ending up stuffed in a trunk: hardly a fairy tale kind of life.

"So Trayla Trash isn't with Brian," I said, more to reassure myself than anything.

"No, princess, she's not hanging with anyone but the Big Guy Upstairs. Or maybe the Dude Down Below."

"Andrea? What trailer trash are you muttering about and why would you think she was with Mr. Malone?" My mother appeared at my side, and I raised a hand in the universal "hush" sign.

Though she clearly looked annoyed, she obeyed.

And I sorted out the million questions in my head, asking the first one that made the jump to my lips: "Are they sure it's really her?"

"They've taken her to the morgue for a positive ID, of course, but all signs point to her. They've got her prints on file, according to Rob—um, my contact—and he sounds sure enough. So, yeah, Kendricks, I think the poor girl's done her last lap dance," Allie said, though she wasn't joking around.

Neither was I.

"I can't believe this. None of it makes any sense." I felt too loopy to stand, and dropped onto the sofa, at which point Mother settled down beside me and put a hand on my shoulder. "It's too weird to be real. Like a Quentin Tarantino movie."

"Except Brian's gonna wish it was only Uma Thurman kicking his ass when he finally surfaces. This is just crazy, way beyond the time when he took me to Disney World because he wanted a tour of those freaky underground tunnels where they haul the trash so no one in the park ever sees a garbage truck," Allie said and sighed.

Malone took her to a strip club and *to Disney World?*

The things I'd missed.

"You might be right, Kendricks," the Size Two Terror admitted, and my neck hairs prickled at the realization she was hitching a ride on my bandwagon. "This is so not like Brian that I'm seriously starting to wonder if it's some kind of setup. That phone call from him. Are you sure he told you he wanted to split? Is that all he got across? He wasn't trying to send you an SOS? A secret message, like in code or something? Anything strike you as weird?"

A secret message in code? What did she think we did, communicated with smoke signals? Or pig Latin?

All I could tell her for certain was, "Everything about the call was weird. He was stammering"—I squinted, thinking back—"and, even though we had a horrible connection, he sounded scared, like he wanted to cry."

"C'mon, we both know Malone doesn't get weepy," Allie remarked, and I despised her all over again, for thinking she knew him better—which was very possibly true—and for believing even for a second that he could do any of the things he was accused of doing. "Think hard, Kendricks," Allie prodded again, "did he say anything that didn't make sense?"

"You're joking, right?"

I'd been with Brian for four months, and he was a lawyer.

He'd said lots of things that never made sense, mostly work-related terms like "ipso facto," the "veracity prong," and the "Peyton exception," which is usually when my mind started to wander and I'd pretend to listen, nodding a lot for good measure.

"Think about it, Kendricks," she prompted, sounding

edgy. "Nothing he said seemed the least bit off to you? More so than usual, I mean."

Wait a minute.

It was then that I recalled my dream, about the House of Mirrors and seeing Brian and a caped witch offering cabbage soup.

"My mother's homemade cabbage soup," I said, louder than necessary, which earned me an odd glance from Cissy, who started to open her mouth, then promptly shut it again. Probably afraid I'd duct-tape her lips if she interrupted one more time.

"Your mom's soup?" Allie repeated, shifting from edgy to irritated. "Look, Kendricks, I don't have time to chat about recipes. So give me a call if you come up with something better than that. Otherwise, I've gotta go. Old Abe is on a rampage, and I've got to see what I can do to buy time for Malone before the board kicks his tail out of the firm if he doesn't turn up to defend himself and return those docs to the file."

"Allie, wait," I said, but she was already gone.

Still, she'd got me to thinking, and I didn't much like any of the theories I was coming up with.

I set the receiver gently back in its cradle and turned around to face my mother, who sat patiently with hands folded in her lap, waiting for me to give the okay for her to resume vocalization.

"Something's freaky," I said, making the abrupt and nonsensical decision to tell-all, because I needed a sounding board, an impartial ear to assure me I was indeed sane and on the right track.

"Freaky can be relative," my mother stated, nodding.

"Do go on." She tilted her head, as she'd done while studying my painting. I'm sure she'd found its abstract streaks far more understandable than me, her own flesh and blood.

"No one's seen Brian since Saturday night when he purportedly left The Men's Club in the company of an, um, exotic dancer." I managed to say it all in one breath, without blushing or collapsing into an embarrassed heap.

"I see." She didn't flinch. Didn't blink.

I swallowed a little extra air as backup and pushed onward. "His car turned up early this morning in a no parking zone at the airport with a dead woman in the trunk." I wet my lips. "The exotic dancer in question, or so it appears."

"You're imagining something has happened to him, aren't you?" she asked, her eyes pinning down mine with stealth-bomb accuracy.

I felt that horrible surge that comes before I start to cry, but I didn't aim to break down in front of my mother. Crying could wait. Finding Brian couldn't. And, perhaps, there was some way she could help me out. Being the Queen Mum of Dallas Society had its privileges, and she was a champion string-puller.

I gulped down any pride I had left, deciding to come clean with her, no matter what it cost, mostly in terms of my judgment (or lack of it) and Malone's reputation.

"I'm frantic," I admitted in a whisper. "And I don't know what to do."

"So it seems Mr. Malone has got himself into quite the conundrum." Though her eyes narrowed the tiniest bit, my mother's expression changed not a fig.

"A huge honking conundrum," I said, unable to dis-
agree.

"How did this come about?" she inquired. "Did he lose
his mind? Was he possessed? Did he suffer amnesia?"

"I have no idea," I said, thinking, *Take your pick.*

"What does Ms. Price know about all this?"

"The same as I do. That the police want to find Brian
and question him about the dead girl in his trunk, but no
one seems to know where he is, and I'm more confused
than ever since he called me last night and told me he
wanted space and to apologize to you for missing the party
because he loves your cabbage soup." I dropped my head
in my hands and moaned loudly, which felt pretty damned
good and necessary. "I don't know what's going on. It's
insane . . . it's beyond reason . . . it's . . ."

"Utterly preposterous," Cissy finished for me, and I
raised my suddenly tear-filled eyes to meet hers. It was
I who blinked first.

"What did you say?"

"I said"—she spoke slowly, which made for easy lip-
reading—"it's not possible that Mr. Malone would tell you
such nonsense."

Was she high on Joy perfume?

I didn't get it.

My mother had been on Brian's case for months about not
putting a ring on my finger even though he stayed over at my
condo—which she learned about from Penny George, my
neighborhood snitch—and suddenly she was at his defense?

I swallowed, processing this bizarre turn of events, afraid
to say too much or I'd spoil the moment. Still, I couldn't
help myself.

"Okay, what's going on? You've hardly been Malone's biggest cheerleader, yet you believe that he couldn't have done those things? You agree with me that something's wrong, and he's found himself in some kind of sticky situation he can't extricate himself from?"

She sighed. "Whatever I think of Mr. Malone's etiquette in wooing you, I don't for a minute believe he's a bad man. In fact, just the opposite, or I wouldn't allow your relationship to continue."

Wouldn't *allow*? Who was she kidding? Like she had control of my life any more these days than she had when I'd refused to debut.

"Besides, it's highly unlikely that Mr. Malone would tell you he loves my cabbage soup. If he did, he was pulling your leg."

"Pulling my leg?" As in joking? Brian sounded anything but comical when he'd called the night before. He'd sounded dead earnest.

"Yes, teasing you, Andrea. Messing with your head. Playing mind games." She crossed her arms and leaned back against the sofa, wearing a smug expression that said, *Oh, boy, do I know something you don't know.*

My last nerve twanged like the guitar strings in a country western song. "Whatever you have to say, cough it up." Or I'd be tempted to take hold of her pearls and twist until I forced it out of her. I was sadly lacking in patience at the moment. "Before Christmas, if you wouldn't mind," I prodded her.

Mother performed her usual delay tactics, plucking nonexistent lint off her tweed jacket, giving a little flip to her bobbed blond hair, finally coming out with, "My darling child, your Mr. Malone and I have had occasion to chat about many things outside your earshot, some of which concern you and others that have nothing whatsoever to do with you." As I opened my mouth to ask what, she raised her hand to hush me up, just as I'd done with her. "On one such occasion, we discussed allergies. He's allergic to bees, did you realize? Said he swells up like a basketball, apparently. If he doesn't get to an E.R. so they can treat him with those anaphylactic pens, he's a goner."

Bees?

My response was to stare at her, agog, because I hadn't known, though I wouldn't have admitted that to her if my life depended on it.

"What brought this up?" I managed to croak, once I'd gotten over my initial shock at the idea of Malone sharing secrets with Cissy.

She smoothed a hand over her skirt. "I shared with Mr. Malone that I once had a Polish nanny who used to make cabbage soup, which she forced upon me as a child." Her heart-shaped face puckered. "That horrid stuff nearly killed me. I had the most severe case of hives. I missed Kitty Barstow's fourth birthday party, and I was devastated."

Good Lord, were those tears in her eyes?

"So I would never even joke about making cabbage soup." She shuddered. "Even the thought of it makes me queasy."

"You're allergic to cabbage?" I'd never heard of such a thing. *Was* there such a thing?

She nodded. "And Mr. Malone knew it, so if he told you

he looked forward to eating my cabbage soup, he must've been delirious, or it may have been intentional."

Like he was trying to tell me something?

Just as Allie had suggested.

The wheels in my head started spinning so fast I could hear the grinding, and it wasn't an unpleasant sound, not when I realized what this meant.

Malone needed me.

He'd hoped I'd be smart enough to figure things out, and I had. Well, a little anyway; enough to be sure he was in a very bad spot.

And help him, I would.

"Let's go, Mother," I said, and got up from the sofa to hunt down my purse.

"But I only just arrived, and we haven't even talked about the menu for the dinner, and it's on Wednesday—"

"That's too bad," I cut her off, having located bag and keys. I even fetched her cloak off the back of the couch and handed it to her. "Because I've got somewhere to go, and I want you to come with me."

"Why?"

"I need a wing man."

"A wing man?" I could see the alarm in her face, surely flashing back to the last time this situation had arisen; only it had been Mother asking the very same question of me. "What on earth for?"

"Breaking and entering," I told her honestly as I hustled her toward the door, giving her pause to grab her umbrella before we headed out into the storm, both on the literal and figurative front.

Our destination: Brian Malone's.

My mission: to pry where no girlfriend had pried before.

I wanted answers, and I aimed to find them, whatever it took.

Chapter 12

 I hadn't been over to Malone's apartment much, maybe twice in the four months we'd been going out.

Mostly, he came over to my place, probably because I was usually there. When you worked from home, it meant you were often, well, *home*.

It wasn't that he lived far away, as it was a pretty straight shot over to his building. He lived in Addison, a next door neighbor to my North Dallas suburb, so we were kissing cousins, locationwise.

The main reason why we didn't spend time at Malone's had to do with something more, er, olfactory.

I had a pretty good recollection of precisely what it was after I'd located the key in the hiding spot Allie had spilled the beans about (yep, there it was, wedged in a missing chunk of wood in the frame overhead), unlocked the door, stepped over the rolled-up newspaper on the doormat, and entered.

My nose wrinkled as it hit me.

Eau de Sock.

That was it.

The stench.

No matter how clean the place was—and it was meticulous—the air held an odor of sweaty athletic sock. Don't ask why. Malone didn't smell like that, and I know he did his laundry regularly. Brian had suggested the last tenant wore the same pair of socks every day without washing them, until the stink had killed him. My guess was some kind of mold, growing somewhere behind the walls or in the vents, unseen and deadly.

Yeah, I watched the ten o'clock news and saw the stories about mold driving people out of their million dollar mansions, giving kids asthma, knocking the elderly unconscious, even making Fido's fur fall out.

The government was so worried about terrorists and nuclear weapons they didn't realize we could all be picked off slowly but surely by the fungus among us (try saying that three times fast without tongue-tripping).

"So this is where he lives when he's not at your house?" Mother tiptoed in behind me as I shut the door and hit the light switch.

We'd both trailed in a good bit of the outdoors, despite wiping our shoes on the welcome mat. The rain dripped off my slicker and Mother's cape like the proverbial water off a duck's back. If any of the gang from *CSI* dropped by to collect trace evidence, the muddy imprints of my sneakers and Cissy's chi-chi boots would blatantly link us to the scene of the slime.

"Honestly, darling, I had hoped for so much more. Mr. Malone could use a good interior designer." She sighed and gestured around us. "What do you call this style?"

" 'Penitentiary Spare,' " I managed to joke, even though my humor seemed to fall flat of late, as there was little to joke about.

"And what on earth is that odor?" she said, loudly sniffing, the first thing I'd thought when I'd ventured into Malone's apartment initially, though I'd been well-bred enough to keep it to myself.

Cissy had no such compunction, since Malone wasn't even around, and I was her daughter, which meant rules about manners didn't always apply.

"I don't know," I told her. "Brian thinks someone died here without ever washing his socks. I figure toxic mold lives in the walls."

"Good Lord, I understand now why he spends so much time at your place. Not that I approve of cohabitation, even for health purposes," she explained, if that constituted an explanation. "Besides"—she glanced around her, looking down her nose at the sparsely furnished bachelor pad, mostly done in early IKEA—"your decor is so much cozier."

Cozier.

As in, less than a thousand square feet, jam-packed with the things I loved, collected through the years, some inherited (like the hope chest that served as my coffee table and the Eastlake bed I slept in); others I'd picked up at rummage or estate sales, consignment stores, or antique malls, whenever something struck my fancy. I was good at refinishing, too, when I felt like inhaling fumes from paint stripper.

Argh.

There was that word again.

Stripper.

Though it was worse, wasn't it, when preceded by "dead" as opposed to "paint"?

Which reminded me why I was there.

I had to find something that shed light on where Brian was and what trouble he'd gotten himself into. He was so organized, so on top of things; it was hard to believe he'd vanished without leaving a clue of some sort. If only I could get my hands on his day planner, I'd have it figured out in a jiff. But if it were in his briefcase, which he normally locked in his trunk, I was screwed.

So I started with the obvious.

He kept a calendar on his refrigerator, and I headed there first, sure that if he'd intended to skip town with Trayla Trash he would've jotted down a note in the appropriate square. Brian planned for everything. That boy left little to chance.

I could think of a million such examples.

He had extra batteries for his flashlights and checked them regularly; ditto his smoke alarm and carbon monoxide detector.

He had a AAA-approved emergency kit in his trunk (which obviously had not helped Trayla), and he carried granola bars in his briefcase so he'd have something to eat if he found himself stuck in a disabled car or elevator.

He kept packets of Shout Wipes in his desk drawer at work in case he spilled his lunch on his tie.

When he first spent the night at my condo, he'd come armed with a brand-new toothbrush.

I could go on and on, but I won't because I had a job to do, and I didn't want to hang around long enough to get into a sticky wicket.

With eagle-eyed intensity, I studied the month of October, seeing a notation for a dental appointment, the occasional Monday night poker game, a Bar Association dinner, and my birthday—the date of Cissy's dinner party—circled with a heavy hand in red pen.

It was enough to make my heart leap.

He also had the weekend blocked off with "Andy's Surprise!" stretched from Saturday through Tuesday.

What had he planned? I wondered.

A trip somewhere outside the city limits? To a quaint B&B? A hotel room here in town, where we could pretend we were alone and miles away from every stressful thing?

Though I'd never know, would I, unless I located a phone number with a reservation code or a pair of plane tickets? If they existed, he'd doubtless stashed them in his day planner or in the pocket of his briefcase.

I wondered if the cops had found his attaché in his trunk, along with his potentially murderous Calloway clubs and the alleged dead stripper?

Oy.

"What should I be looking for, sweetheart?" my mother asked, and I jumped, as she was standing right behind me, glancing over my shoulder. "Should I be going through his sock drawer?"

His sock drawer?

"Mother, no, for Pete's sake."

The last thing I needed was Cissy rifling through Malone's underwear. God only knew what she might find.

"Well, I haven't a clue what's expected of me. Whyever *did* you drag me here, darlin'?"

Okay, so I hadn't made her part in this scenario very clear.

I turned squarely to face her. In her dark cape and boots, she resembled a London bobby. All she needed was a baton to whack the bad guys. Though she did have that wicked umbrella.

"You're the lookout," I told her as her brow settled into vague lines of puzzlement. "You need to keep watch for anyone who might surprise me while I'm poking around."

Namely, reporters or the police.

I had been pretty surprised not to see a squad car or a camera crew from one of the local stations positioned in the parking lot when we'd arrived, as I figured they'd be staking out the apartment, waiting for Brian "Most Wanted" Malone's return.

But Mother and I had encountered no one on the way into the building. The cops were likely still focused on Brian's car and the body, which inspired hope that our luck would hold for a few minutes more.

"So you want me to stand in the hallway?" she asked, swinging said umbrella in the direction of the door. "What am I supposed to do? Whistle? Intercept and distract until you're done in here?"

Did she think this was *Mission: Impossible*? Did she expect an instructional tape that would self-destruct?

Yeesh.

I took her arm and guided her toward the door, telling her, "Just sit out there, um, reading the paper."

I saw the huge Sunday edition of the *New York Times* lying like a log on the kitchen table, where Allie had apparently deposited it after coming over and letting herself in yesterday.

The latest *Dallas Morning News* had replaced it on the doormat, and I plucked that from the floor as I nudged Mother into the apartment's corridor.

"Use this." I pushed it into her hands. There was a chair set near a plant a yard or so away, between Brian's apartment and his nearest neighbor. "Take a seat and act casual. If you see anyone approaching Brian's door, um"—I was going to say *Call my cell,* but Cissy hated using hers and rarely carried it anywhere—"how about you scream or something."

"Scream what?"

"I don't know. Does it have to be something in particular? Can't you just holler like Fay Wray in *King Kong*?"

Mother did her best "miffed" expression, and it was a doozy. "Ladies of my age do not holler, Andrea. I don't expect to be palmed by an oversized ape, nor am I a barefoot illiterate in overalls minding my sill in the wilds of Appalachia."

So I guess I couldn't ask her to squeal like a pig, huh?

"Just make like you've seen a mouse, okay?" I suggested, assuming she could handle that bit of stage direction. I'd watched her freak out at the sight of a tree roach nearly the size of a mouse, and she'd managed a pretty good Janet "I'm Getting Stabbed in the Shower" Leigh impression.

"A mouse?" She shook her head. "No, I don't think so."

What the heck did she want? A Hollywood screenplay and Spielberg calling "Action"?

Perhaps she'd go for something more John le Carré, words a spy might say. "Try, 'The eagle has landed,'" I said.

She tapped a manicured nail to her chin. "Sweetie, I'm just not feeling it. Besides, it's already been done to death."

Who'd she think she was? Katharine Hepburn?

I choked back what I really wanted to tell her, offering instead, "How about shouting 'Fire'? It does wonders for crowded theatres."

"Hmm." She paused. "That's not bad." She gave a slow nod. "It's succinct, yet powerful. Perfect," Mother said. "I can work with that."

"Great." It took concerted effort not to roll my eyes.

Cissy gazed off somewhere in the distance, obviously a thoughtful moment to get into the skin of "woman pretending to read paper who shall shriek 'Fire' hellaciously should anyone approach forbidden door"—my mother had a bit of the Method actress in her, dating back to her college days at SMU.

She was heading over to the chair by the ficus when I did an about-face and slipped back into Brian's lair.

I shut the door behind me, dead-bolted it for good measure, then surveyed the space around me, feeling determined. I didn't like feeling helpless, and the best antidote for that was actually *doing* something.

I wasn't sure what I might find that could give me answers, or if there even were any hidden around his apartment, just waiting for me to stumble upon them. But, having seen the way he'd marked the calendar for my birthday-related events, I felt strongly that Brian was in trouble by chance, not by choice.

All rightee.

I rubbed my hands together.

Time to snoop.

Although, it's not like I was snooping the way a nosy girlfriend would.

Contraire, mon frère.

This particular invasion of privacy was purely beneficent. So it wasn't the Woodward and Bernstein "we must expose evil" type of investigating, but rather a kinder and gentler "must go that extra mile to get Malone out of deep doo-doo" sort.

I had myself fully convinced of that by the time I started pulling open desk drawers and shuffling through the contents, finding more signs of Brian's compulsive organization: neatly stacked boxes of binder clips and rubber bands, extra pens and reams of paper, a paperback dictionary, staplers (did he really need three?), a spare cartridge for his laser printer. But nothing that would explain his disappearance, unless he'd had a savage tiff with one of the sales people at Office Depot.

Any business-related files he kept at the office—or in his briefcase—so the manila folders arranged alphabetically mostly dealt with his personal life: credit cards, health and car insurance, bank statements, utilities, and other mundane items that concerned activities of daily living.

I saw no sign of the paperwork relating to the criminal case that Allie had been pissing and moaning about, which meant Brian had taken the documents with him; perhaps the police had turned them up in his car.

The only thing of consequence I tripped over was his address book.

I did a fast flip to the M's and noted his parents' address and phone number in Chesterfield, Missouri. Had the cops called them already? Told them their son was tangled up in a stripper's death?

Yipes.

I prayed that hadn't happened. If they should hear about Brian from anyone, it should be me.

So I pocketed the address book.

I would call them later. I didn't have any idea what I'd say, but I'd think of something.

The desk having yielded next to nothing, I moved into the galley kitchen, checking drawers and cabinets, quickly realizing that he—a single guy—was better stocked than I in so many departments: cutlery, cooking utensils, baking pans, even a collection of olive oils that would've made Julia Child drool.

He had *The Joy of Cooking* and assorted other cookbooks stashed in a cabinet above his fridge, which made me suspicious. If Malone could cook, he hadn't spilled those fava beans, not to me. All I did know was that he could make toast or grill a cheese sandwich when the situation called for either; and, at my place, that was about all one could do.

I seriously pondered if Brian had a talent I hadn't been privy to, and, if so, I was pea green with envy. I lacked all but the most basic of culinary skills, which explained why the sum total of my cookware consisted of a cookie sheet, should I have a craving for slice 'n' bake; the single mixing bowl I used to make salad; and a spatula to flip aforementioned cookies. Not exactly the Cordon Bleu.

Still, if he'd ever said to me, "Come over to my apartment, and I'll whip up a couple pecan-encrusted chicken breasts with spinach orzo on the side," I would've hightailed it to his place, stinky sock smell or not.

Had he ever cooked for Allie?

My neck tensed at the very thought, and I felt a stab of jealousy, as I had when she'd mentioned things they'd done together that had nothing to do with me.

I didn't like knowing they'd once shared a lot more than spit, even though I had a past of my own (not that I was ever promiscuous, just to be clear). I'd explained my "don't ask, don't tell" rule early in the relationship, to keep us both from bringing up old baggage that might—no, that almost certainly would—hurt the other somehow. No one wanted to be reminded of those who'd come before, although one could always hope there weren't too many; particularly in this day and age.

But back to Brian's past loves.

I was aware that the Blond Menace had been his girlfriend and his colleague, which had given her greater access to his life than I had, something I hadn't dwelled on much before. Until these last few days when I'd begun to doubt how well I really knew Malone. How much I trusted him.

How much he trusted me.

Focus, Andy, I told myself, because I hadn't come over just to ponder the cracks in our relationship. Brian needed help—I'd convinced myself that's what the indecipherable cabbage soup comment meant—and I couldn't let him down.

I started to the bedroom, stopped and cocked my ear toward the door, thinking I'd heard the sound of voices.

I waited a minute.

Wondered if I should check on my mother.

But all seemed quiet on the ficus front.

So I ventured into Brian's sparse sleeping quarters, which consisted of a white IKEA bed, matching white dresser, a beat-up leather club chair, and a closet with shuttered doors. I stood just inside the doorway for a moment, not sure of where to begin since I had no clue what I was searching for.

I checked the dresser top first, finding little there of interest besides a silver dish filled with change, a wooden box stuffed with receipts, and several framed photographs. One picture was of the two of us at the sculpture park, and another of a salt-and-pepper-haired couple posing with a pair of golden retrievers, who presumably were his parents (the people, not the puppies).

I picked up the latter and studied it for a moment, staring at the faces, wrinkled up with big grins. I could see a bit of Malone in each of them. He had his mother's brown hair and bright blue eyes, and his father's lean build.

Odd, but he didn't talk much about them, and I was always whining to him about Cissy. I didn't know what his folks did for a living, if they were retired; perhaps because I'd never asked. Malone just wasn't that great at volunteering personal information. If I wanted scoop, I had to pry it from him.

I made a decision then and there to ask him about his

family at my first opportunity, once he'd been found and things had returned to normal.

Not that I ever strived for normalcy, but it sounded good in this instance, far better than this craziness.

Where to? I asked myself, wondering if this little jaunt wasn't a lost cause.

What could Brian have left behind that would point to where he'd gone? I mean, how could he have anticipated anything that had happened the night of the bachelor party when he somehow got tied up with Trayla Trash?

Because if he'd had any inkling, surely he would've told me, "Andy, it's going to look like I've run off with a stripper, only I haven't. And when she's found wrapped in a tarp in the trunk of the Acura, left in a no-parking zone at the airport, the truth won't be anything like what it seems."

So if I could just scratch the surface to find what was beneath.

Then, voilà!

Mystery solved. Brian could come home.

If only it were that simple.

Doing my best Miss Marple routine, I continued my snoopfest, shoving my hand between bed frame and mattress, where I'd hidden my diary as a kid. I didn't have to probe much before I ran into the spine of a book.

I took a seat on the edge of the bed and flipped through the pages of a journal, mostly blank, though a handful in the front were filled with doodles and scribbled poetry. At least it appeared to be poetry, a mixture of badly rhyming sonnets and haikus.

I realized they weren't meant for my eyes, or Brian

would've shown them to me; but I couldn't help reading one haiku written next to the barely decipherable rendering of a milk carton with EXPIRED scrawled across its label.

rectangular box
some kind of goo leaking out
maybe it's rotten

Oh, God. I smiled.

It was dreadful, but I loved it.

More so because I had no idea Brian released his creativity this way, using words where I used paint. He'd never mentioned writing, and I wondered why. Was he embarrassed? Did he imagine I'd laugh at him? Did he not feel safe enough with me to share something like this?

Or maybe he just wanted his privacy, something I could relate to well enough.

As much as I ached to hold onto the book, I put it back in its hiding place. I wanted it to be there when he returned, so he could add more awful haikus to it. Maybe write a poem about me someday.

I zoned in on the sock drawer. I had to give my mother credit for the suggestion. Honestly, who didn't keep little things hidden beneath their panties or knee-highs?

I had jewelry stashed in mine—a small jewelry box that held the diamond ear studs Mother had given me when I'd turned eighteen, along with some antique rings I'd inherited from my grandmother.

I slid open Malone's topmost drawer, revealing a plethora of Gold Toes and a half-dozen neatly folded pairs of preppy boxers. Feeling like a sneak, I gently ran my hand through the sea of socks, finding zilch. Then I slipped my fingers beneath his underwear and encountered something hard.

I palmed it, drew it to eye level and stared, my breath quickening.

It was blue.

And square.

A box from Tiffany & Co., a sight my mother had taught me to appreciate early on, and I still couldn't stop the catch in my heart when I saw one, even if I had done my damnedest to ditch the "born to debut" attitude long ago.

Did I think this had anything to do with Brian and the dead stripper?

Of course I didn't.

Could I put it back without opening it up to see what was inside?

Absolutely not.

Pulse thudding in my ears, I plucked off the blue lid and saw what I imagined I'd see: a second box, this one velvet with a hinge.

Of course, I opened that, too, and my breath caught at the sight of its contents.

Wedged comfortably amidst the satin lining were two rings.

One was a full circle bead-set diamond band; the other, a simple band in matching platinum.

They had that antique look I loved and were gorgeous enough to make me gasp, no matter that I didn't really care for jewelry.

My brain tried valiantly to assimilate the facts as I saw them.

My serious boyfriend of four months (and let's forget that he dumped me, because I didn't believe it).

Crazy about each other (well, I was about him, and I assumed he felt the same about me, or at least he had before the "stripper incident").

Tiffany box hidden in sock drawer.

Wedding bands.

Could it be?

As usual, my mind leapt to conclusions, unsupported by physical evidence, based solely on conjecture: Brian had elopement on his mind, forgoing the engagement thing entirely.

He wanted to marry *me,* not some fly-by-night floozy. (I couldn't for a minute buy that he'd pondered jetting to Vegas for a quickie wedding to Trayla Trash.)

Except there was a slight catch in any dreams of our getting hitched, the biggest obstacle being that I had no inkling where Brian was.

On impulse, I plucked out the band with the diamonds and slid it onto the third finger of my left hand, though it didn't fit, being at least two sizes too large.

Hmm.

It would probably perfectly suit a more robust bride, however, say, Eleanor from Pittsburgh? That wedding was mere weeks away, and Malone was Matty's best pal.

Fudge.

Cue lightbulb moment.

Matty had told me that Brian was holding some "important hardware" for him, and the rings no doubt were it.

Oh, waitress, I'll take that reality check, please.

Duh.

How dopey could I get? Imagining Brian's birthday surprise for me might be wedding bands and plane tickets to Vegas so we could be joined in holy matrimony by an Elvis impersonator.

So much for my postcollege declaration that I was "Miss Independent" and might never tie the knot, huh? Though I realized this sudden epiphany about Malone had come when I felt so close to losing him.

Why was that always the way?

With a sigh, I slipped the ring off, put it back in the box then stuck the box in the drawer just as I'd found it, feeling a prick of disappointment, despite telling myself, *Your day will come, Andrea Blevins Kendricks.*

And maybe it would, once I was with Malone again.

Without further ado, I continued my poking, even glancing through the old *Smithsonian* magazine lying at the foot of Brian's bed, pages dog-eared at articles about poisonous jellyfish—ooh, they were pretty!—the unsolved art heist at the Isabella Stewart Gardner Museum in Boston with lots of color photos that I wished I had the time to pore over—and something on Lewis and Clark.

I tugged open the slender drawer on his nightstand and found a card addressed to me, which I drew out of the envelope.

The front depicted Frankenstein and the Bride of Frankenstein, and inside it read: *We were made for each other.*

Below that, he'd scrawled, "So true—opposites attract,

so they say. You're as open as the sky, and I'm steady like the rain. I love you, babe."

That was beautiful.

Way better than his poetry.

A gentle sigh escaped my lips, because it's what I'd needed to hear, however the message was delivered.

Brian loved me.

The rest was madness.

If only I knew how to fix it. My daddy was always so good at that, setting things to right, but I'd always seemed to make messes of everything.

"Trust yourself, pumpkin," he would've urged me, certain I could do anything if I put my mind to it.

So I put my mind to it now.

I kept the card, because I needed it; shoved it down in my bag so I wouldn't lose it while I tossed the living room, looking for my elusive Holy Grail; which is when I heard a thump against the apartment door and noises in the hallway.

I edged nearer the door, detecting the scuffle of feet and the muffled baritone of a male voice saying something akin to: "Lady, put it down now."

Followed by my mother's drawl, raised to ear-splitting decibels, yelling, "Fire, fire, fire!"

I hurried over to the peephole, squinting out to see a pair of men in blue uniforms wrestling with Mummy Dearest, who appeared to be using her umbrella to block their way to the door.

Oh, crap.

The fuzz had landed.

And I was trapped.

Chapter 13

 I'd never imagined my life could get any more pathetic than rifling through my missing boy-friend's boxers.

Incredibly, it did.

Is there such a thing as reaching the depths of patheticness? And I must've taken the elevator, not the stairs, because the trip was very quick.

Mother and I ended up at the Addison police station after a joyless ride in a cruiser that smelled of sweat and pine deodorizer, which wasn't much of an improvement over Eau de Sock at Malone's apartment.

A pair of detectives from the Dallas P.D. joined our little coffee klatch in the office of the City of Addison's police captain. The only thing that was missing was actual coffee, which no one had offered us, though I didn't often drink the stuff myself and imagined whatever they served here had to be pretty bad.

No Miranda warning had been read to us—which left me feeling oddly disappointed—because we hadn't been arrested, just asked to "come down to the station" so we could explain why we were in Brian Malone's abode, particularly since the Dallas P.D. so desperately wanted to chat with him.

The Addison patrolmen who'd shown up at Brian's place—thanks to a phone call from a neighbor—assumed at first that I was a reporter, since local journalists had apparently been nosing around the building since the story broke about the dead stripper in Brian's car; though Mother had generously volunteered that I was Brian Malone's girlfriend and that we had entered his apartment with a key, so we'd done nothing unlawful.

Great defense, Ma Barker.

I figure it was the "Malone's girlfriend" part that had pricked their ears most, considering his name was all over the morning news and had surely been broadcast over the police band.

We were assured that we didn't need to lawyer-up, which didn't stop Cissy from dropping the name "J. D. Abramawitz" enough times to ensure we were treated with kid gloves—meaning, no one had been frisked, bopped with a baton, or handcuffed—which confirmed that they didn't really want *us,* per se.

They seemed more interested in playing "Where's Waldo?" Or, rather, "Where's Malone-o?" Even after I insisted I had no clue where he was hiding—if that's what he was doing—and how badly I wanted to find him myself.

I had high hopes that I could convince the police that

Brian was a victim of circumstance and possibly in grave danger, something I made clear to them from the get-go. Only my pleas fell on deaf ears.

Just minutes into our impromptu gabfest, I realized quite clearly that Brian's well-being wasn't foremost on their minds. They saw him as a suspect in a heinous crime, nothing more and nothing less.

"So he called you last night?" one of the Dallas detectives asked—a fellow with dark curls and a stocky build who introduced himself as Duane Swiercynski. I'd already nicknamed him "Starsky," as it was a whole lot easier to handle. "What exactly did he say?"

Like it hadn't been embarrassing enough repeating his "I hereby dump thou" message to my mother.

So I repeated the conversation, as close to word-for-word as I could recall.

I explained, too, the part about the cabbage soup, what I thought it meant, and how Malone had marked off the coming weekend on his calendar for my birthday, which merely earned me long, silent stares and got my hackles up.

I wasn't a liar, but they sure didn't seem to believe a thing I said.

Cissy appeared upset enough to rap them all upside the head with her umbrella, and I'm sure she would have if they hadn't confiscated it from her after the brouhaha in Malone's hallway when they'd threatened to cuff her (while Mother threatened to report their bad behavior to the pearl-wearing mummy of the president, which no doubt had them shaking in their cowboy boots).

The blond Dallas detective set his hands on his knees

and leaned toward me. Let's call him "Hutch," because his name, like Starsky's, had more consonants than any *Wheel of Fortune* puzzle, and I wasn't sure I could pronounce it without tripping over my tongue.

"So, Ms. Kendricks," Hutch drawled, "you believe your boyfriend is in peril, and he conveyed this to you through a phone call where he noted that he wanted space and mentioned your mother's homemade cabbage soup. Did I get that right?"

"My mother's allergic to cabbage, and Brian knew it," I told them, eager to get this ironed out so they'd grasp the concept that Malone needed their help, not an all-points-bulletin. "Don't you see? He was trying to tell me he's in trouble. He was stammering, too, and he only does that when he's under extreme stress. Plus, I found a birthday card he meant to give me, signed, 'I love you.'"

"A birthday card?" Hutch looked ready to laugh.

"Yes." What? Were they hard of hearing?

"Anything more substantial to go on than that, little lady?" Detective Smart-Ass asked.

The "little lady" bit nearly made me spit nails.

"Malone could be as dead as that stripper, but none of you seem to care a fig about that, do you?" I came up out of my chair. Only Mother's arm kept me from leaping atop the blond cop and pulling the rug off his head.

My God, didn't they get it?

My boyfriend might already be dog meat, yet they couldn't see any further than Trayla Trash.

"Should I go over it one more time?" I volunteered, my teeth gritted.

The Addison police captain—a woman with steely gray

hair and a seemingly permanent frown—sighed her disapproval. "If you don't mind, Miss Kendricks, we'd prefer not wasting time yammering about stuttering and Hallmark cards. There's a lot at stake here, and we can't do much good if you won't cooperate with us."

A lot at stake? Isn't that what I'd been trying to tell them?

If they wanted cooperation, they weren't doing much to invite it.

Was it improper to bark at people with badges? Because I was on the verge of a warning growl before I bit them all in the ass.

What kind of proof did they require to rest assured I was being as forthcoming as all get-out? A promise to turn over my firstborn to be raised by drill sergeants at the Police Academy?

"What makes you think I'm hiding something?" I demanded, because I didn't appreciate being second-guessed.

Heck, I'd even clued them in to Malone's trip to The Men's Club with Matty and each potential misstep that had followed after. Figuratively speaking, my pockets were empty. They could turn me upside down and shake me, and only lint would fall out.

"I don't believe you're being candid with us, Ms. Kendricks. I think you're protecting your boyfriend." The police captain folded her arms on her desk and stared at me sternly, like she could hypnotize me into submission. "This will go a lot faster if you share everything you know about Mr. Malone."

Share everything I knew?

Like Brian's favorite food, which was toasted ravioli; some kind of St. Louis specialty. Or maybe they'd like to hear his favorite color, which I pegged as navy blue, judging from the hue of most of his suits, though I wasn't a hundred percent on that. Oh, oh, or the unimaginative name he'd given his Acura? Red Car.

Because I had zip to give them regarding his whereabouts. If I knew where he was, why would I have been snooping around his apartment, with my mother playing palace guard in the hallway?

"Were you aware that Mr. Malone was involved with the murder victim?" Hutch of the blond hair and scraggly mustache asked.

"You're talking about the stripper from The Men's Club, Trayla Trash, right?" I said, earning me a pair of raised eyebrows. "That's who you found in his trunk, isn't it?"

I didn't add that I knew she'd been beaten with a golf club, which may or may not have been a Big Bertha. Like Mother had always said about sequins, sometimes less was plenty.

Hutch cleared his throat and tucked a finger beneath his collar, neck turning ruddy, probably wondering how I knew as much as I did. "Uh, we haven't released the name of the victim to the public yet, ma'am, and the fact that you're familiar with one of her known aliases makes me wonder if you haven't had a little chat with your on-the-lam boyfriend."

Known aliases?

Not stage names?

Sounded like there was more to Trayla Trash than her skimpy costumes.

"Like I told you, I haven't chatted with Brian, not since Saturday afternoon, and, for the record, I don't believe Brian was involved with Ms. Trash, not in the way you imagine," I said firmly, my cheeks tight and angry, doubtless reflecting the expressions on their similarly unsmiling faces. "He wasn't dating her or anything."

"Do you realize his business card was found on her person?" Hutch pressed me, and I did a double take.

"On her person?" I repeated. "But wasn't she found buck-naked?"

Was his card stuck in a pocket that wasn't really a pocket?

Oh, my.

"Seems like you know an awful lot about the crime scene, little lady." The cop I'd dubbed Hutch obviously relished the role of bad cop. Or "worse cop," anyway.

"I only know what I saw on TV," I shot back.

"We'll be looking into Mr. Malone's finances," Hutch continued, "and if we turn up anything that ties him to our victim, he's up shit creek without a canoe, much less a paddle."

"Are you suggesting he gave her money? Because he didn't," I insisted. "He was paying off his student loans and what he borrowed for the Acura, so there's no way he could've sprung for so much as a tassel of her bimbo attire."

I nearly bit my tongue in two to keep from snapping at the not-so-nice officers.

"He didn't pay for her tassels, huh?" Hutch said, and gave Starsky an exaggerated eye roll to the effect of *How stupid are chicks?* without having to utter a word.

I sat on my hands to keep from swinging a fist in his direction.

This was getting me nowhere. I had to calm down. I had a few questions of my own that I wanted answered, and I wasn't about to let their rude behavior stop me.

"Can you tell me if you found his day runner or his briefcase?" I asked, as benignly as possible. "He might've had some documents with him that could help us figure out why he's missing. They have to do with a case he's involved in. And what about blood? Did you find any of his in the car? Was there any sign of a struggle?" My voice rose, exposing my fear, and I had plenty to go around. "Were his keys in the ignition? Was the seat set back or moved up, because then you'd know if he was driving or not, right?"

Again, the police officers shared a communal glance before the cop with dark curls crossed his arms over his chest and dared to address me.

"Whatever we found in Mr. Malone's car is part of our investigation and not for public consumption." Detective Starsky scratched his throat, and I noticed he had inky hair poking out of his collar. "We're not fond of sharing information with the girlfriends of suspects."

"So now he's gone from a person of interest to a full-fledged suspect?"

I didn't like where this was going. No one seemed to be listening to my pleas that Brian needed a hand, not handcuffs.

"Your boyfriend is on the defense team in a high profile money laundering case, were you aware of that, Miss Kendricks?" Starsky asked. "Because we're just wonder-

ing if he got a little cozy with his firm's client, maybe took
something that wasn't his and ended up in over his head."

Just what were they implying? That Brian was crooked?
That he would jeopardize a case and his firm's reputation,
not to mention his life, by playing dirty?

"Brian's one of the best young defense attorneys in the
city," I said, talking faster than I meant to, barely keeping
my tone civil. "He handles lots of criminal cases, plenty
of them high profile, but he would never take money that
wasn't his."

Starsky squinted. "I didn't say he took money."

"Then what—" I stopped myself before I finished.

Yikes.

Did they mean Trayla?

Did they honestly believe Brian stole a stripper from a
money laundering client?

I would've laughed had I not seen how serious they all
looked.

"Detectives, if you'd allow me." The gray-haired captain cleared her throat, and the pair of Dallas cops re-
sumed their deadpan expressions. She turned her beady
eyes on me. "The Addison police are fully cooperating
with the City of Dallas in this investigation, and we'd like
to do whatever we can for Mr. Malone, being that he lives
in our jurisdiction. But we can't assist him if we can't
speak with him."

I felt like water left to boil on the stove for too long,
steaming up a storm and ready to overflow my pot.

"For the tenth time, I don't know where he is!" I
snapped at them all, clenching my hands into fists. "I wish
I did, but I don't." I uncurled my fingers and turned my

palms up. "Nothing. That's what I've got," I assured them, feeling on the verge of tears, because I hated being so impotent while Brian seemed to have his whole world caving in on him. "I swear on my mother's life."

"What a lovely sentiment, dear heart," Cissy said, a dry edge to her drawl, and she patted my thigh.

"Miss Kendricks"—it was apparently Starsky's turn again—"we don't want to harm your boyfriend, we just need to have a conversation with him. So don't cover up for him and assume you're doing him any favors. You're not."

"My daughter is not hiding anything, nor is she a liar." My mother bristled, squaring her shoulders and lifting her chin.

Them's fighting words, I thought. *Go get 'em, Her Highness of Highland Park! Let the bloodletting begin!*

"If she had anything to confess, she would," Cissy insisted. "So why don't you go about your business of finding poor Mr. Malone instead of harassing law-abiding women, particularly one who keeps the mayor's number on her speed dial."

Damned if that didn't earn us a trio of dirty looks, but I was very proud of Mother for standing up to them, even though I had a fleeting fear that we'd be sent to solitary and made to live on bread and water while they detained us, without allowing us the usual phone call to summon Cissy's armada of attorneys.

Well, hey, I'd seen plenty of "when good cops go bad" stories, where some poor sap out for a stroll past curfew in New Orleans got clobbered, or a housewife making a nighttime dash to the twenty-four-hour Walgreens got arrested for a DUI because she had Nyquil in her system.

I briefly envisioned my life behind bars and how I'd get along without a lid on my metal toilet. Maybe Martha Stewart could give me decorating tips. Then I tuned back into the conversation at hand and realized my mother wasn't letting up.

"Mrs. Kendricks, if you wouldn't mind, we'd simply like your daughter to—"

"Andrea has nothing else to offer, though you don't seem to understand that," Cissy cut Starsky off cold and continued her defense. "You seem to have glossed over the fact that Mr. Malone is obviously caught up in some kind of ungodly mess, and Andrea and I are both worried sick about him. He's an upstanding young man and a fine lawyer at one of the most respected firms in the city. He's not a wastrel and certainly not a killer."

I blinked, hearing her say those words, knowing they must be true, as my mother wouldn't fib to the police.

Holy cannoli.

Cissy had vouched for Malone. She, at least, believed me.

If I hadn't heard her with my own ears, I'd figure I was hallucinating.

Forget all those "milk for free" lectures. My stickler-for-manners mother had climbed the fence and jumped into the pasture with me, stepping right into a minefield of cow patties in her black Chanel boots.

"Yeah," I chimed in. Well, more like croaked. "Malone wouldn't hurt a fly. If you knew him, you'd realize he's one of the good guys."

"Perhaps you could advise him to turn himself in, Miss Kendricks, and then we'll see what we can do," Starsky said with a saccharine-sweet smile, doing his best "good cop" imitation, which pretty much stunk.

"Why should I do that, if you're only going to arrest him?" I shot back.

"We're not going to arrest him if he didn't do anything wrong," Hutch said. "But if he did, well, he'll have to face the consequences." He shrugged in an exaggerated way, encouraging me to imagine the worst.

So I did.

"You'll probably interrogate him for hours without anyone knowing where he is, deprive him of food, water, and an attorney, and get him to make a bogus confession when he's too delirious to know better." I glared at all of them. Blame it on my spirit of anarchy, at least at the moment, since none of the White Hats seemed to care that Malone needed saving, not skewering. "Once you've set your sights on a suspect, you stop looking for anyone else, and I won't let you railroad Brian, not when he didn't do anything wrong except try to take a friend out for a good time before he ties the knot."

"Ms. Kendricks, maybe you should consider that your relationship to Mr. Malone could make you a person of interest as well," Steel-haired Girl Cop said in a brittle tone, as if that was going to make me cave.

Please.

I'd survived worse threats from Cissy (with far more frightening consequences). I didn't crumble easily.

"Maybe you should consider that one of my best friends is a reporter," I said, perhaps unwisely and not quite accurately, as my buddy Janet Graham was the society editor for the suburban *Park Cities Press*, not a crime writer for the *Dallas Morning News.* "I'm sure she'd be happy to do an exposé on abuse of power at several local police departments."

"Are you claiming abuse, Ms. Kendricks?" That damned blond detective looked ready to pounce.

"I'm not exactly feeling the love," I snapped, regretting my choice of words the moment they flew out of my yap. Since when had I turned into such a smart-mouth? Oh, yeah, since I'd left the birth canal.

"I think we're through here," Cissy interjected and rose from her seat, reaching down for my arm, urging me up. "As you told us we could leave at any time, I believe now is the time. Andrea?" She dragged me toward the door, though none of the three police folks had budged an inch. "If you have any further questions, you know how to reach us. Or better still, if you need to converse with us further, why don't you arrange it through Deputy Chief Anna Dean at the Highland Park P.D. I've co-chaired plenty of Widows and Orphans fund-raisers with her, and I'm sure she'd be delighted to do me a favor."

You go, Mummy Dearest, I silently cheered.

Then I followed on her boot heels, nearly bumping into her backside when she stopped abruptly, turning around for one last hurrah.

She held up a finger, a brilliant smile on her puss. "Oh, and which one of you nice police people would like to drive us back to Mr. Malone's apartment? I left my Lexus in the parking lot."

Within five minutes, we were ensconced in the backseat of an unmarked Dallas police car with Hutch riding shotgun and Starsky at the wheel.

Not two words were exchanged in the brief time it took to get from the Addison P.D. to Malone's building. I'd half expected another lecture from Frick and Frack en route, reminding me it was my civic duty to rat out my boyfriend's hiding place, but they remained thankfully silent, checking the screen of an on-board computer.

The rain had stopped, though the windows sweated with condensation from the still humid air.

A van with the Channel 8 logo filled one of the parking spots, and, upon approach, I saw one of the omnipresent blond reporters from the station sticking a microphone in the face of a woman walking a dog.

Ah, what a thrill, I thought with a shake of my head, *getting your fifteen minutes of fame while your pup took a dump.* I could already hear said neighbor telling Susie Reporter things like, "He was always so quiet. He seemed like such a nice guy. I can't believe he's a cold-blooded killer."

Oy.

Cissy pointed out her champagne-hued Lexus sedan, and Starsky slid neatly into the empty slot beside it, thankfully nowhere near Ace Girl Journalist, her camera crew, and the small crowd beginning to gather around them, eager folks all hoping to get their mugs on the six o'clock news.

"All right, duchesses. There you go," Hutch said, as the car stopped, though neither detective made any move to let us out.

My mother cleared her throat less than discreetly, as if that would remind them of their manners. Instead, our holster-wearing escorts sat lumplike in their respective seats, proving that chivalry was indeed dead, or at least dormant.

At least the unmarked car had handles on the back doors, unlike the Addison P.D.'s squad car, which kept prisoners—and girlfriends and mothers of persons of interest—trapped in the rear seat.

Before I made my escape, Hutch shoved a business card at me and said, "Be smart, Ms. Kendricks, and give us a call if you learn something."

I took the card, but rebelliously thought, *Like hell I will.* What kind of woman turned in her man to the fuzz?

It was quite apparent that the police were after Malone to crucify him, not set him free from whatever spider's web he'd gotten himself caught up in. Not that I had great insight into police procedure, but it seemed to me that once they had a suspect in mind, they didn't often waver from that course.

And I wasn't about to see Brian go to jail for a crime I was sure he didn't commit. Not if I could get to him first.

Which I would. Somehow.

I just wasn't so sure what path I'd have to take.

I figured I'd ring my good friend Allie and apprise her of Mother's and my detainment in Addison, just as soon as I departed the detectives' company.

As if by osmosis, the cell in my bag started ringing as I put shoes to damp gravel and slammed the car's rear door. I stepped away from the unmarked vehicle, which began to slowly roll away, and retrieved the gadget with the irritating ring tone, seeing an unfamiliar number as I flipped it open and answered, "Hello?"

I heard a strangely garbled voice. "Andrea Kendricks?" it asked.

"Uh-huh. Who's this?" I couldn't even tell if it was male or female. Sounded like someone was talking through a dish towel.

"You still missing your boyfriend?"

"What? How do you know about that?" I asked—the first thing that popped out of my mouth.

"If you want him back alive, shut up and listen, and don't call the media or the police. You understand?" the barely discernible voice demanded, and a frisson of fear shot through me so that I couldn't have spoken if I'd wanted to. "It's up to you, okay? Pay us the money or you're gonna find pieces of your boyfriend all over New—um, Dallas. I won't waste a bullet. I'll just sharpen my knife. And I'd hate to get blood on his pretty pink shirt."

Despite my cotton-dry mouth, I got out, "What do you want from me?"

"We want $212,000 in cash by midnight tonight. We'll take it in Benjamins. You deliver it. No one else. We know what you look like, so no funny business. Got it?"

I whispered, "Yes," because it was the only answer that seemed fitting. I was already picturing a blade being sharpened, like on those Ronco commercials for Ginzu knives.

"Be a good little girl, and he won't get hurt, okay? We'll contact you soon with instructions."

"Wait," I piped up. "How do I know that you have Brian? Let me talk to him. Hello? *Hello?*"

But there was nothing; merely dead air.

It took a moment for the gist of the phone call to register; then a wave of panic filled my chest, and I could hardly catch my breath.

Someone had Malone, and they wanted a ransom?

I wished I could've laughed this off, but my gut told me it was real enough. Why else would the bad guys phone me unless they'd found out who I was from Brian?

Unless they knew I was someone with access to money (and I was, courtesy of my generous trust fund from Daddy, though it's not like I kept it in a piggy bank).

Hell's bells, this couldn't be happening.

What kind of nightmare was I trapped in?

If I lived on Elm Street and Freddie Krueger was my next door neighbor, things would surely seem rosier than this.

Tears stung my eyes, and I bit my lower lip to stop its trembling.

Just when I thought nothing worse could possibly happen, it did.

It already had.

Chapter 14

Malone had been kidnapped?
Was it possible?

Or was it a horrible hallucination, borne from inhaling an overdose of Eau de Sock while at Brian's place, when I should have worn the OSHA-approved gas mask?

But the call was real enough.

I'd heard it with my own reliable ears, and the way my knees shook attested to its authenticity as well.

What the devil was going on?

My boyfriend was being held hostage.

No wonder he couldn't be found. He was probably imprisoned in some madman's basement, chained to a radiator, made to lap up fetid water from a dog bowl.

So I'd been right in thinking someone else was responsible for his vanishing act. I'd believed all along there was an outside force involved, and now I knew for sure there was, which scared the hell out of me, like nothing else.

I tasted fear in my mouth and looked up, watching as the cop car pulled away and out of the parking lot, panic filling my chest as I realized I couldn't tell them about the threat to Brian's life.

Could I?

If you want him back alive, shut up and listen, and don't call the media or the police, got it?

I got it all right.

No cops.

No reporters.

Unless I wanted Malone carved up like a Cobb salad.

If anything happened to him and I was responsible, I would never forgive myself.

A soft touch on my arm startled me, and I glanced up at my mother, standing at my elbow with a worried look on her face.

"Is somethin' wrong, Andrea sweetie?"

I couldn't meet her eyes, and instead fumbled with my cell, afraid to drop it in my bag for fear I'd miss another call from the bad guys, though they wouldn't phone again so soon, would they?

Regardless, I hung onto it, despite my shaky grip and fingers suddenly slick with sweat.

"Andrea, whatever is the matter? And don't try to tell me it's nothing. You look whiter than Bunny Beeler's new porcelain veneers." She had her car keys in one hand, but reached for me with the other, tucking her thumb beneath my chin. "Who was that call from? Was it about Mr. Malone? Is he injured?"

The last time I'd broken into tears in front of Cissy was . . . well, I couldn't remember when. I tried to avoid that kind of situation if I could. There was something bred into me that always made me want to buck up, grin and bear it, never let 'em see me sweat.

Though this was different, wasn't it?

I wondered if my daddy would have pearls of wisdom for a situation like this, some down-home advice to get me through this; because I couldn't think of anything offhand that would make me feel less than frantic.

The trembling in my legs increased, and I felt the rest of my body shudder, dying to join in and collapse in a heap.

"Sweet pea, answer me. Did someone give you bad news about Brian? Well, worse than what we already know, of course, what with the police thinking he might've killed that erotic dancer."

Erotic dancer?

I wanted to correct her, but my teeth started chattering, and I couldn't form a single word.

"Andrea, please, you're scarin' me." My mother's pale blue eyes bored into mine, the worry in them palpable, and I bit the inside of my cheek as I fought to get control of my emotions.

"It's bad," I said, voice catching. "Really bad."

I saw my mother glance around us, at the crowd gathered around the reporter, still interviewing neighbors from Brian's apartment complex.

"In the car," she commanded, obviously sensing I was on the verge of hysterics. She guided me toward the passenger door of her Lexus, hustled me in and then quickly appeared in the driver's seat, starting the car and turning on the heat, though I was perspiring like a marathon runner.

"What can I do, sweetheart?" she asked, leaning nearer

so that I caught a huge whiff of Joy. She took my hand between her powdery soft ones and patted. "If you'd tell me what it is, perhaps I can help you. Was that Mr. Malone on the phone? Do you know where he is?"

"No," I said, a tiny pathetic squeak. "It wasn't Brian."

She laced her fingers through mine and squeezed. "Whoever it was obviously scared you to death. You're positively clammy."

"I am scared to death," I whispered, the blur of tears in my eyes. "I'm afraid for Brian."

"Sweetie, talk to me, or I can't fix it," she said in that soft way of hers that could so often make me do things I didn't really want to do. "Don't shut me out."

I could keep this to myself, try to handle it on my own, but I didn't like that option because I wasn't sure I could do it without sacrificing Malone. I couldn't afford to screw up, or he might be sliced and diced.

As far as I could see, there was no choice but one. So I made the decision then and there to confide in my mother, to trust her, because I wasn't sure what else to do and I couldn't go through this alone. I needed guidance, a plan, some kind of strategy.

Though Cissy had done her fair share of playing diplomat and defusing potential blow-ups when it came to self-absorbed socialites on committees, I wasn't sure how much she knew about freeing a hostage.

But she was dating a man who might well have a smidgen of experience in that area.

"I think I should talk to Stephen," I told her; hardly able to believe I was uttering those words, particularly after our uncomfortable conversation at brunch yesterday. But

Mother's beau had a military background, which doubtless had prepared him on how to get out of situations as
sticky as this.

Besides, I couldn't fathom where else to go, who else I
could turn to.

Stephen Howard was my only hope.

"You want to discuss whatever's bothering you with
Stephen? *My* Stephen?" She looked puzzled and pleased
all at once. "Are you still upset about my traveling with
him to Vegas? Because if that's adding to the state you're
in, well then, my darling, consider the trip cancelled."

*Good Lord, did she think everything revolved around
her?*

Yep, my boyfriend was being held at knifepoint under
threat of death, yet I was more miffed that my mummy
planned to fly to Sin City with a man she wasn't hitched to.

Okay, that was probably an unfair assessment, but I was
feeling pretty discombobulated at the moment, so forgive
my snarky mood.

I managed to answer calmly, "Mother, no, it's not about
you at all. It's about Brian and what he's gotten himself
into. He's in real trouble."

"I know, darling." She cocked her head. "They found a
murdered girl in his car trunk, which I'd hardly call a picnic."

"Brian didn't murder that woman, and just because she
was found in his car trunk with his business card doesn't
prove a thing, no matter what the police seem to think," I
sniveled, whining like a three-year-old.

"I'm sure he didn't kill that girl, my goodness," she
said, all wide eyes and fluttery lashes. "Though his being

innocent doesn't explain why he's hiding, which tends to make one wonder what kind of situation he's tangled up in. Not that I'm implying anything."

Whoa, Nelly.

What had happened to *He's an upstanding young man and a fine lawyer at one of the most respected firms in the city?*

In addition to wanting to cry, I suddenly felt the urge to kick something, and I didn't even have PMS. Everything was such a freaking mess.

"Mother, Brian's not hiding, he's been kidnapped," I wailed in a most indelicate manner, not caring about the sobs that shook my voice. "So, it's not fatherly advice I want from Stephen, and I don't need you being judgmental about what they found in Malone's trunk. Someone's got him, and they want a wad of cash by midnight or they'll cut him up in a million tiny pieces!" I finished with a strangled cry, which is when the tears began to fall in earnest.

"For heaven's sake, Andrea, why didn't you say so in the first place? You do tend to run in circles sometimes."

I ran in circles?

Oh, boy.

I couldn't even manage a biting retort, not in the midst of my meltdown.

For a minute or two, I boohooed with the best of them, before the waterworks started to dry up and I wiped my nose on my cuff.

"Oh, Andrea, honey, no." My mother promptly withdrew a clean and pressed (and monogrammed) handkerchief from her bag, handing it over. "Now blow."

In my family, a proffered hankie was often given in lieu of a hug.

Call us sentimental.

So I honked my horn into the hankie and blotted at my soggy eyes, pulling myself together so I could repeat the kidnapper's ransom demand.

Cissy kept her lips zipped as I rambled; though, when I'd finished, she further cranked up the heat in the Lexus, as if she could sweat the fear out of me. Then she unsnapped her rarely used cell phone from its compartment in her purse.

"What are you doing?" I asked, hoping to God she wasn't calling Anna Dean, the deputy chief of the Highland Park Police, or one of her society reporting cronies at the *Dallas Morning News*.

She gave me a "hush" look as she dialed before she uttered sternly but sweetly, "Hello, Stephen? Can you meet me at the house in, say, twenty minutes? Andrea has something serious to discuss with you . . . Oh, you did? On the radio?" She lowered her voice, as if I wouldn't hear. "Yes, it's about *that*. And thank you." She blushed, the flicker of a smile on her lips as she added, "Yes, me too. See you soon."

I stared at her for the longest moment, thinking that in the good old days it would've been my daddy she'd been talking to in such an intimate tone. It would've been my father whom I'd run to, since he could solve any problem, no matter how big.

But Daddy was gone, and I needed a cooler head to prevail.

Stephen Howard would have to do.

"Better now?" she said, and I nodded, pressing the used kerchief back into her hand. "Good girl."

Be a good little girl, and he won't get hurt, okay?

I recalled the mumbled voice again and shut my eyes, pressed my hands between my thighs to still them.

Mother put the car in gear and started driving.

All the way south to Highland Park a million questions flitted through my mind. Why would someone do this to Brian? How could I get $212,000 in cash—and Benjamins, mind you—together before midnight? Would they really kill Malone if I couldn't?

"Who would want to hurt Mr. Malone?" my mother said at one point, surely sensing the direction of my thoughts. "Perhaps he helped send some nasty fellow to jail and the family wants revenge."

My God, did she think this was a rerun of *Law & Order*? Or a late night showing of *The Godfather*?

"That doesn't happen in real life," I told her, leaning my forehead against the cool window. "Not unless you're in the mob."

"He's a defense attorney, isn't he?" she replied, doing her superior mother thing again. "Surely he's dealt with his share of lowlifes." She tapped a finger against the steering wheel, ticking off: "Murderers, killers, rapists, kidnappers, embezzlers, child molesters. Could be that one of them wasn't happy with his work."

"You watch way too much cable," I groaned.

"Well, it's too bad you don't have cable," she came back at me. "Because if you saw a few episodes of *Court TV*, you'd realize I was right. It happens all the time."

"I have better things to do than flip through four hundred

channels of television." I sat up straight and sniffled. "Besides, there's never anything worthwhile on."

"I think you'd take back that remark if you ever watched the History Channel or A&E," my mother insisted. "And *Oprah*. That woman can make finding the right bra seem fascinating, although I wish they'd quit dressing her in such tight pants. Sometimes she looks like a stuffed sausage."

The world's richest woman looked like a stuffed sausage? *Lord have mercy.*

I laughed, despite myself.

Sweet black-eyed peas, the things that came out of Cissy's mouth! The unbelievable non sequiturs! Someone should bottle it and offer it up as a substitute for antidepressants.

"What's so funny?" she asked as I suffered through a fit of giggles.

"You," I said when I'd settled down enough to speak.

"My dear," she said, completely serious, "I think you need a Valium."

I wanted to hug her, throw my arms around her and squeeze, although I didn't, and not only because she would've lost control of the wheel and driven us into a fence.

Instead, I sighed and leaned back in the seat, listening as she began to hum a tune I didn't recognize at first, then realized it was Patsy Cline's "Crazy," which made me grin on the inside.

If "crazy" didn't define my life—heck, my entire world— I didn't know what word would.

My mother was clearly insane (okay, eccentric, at the very least).

I couldn't call myself "rational" or "grounded" without crossing my fingers behind my back and hoping my pants didn't ignite spontaneously.

But then again, how could I keep a sense of humor—and a sense of hope—with all that was going on if I weren't a little nuts?

"Thank you," I whispered, though I'm not certain she heard me.

She hummed like a fiend, absolutely unaware of what she'd done for me, just by being there.

When we finally pulled up in Cissy's driveway, I had pulled myself together.

I didn't necessarily feel able to leap tall buildings in a single bound, but I could handle this. I could do what must be done to set things straight.

Stephen's blue Chevy pickup sat near the pair of white-washed terra-cotta lions that perched upon the front stoop, and Mother settled her car in behind his. The front door came open as we parked, and I saw Stephen step outside, hands on hips, waiting.

I stared at him and swallowed hard, deciding he looked as capable as anyone. Maybe not as physically sturdy as my father (whom I'd never have called slim), but someone used to being leaned on, just the same.

And, boy, did I need to lean.

Cissy came around to my side of the car. As I shut the door, she took my arm, guiding me toward the house.

She said hello to Stephen, as did I, and he didn't ask any questions, not then, but merely fell into step behind us. My lifelong fairy godmother and Mother's longtime social secretary Sandy Beck popped into the foyer as we entered, and Cissy suggested she bring us a tray of hot tea and cookies.

I guess it couldn't hurt to have a little Pepperidge Farm fortification before the powwow.

Mother shepherded Stephen and me toward the downstairs den, a warm room with high beamed ceilings, dark patterned rug, and overstuffed furniture that looked like it could swallow you whole. There were books filling shelves that lined the walls, ones I knew had been selected more for the color of their leather spines than for their contents. Cissy's decorator had basically bought them by the foot.

The "real" books, the beloved tomes my father had often read from aloud at night before I went to bed, those were stored upstairs in his well-preserved office, a room my mother hadn't touched since he'd died except to allow the housekeeper to clean it.

Mother took off her cloak and settled me down beside her on the sofa, while Stephen perched on a nearby club chair, its cushions so plump they nearly engulfed him.

Cissy and her beau engaged in small-talk, at first, about how much we'd needed the rain and how nice it was that the Dallas Zoo would be borrowing a pair of pandas from China in the spring.

I sat and listened, doing my best just to breathe; to demonstrate a calm I didn't feel, like sitting around, plotting a way to get my boyfriend out of his kidnappers' clutches was an everyday thing.

When Sandy brought in the tea and cookies, my mother and her dude got suddenly quiet.

"I'll leave you all alone to talk," Sandy said, drawing

her pink cardigan closed, her comfortably creased face turning briefly to me. "If you need an ear, Andy, I'm always here."

"I know, thank you," I told her, realizing full well that my mother would fill her in soon enough on all the details. Sandy knew more secrets about my family than anyone, and she would take them to the grave, I was sure. Another reason we adored her.

She shut the heavy paneled door on her way out, and Mother poured a cup of tea and passed it over. Earl Grey. Straight up. No sugar, no cream. Just the way I liked it. The first sip warmed my insides, all the way down to my belly, and I appreciated the heat of it, despite how damp I felt on the outside, with the rain and my nervous sweat.

Once Stephen had a cup, too, and Cissy had prepared one for herself, she verbally nudged me. "Go ahead, Andrea. Tell him everything and don't leave anything out."

So I set down my tea, afraid my hands would shake too much not to spill, and wiped my palms on my thighs, before I raised my gaze to meet the man's weathered face and calm blue eyes.

"It started on Saturday night when Brian took Matty to the strip club for a two-man bachelor party . . ." I began, and I didn't stop until I'd gone over every detail I knew of what had transpired since that fateful evening.

I shared the fact that I'd gone to The Men's Club myself to talk to Lu McCarthy, the barmaid who'd known Trayla Trash and who'd supposedly witnessed Brian leaving the place with the stripper. I noted the piece on the news about Brian's Acura being found at Love Field with Trayla wrapped in a tarp in his trunk, and how I was sure that his business card being found with her meant someone was trying to frame him.

I explained that Brian was a wanted man and that I'd dragged Mother over to his apartment so I could comb the place for clues, resulting in an invitation to the Addison P.D. for a chat when we got caught red-handed.

If Stephen was shocked by any of it, he didn't show it. His expression remained sober; I didn't ever see him flinch.

I mentioned that Allie had been looking for papers from the office Brian had taken with him regarding a criminal case they were helping to prepare for trial.

Ultimately, I spilled all about the phone call on my cell, the one with the garbled voice demanding $212,000 in Benjamins by midnight or else Malone would be chopped into a million pieces.

When I was done, Stephen unloaded some follow-up questions, as in, "Who did you talk to at the strip club?"

I told him: the hostess inside the front doors, the bouncer, Lu McCarthy, and Cricket the bartender.

"Did Brian discuss this latest case with you?"

No, he hadn't.

"Did his alleged kidnappers let you speak to him?"

No, they didn't.

"Did they offer any proof they've got him?"

That one made me squirm.

Okay, they obviously knew I was his girlfriend, which wasn't something they would've found out about on the news. Either Brian had to have let the cat out of the bag or else they'd done a fair amount of digging.

I was about to tell Stephen *Nope, no proof* when I re-

membered the remark about getting blood on his pink
shirt.

"They know what he was wearing that night," I said.

"That doesn't mean they have him, Andy."

Surprise, surprise. The ex-IRS agent was a pragmatist.

Only I wasn't feeling all that practical at the moment. I
was running on high octane emotion.

"Where else could he be?" I said, not a little impatiently, because the idea that someone had snatched Brian
from The Men's Club explained his absence, and it was
far better than believing he'd left me for a stripper whose
head he'd later bashed in before stowing her in the trunk
of his illegally parked car, for Pete's sake.

"Andy, we should take some time and look into this,"
Stephen said, but I wasn't having it. I wasn't risking Malone's life for mere money.

"I want him back," I insisted, "so help me do that,
Stephen, please."

He glanced at my mother before giving me a slow nod.
"Okay."

"Where do we go from here?" I demanded, the pitch of
my voice strained. "What do I say when they phone
again?"

My fears out in the open, I sat still and waited.

"I could hire someone," my mother said to Stephen,
barely raising the soft drawl of her voice. "A private in-
vestigator. This kind of thing is too dangerous for Andy to
be involved in."

"I don't think we should bring in an outsider," I said, re-
jecting her very generous offer. "Besides, they want me to
deliver the cash, not some stranger."

"The girl's right, Cissy," Stephen agreed. "They obviously know who she is and what she looks like."

My mouth went even drier at the way he put it so bluntly, and I imagined the evildoers spying on me, maybe even hiding behind the bushes and taking pictures of me and Malone.

Stephen went on: "If they've really got Brian, we've got to play by their rules, within reason." He proffered his palm. "Let me see your cell, Andy."

Without hesitation, I removed it from my bag and handed it over. He squinted at the tiny screen, obviously hunting down my recently received numbers, before he hit a button and held the phone to his ear. Doubtless doing what I should have done: dialing back the phone the kidnappers had used.

I scooted to the edge of the sofa, hands between my knees, holding my breath.

"Gotta be a pay phone," he said, frowning, and took a moment to pull a tiny pad and pencil from his breast pocket to jot down the number. "I'll see if I can't find out where it's located. A reverse directory should do the trick." He returned the phone, which I set in my lap.

"What should I do now?" I asked him. "Shouldn't I be working on getting the money, or boning up on ransom drop etiquette?"

"At least you've still got your sense of humor." He shot me a tight smile. "Give me a minute, will you? I need to think."

Stephen rose from the chair, walked over to the shuttered window and stood there a long moment, peering out. When he was done contemplating, he extracted his cell phone from the pocket of his tweed jacket and excused himself from the room.

I glanced at Cissy, who seemed not at all disturbed by his behavior, but instead continued sipping her tea, pinky extended in the manner of well-bred ladies.

I caught my hands between my knees, determined to rein in my impatience, wanting to remind them both that the clock was ticking.

It was nearly noon, and I had but another twelve hours to figure out what to do or Brian might not live to see to-morrow.

I bit the inside of my cheek so hard I tasted blood, and still I stayed cool, didn't scream, ignored the ticking of the clock on the mantel, the noise infinitely magnified.

Just when I thought I couldn't stand another moment more, Stephen reappeared in the den, closing the door behind him. He came around the sofa and paused across the coffee table from where I sat.

"I think I know how we can handle this without anyone getting hurt," he said. "I've got a few things to take care of with an old buddy who used to be a Treasury man, so give me an hour or two, and I'll be back. These people—whoever they are—don't sound like seasoned criminals, or else they'd be asking for wire transfers to accounts in the Caymans, not cash." He rubbed his jaw. "They also wouldn't ask for 'Benjamins,' Andy. That's Hollywood's idea of a ransom. The denomination's too large. They sound like greedy SOBs who spotted an opportunity and figured they'd bleed a local heiress for a chunk of her trust fund without anyone getting hurt."

Seasoned criminals or not, they had my boyfriend and

weren't going to let him go until I paid them off. Which meant I had to get my hands on a lot of greenbacks. Local heiress that I was, I still didn't have 212,000 bucks at home in my cookie jar.

"So what about the money?" I asked him, thinking maybe I should get my portfolio manager on the horn and order him to dump some stocks pronto.

"I've got that covered, Andy. Trust me."

"Where'll you get that kind of cash?" Had the caffeine in the Earl Grey made him dizzy? "You plan on breaking into the Treasury?"

I was joking, but Stephen didn't laugh.

"Something like that," he said, like a man with a secret. "Hang tight until I'm back. Can you do that?"

Like I had the strength left to fight.

I sighed and told him, "I'm not going anywhere."

Really, what choice did I have?

Chapter 15

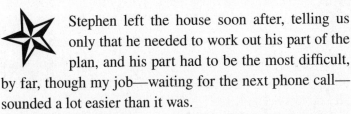Stephen left the house soon after, telling us only that he needed to work out his part of the plan, and his part had to be the most difficult, by far, though my job—waiting for the next phone call—sounded a lot easier than it was.

Before he split, Mother's beau did his best to calm my nerves, telling me not to worry about the cash, to concentrate on the phone call and anything I could remember about it.

I wondered if we could tape the next conversation, or trace it, but Stephen had explained that without some kind of spy gear to pick up the signal, there wasn't much chance of recording anything; and if they used another pay phone, it wouldn't give us much to go on anyway. So I was to pay attention, write down any instructions they gave me, and stay put at Cissy's until he returned from his mission.

I didn't argue with him, though we did have a brief debate about getting the police involved. Stephen was of the notion that the cops could handle such a situation discreetly, but I didn't have the same kind of faith, not after the morning's session with Starsky and Hutch. They were foaming at the mouth in their eagerness to interrogate Brian about Trayla's death. They hadn't listened to me then, so why should I think they'd believe me about this? They'd likely assume I was trying to distract them from looking at Brian as a murder suspect.

Besides, the voice on the phone had said "no cops," and I wasn't going to cross the bad guys, whoever they were. So far as I was concerned, this was all too real, and I wasn't even thinking in terms of a hoax.

I mean, seriously, who was warped enough to pretend to have kidnapped someone? Weren't there easier ways to get money? Say, robbing a bank? Hooking a chain around an ATM and dragging it from the bumper of a rusty pickup truck?

I was doing my best to ponder the "who" part of the equation, as in who would have taken Brian? And why? Unless it had always been about the ransom. But, if it were, why had they waited more than a day to call?

Stephen had surmised that the kidnappers were well aware of who I was and the fact that I hadn't exactly sprung from impoverished roots. "My God, Andy, anyone who Googles your name will see the word 'heiress' pop up over and over," he'd said. "It's not a secret that you come from privilege."

Yet another black mark against my being raised in "the

bubble" of Highland Park. If I'd come from po' folks, maybe none of this would've happened.

"But why not take me instead?" I'd asked, jerking my chin toward Cissy. "Mother would've paid far more than two hundred thousand to get me back. They could've asked for fifty million, and she would've ponied up." I met her eyes. "Wouldn't you?"

Pregnant pause.

"Mother?"

"Of course I would, sweetheart, whatever they wanted," she'd assured me, after my heart skipped a beat as she hesitated, like she'd needed the chance to stop and consider it.

It was great to know where I stood.

Yeesh.

"There'd be less press interest with grabbing Malone," Stephen had explained. "And he's the perfect form of leverage. The man you love. Someone could have been following you and Brian for a while, figuring out a time to nick him when he was alone."

Like when he'd taken off backstage after Trayla?

Which had me pretty well convinced she'd been the bait that had gotten him snagged. Though why had he chased her in the first place? Okay, she was pretty enough, from what I'd glimpsed in the snapshot taped to her dressing room mirror, and she was plenty stacked. But it's not like pretty girls weren't a dime a dozen in Big D, and most of them didn't take off their clothes for cash.

There was something big I was missing, and I hadn't an inkling what that was.

Besides, why would they kill Trayla if she was part of the scheme? Because it didn't sound like a logical ending.

Unless she'd flubbed up somehow or had threatened to go to the cops. Was she behind his call to me? But why the fictional breakup message? To make sure I was really his girl? To confirm it was my number?

Something about that felt wrong, but I wasn't sure what.

I still had too many questions and was sorely lacking in the answer department.

"If they wanted to keep the press out of it, they're doing a piss-poor job," I'd suggested to Stephen, "what with the police finding his car parked at Love Field with a dead girl in the trunk."

I cringed as the image of a figure wrapped in tarp flashed into my head.

"Probably why they contacted you when they did, Andy. Somehow, they screwed up and the girl was killed, so they covered their butts by pointing the finger at Brian, only now the police are looking for him, too. Whoever snatched him must've realized they'd better do the cash exchange pronto, hoping you'd be compliant and they could grab the money and clear out before they attracted the attention of the boys in blue."

Okay, I'd buy that.

It was as good a reason as any, I supposed. Though I couldn't say I felt better, knowing the bad guys had taken Brian instead of me. Malone was a great guy. I couldn't imagine him harming a flea, much less a human being, so it drove a knife in my heart, thinking he was afraid or even injured.

How could anyone do anything so awful as to kidnap another human being?

I just didn't get it.

But I'd grown up in a sheltered world, one pretty much devoid of ugliness, so I was having trouble grasping the situation.

I felt a little like I had when my father died, as though someone had pushed the Pause button on my life, and I couldn't see past the hurt of the moment. I couldn't laugh, couldn't smile, because inside I was numb, too stunned to do much of anything.

Maybe that was how we dealt with pain and grief, by temporarily suspending our emotions and our daily routine, by zoning out so that our minds and hearts didn't have to process the devastation and fear. Otherwise, how could we go on?

"Andy."

A soft voice drew me out of my maudlin meanderings.

"Please, child, you have to eat something," Sandy Beck, my fairy godmother, urged, as I hadn't touched the tuna sandwich she'd made me for lunch.

"I'm trying," I told her, and forced myself to take a nibble as Mother watched with her eagle eyes from across the table.

Tuna was normally a favorite of mine—despite my dislike for most fish—but I had little appetite at the moment. It was difficult to eat and think at the same time when I had so much on my mind.

There was something I needed to do, and I'd been avoiding it. I had the address book I'd taken from Malone's desk, opened to the page with his parents' phone information on it, and I had Mother's portable phone in hand, only I had to work myself up to it, because I had no earthly idea what I'd say.

Had the police called them already? Were they packing their bags and heading to the airport to fly from St. Louis to Dallas?

Or would I be their first-alert, the alarm bell that caused their hearts to stop when I told them their son was in serious trouble?

I couldn't decide which was worse.

"If it were me, would you want Malone to call you?" I asked Cissy, and told her what I aimed to do.

"Yes," she said. "I would."

Which gave me a much needed nudge, although I still wasn't all-fired certain what I'd say.

I sucked it up and dialed the ten-digit number for Chesterfield, Missouri, holding my breath as I counted one ring then two.

When I caught the click of the line being picked up, I braced myself for a motherly tone, chirping, *"Hello, Malone residence."*

But I quickly realized I had their voice mail, and it wasn't a woman but a soothing male voice that delivered the message:

"Sorry we can't take your call, but we're on a retreat. No TV, no laptops, no phones, just a lot of love and heavy petting. If you need to reach us, Pam's holding the fort at the office and she'll help you till we're back. Until then, woof-woof and ciao."

Woof-woof and ciao? Love and heavy petting?

What was going on there in the St. Louis suburbs?

Sounded kinky enough for Maury Povich.

I guess I could've written down the office number delivered after the greeting, but I didn't. Instead, I hung up as fast as I could, relieved that my first communication with Malone's parents wouldn't be about his dire circumstances.

My mother gave me a look. "Well?" she said.

"They're out of town," I told her. "On some kind of retreat with no phones, TVs, or laptops."

"Maybe it's for the best."

I nodded, hoping Malone would return, clear things up with the cops, and get his life back in order before his parents came back from their trip and learned that anything had ever been wrong.

"Would you like a piece of pie, Andy?" Sandy asked, getting up from the table and clearing our plates, though no one had done much eating. "I've got some apple left from one I baked this weekend."

"No, but thanks." What I needed was something Sandy couldn't warm up in the oven.

I had my cell phone on the table, and I stared at it, my concentration so intense I jumped out of my skin when it actually rang.

Cissy let out an audible gasp, pushing a pad of paper and pencil in my direction as I snatched up my cell and flipped it open, my pulse pounding ferociously. I didn't bother to catch the number on the screen, knowing in my bones it was them, the bad guys. I could sense the evil emanating through the receiver as I breathed a wary, "Hello?"

"Kendricks? Where the hell are you? 'Cuz you're obviously not home."

Damn.

It was evil all right, just not the kind I'd expected.

"No, Allie, I'm not home," I said, my anxiety rerouting in another direction entirely. "I'm at my mother's. What do you want, and make it fast. I'm waiting for another call, and it's important."

I shook my head, and Mother settled back into her chair. Sandy went over to the sink to rinse dishes.

"I went by your condo during my lunch hour, and Channel 8 is on to you, Nancy Drew. Their van has your place staked out, and it probably won't be long until others show up on your doorstep. The helmet-haired reporter was interviewing some woman in curlers and fuzzy slippers."

"Crap," I let slip, knowing exactly who that was. My upstairs neighbor Penny George, better known as Cissy's snitch. I was sure she'd donned her best velour warm-up suit for the occasion and could hardly contain her giddiness as she'd confessed to all that she often saw Malone's red Acura—in which the dead stripper had been found—parked in front of my place.

Could I hope that she rotted in Hell, even if she went to Bible study with my mother? Or was that an offense punishable by a lightning strike?

I groaned, wishing the reporter had talked to Charlie Tompkins, my next door neighbor instead. He was a good ol' Texas boy, loyal to a fault. He would've lied if he'd thought it would help me or Brian.

"I didn't see your Jeep," Allie continued, seemingly oblivious to any noises I made. "So I figured you were hiding out somewhere quieter."

"I'm not hiding out. I just didn't want to be alone.

There's—" I hesitated, not certain of how much I felt like sharing. "—a lot going on."

"I'll say," she piped up. "Your condo's not the only hot zone. Don't you want to know the latest from ARGH?"

"I'm kind of busy here," I told her, wanting to get her off the line, though I did have call waiting. Still, I was hardly in the mood for chitchat with Attila the Blonde, despite our strange bonding of late.

"You're not curious about the fresh scoop on Malonegate?"

Malonegate?

This mess had a nickname?

"Go on." I rubbed my forehead.

"Abramawitz is on to the missing docs," she said without waiting for my answer. "For the Oleksiy case," she explained, in case I'd forgotten, which I had. "I tried to cover for Brian, apologized to Old Abe and mumbled about leaving them at home. I called the prosecutor's office to get another copy of the updated witness list after I got bawled out big-time, but it's better than Bri getting fired. Guess he thought he'd have it back by this morning before anyone noticed; though he didn't quite make it, did he? Goes to prove your theory, doesn't it?"

"Which theory was that?" I'd come up with several variations on the "Malone is missing" theme, so I had no idea which she meant.

"Duh, that Brian's an innocent bystander in this ballooning disaster." She sounded impatient, which seemed pretty much her usual tone of voice. "Look, I know he didn't have anything to do with that woman's death. When we were together, he used to scoop up spiders in Kleenex and deposit them outside, because he couldn't stand to squash them. No way could he hurt a woman, much less bean her to death with a golf club. Particularly with one of *his* golf clubs. I know how he loves his precious set of Calloways."

The cockles of my heart felt suddenly warm and toasty, despite her reference to homicide.

"You believe me?"

"My source at the DPD said the woman found in Brian's trunk wasn't just clobbered with a Big Bertha, her skull was fractured and her face was beaten so badly it looked like pulp. Someone didn't just want her dead, Andy. This was superpersonal."

"My God."

I was truly thankful that I hadn't eaten the tuna sandwich. My stomach curdled at the thought of such violence, of anyone being brutalized like that, though it convinced me like never before that Malone had nothing to do with the woman's death.

"I take back everything bad I said about Brian," Allie went on, and I could do little more than listen and blink. "I can't sit on the sidelines. Hell, this has gone too far already. I need to prove Malone's not a killer."

"You're serious?" Wow. I was stunned, but oddly grateful. I would take all the help I could get, considering the sum total of my posse was my mother and her boyfriend. Not exactly the A-Team, was it?

"I want to peek into Brian's office, though I have to wait until the coast is clear, as it's the center of attention right now. I have to tell you, Kendricks, the more I think about what Brian was doing on Friday, the more I wonder if whatever he's caught up in is somehow related to Oleksiy.

Only, I don't know the connection yet. Give me some time, and I'll figure it out."

Time?

It was less than twelve hours until midnight.

I didn't have much to spare.

I glanced at my mother, reminded of her remarks from hours earlier: *Surely he's dealt with his share of lowlifes . . . Murderers, killers, rapists, kidnappers, embezzlers, and child molesters. Could be that one of them wasn't happy with his work.*

"So you think this might have to do with the witness list?" I asked, to get it clear in my mind.

"Could be."

"You think someone on it wanted to hurt Brian?" The words popped out of my mouth before I could censor them. "Why?"

"Maybe not someone on the list, Kendricks."

Something clicked inside my brain.

A remark one of the cops had made this morning.

"The Oleksiy case involves money laundering, doesn't it, Allie?" I asked her, thinking of Starsky's comment that Brian might have taken something that wasn't his and gotten in over his head.

"It does, yeah." She added in a whisper, as if afraid someone would overhear, "Let's just say that it's a whole different ballgame in this brave new world. With the Patriot Act clamping down on banks, things like gift cards and stolen art are becoming the currency of choice."

I'm not sure what any of that had to do with Brian, but I had a strong sense he'd gotten himself mixed up in something dangerous.

"What if you're right about a connection?" I caught my mother's eye, and she narrowed her brows, listening. "What if Brian starting digging into one of these witnesses' backgrounds and unearthed some nasty worms?"

"I'm already nosing around in that wormhole, Kendricks. When things cool down, I'm gonna have a chat with Malone's secretary."

"Though it doesn't make sense, does it?" I ruminated aloud. "I mean, if he uncovered dirt on a witness testifying against Oleksiy, that'd be good for your side, right? So who'd want to kidnap him? The district attorney?" Even I figured that was unlikely.

"Did you say kidnap?"

Had I?

Oh, boy.

"Geez, Allie, I'm not sure what you mean." Did I want to drag her into this? Was I taking a risk, spilling to Allie? Though she wasn't a cop. She was Brian's colleague, his friend. "Um"—crap, I felt obligated to come clean—"okay, yes, I said kidnap."

"Wait a minute, drama queen. Are you telling me someone's holding Brian hostage?" she jumped on me. "What's going on? I thought we were in this together. Don't hold out on me."

In it together.

How weird did that sound?

Then again, she was already part of this whole sordid mess, and she was the one with the firsthand knowledge about Brian's work, about this Oleksiy case; she was the one who had a contact at the Dallas P.D. It might not be in Brian's best interest to shut her out.

So I blabbed.

"I got a ransom demand," I admitted, "right after Mother and I left the Addison police station."

"Wait a minute, Annie Oakley. You and Mama Kendricks had a run-in with the Addison P.D.?"

Oops. I hadn't exactly filled her in on that either, had I? "It was a big misunderstanding. We'd gone over to Brian's apartment, after some reporters had been poking around, apparently, so a neighbor phoned the cops—"

"Why were you at Brian's?"

"Looking for clues." And finding none, except the birthday card, which was message enough for me. "The police thought I knew where he was."

"But you don't, do you?"

For God's sake.

Et tu, Brutus the Blonde?

"If I knew where he was, do you think I'd be waiting around for his kidnappers to call? You figure I made this whole thing up just for kicks?"

"Hey, tone it down, Kendricks. You don't have to yell at me."

I sucked in a breath, tried to keep my cool. Mother traded chairs for one beside me and put her hand on my shoulder, giving a squeeze.

"You don't think someone's playing you?" she asked. "You really believe that Brian's been kidnapped?"

Tears pricked at the back of my eyelids again, and I fought them hard. I would not crack. There was too much still to do. "I have to believe it, Allie. I have no choice. They said they'd kill him if I didn't pay up."

"How much do they want?"

"Two hundred twelve thousand."

"*What?* That makes about as much sense as Kinky Friedman in the governor's mansion."

Which is exactly what I'd thought, but I figured kidnappers had their quirks, too.

"Why not a million?" she asked. "Or ten mil, while they're at it?"

"I don't know, Allie." *Gee, what was I? The ransom psychic?*

"When do they want it?"

"Delivered by midnight tonight," I informed her, my voice a disturbing croak. "They're supposed to call again with instructions, so I'm practically sitting on my cell phone."

"Did you contact the cops?"

"No!" I panicked at the thought. "They said no police or media, or I'll find pieces of my boyfriend all over Dallas." Well, actually, the voice had said "New Dallas," which was odd, wasn't it? "Then they told me they won't waste a bullet. They'll just sharpen their knife."

"You're joking?"

What did she want? The ransom note recorded on CD for her listening pleasure?

"No, I'm not joking, and yes, that's what they said, and no, I don't know if it was a man or woman, which is why I'm using the plural, in case you're planning to sic the grammar police on me."

"Excuse me for saying so, Kendricks, but those are some crazy-ass kidnappers. Sharpening a knife, saving a bullet, demanding 212,000 bucks from a Highland Park deb who could easily fork over ten times that."

"Debutante dropout," I reminded her, feeling irked that she, a lawyer, didn't have all the facts. "I didn't go through with it."

"But you didn't give up your inheritance, did you?"

I bristled, reminding her, "This isn't about me, Allie."

"Isn't it? You think anyone would've wanted to hold Brian for ransom if you weren't his paramour?"

His paramour?

That was *so* 1930s. Sounded like a word my mother would use.

I figured I'd had my quota of Blondie for the day. "If you want to help Brian, then fine, but I don't need you to make me feel worse," I snapped, earning a curious look from my mother. "Ringing up Malone's parents in Missouri was awful enough," I grumbled. "I'm almost relieved they weren't home, something about petting and woofing—"

"Their animal-psych retreat," Allie interrupted, like a chronic Ms. Know It All. "They do it every fall like clockwork."

"Animal retreat?" Honestly, was it wrong to assume everyone else had gone mad, and I was the last semisane person on the planet?

"Malone's mom and dad are pet psychs."

"Pet psychics?"

"Psychologists," she corrected, and there was no kidding in her tone. "They analyze critters, trying to figure out why Fido's chewing up the husband's shoes or why Fluffy's peeing on the Persian rug. Their motto is something like, 'We'll show your pets how to heal.' If they're off to the boonies for human-canine bonding, they'll be incommunicado for a while. Probably all for the better," she reasoned.

Another bit of Malone's life I'd been left out of, though Allie seemed as well-versed on the subject of his parents as she was on where he hid his extra house key. Damn her skinny self.

Why hadn't Brian mentioned his folks were pet psychologists? Was he too embarrassed to tell me? Or was it just one more thing in his life he'd kept private, like that journal filled with bad poetry and his affinity for *The Joy of Cooking*?

Man, but it was hard to fathom how such a straitlaced lawyer could have been raised by a pair of dog shrinks.

Though one could say the same about me and Cissy, couldn't they? As in, how could such a prissy and proper socialite have reared such an etiquette-impaired society refugee?

"Kendricks?" Allie's voice again derailed my thoughts. "You might want to use your computer savvy and look into this ransom thing. It sounds too hinky to be real."

What did she mean "look into this ransom thing"?

"I don't know what you think I'll find online," I told her. "It's not like lots of kidnappers are doing blogs, and I don't know of any Web sites offering advice for dealing with boyfriend snatchers, like what to say when you make the first contact or what kind of tote to stick the cash in."

"Any reason you're afraid to do some snooping?" Allie challenged. "You don't even need to leave the safety of Mama Bird's nest for that. But handling the kidnappers' demands . . . girl, that's not your bag. On the other hand, I'm used to dealing with dirt-bags face-to-face. They're usually clients," she said and made it sound like a good thing. "Maybe I should go with you on the drop. I'm cool under pressure."

"Thanks for the offer"—surprising as it was—"but you can't, Allie. They want me solo."

"I could hide in the backseat."

I glanced at the clock. I'd already been on the phone with her for too long, and I didn't want to tie up the line, call waiting or not.

"Why don't you leave the ransom to me, all right? You worry about getting into Brian's office. Find a copy of that list. See what you can turn up. Maybe you'll figure out who's got him, and we can nip this whole thing in the bud."

"You're right," she said. "I'm on it."

"Great."

I hung up and set the phone down on the table. My hand was trembling.

"Sweetie? Are you okay?" my mother asked.

"I'm fine." I made a valiant effort to shoot her a convincing smile; but it was a feeble attempt, and I'm not sure she bought it.

What I wanted to do was lay down my head and cry.

Or throw up.

How was I supposed to feel? To react?

My life had come to resemble the plot of a bad crime novel when you strung all the parts together.

Malone was missing, and the cops believed he was involved in the murder of a stripper found wrapped in plastic in the trunk of his illegally parked car. Like that wasn't god-awful enough, there was the phone call claiming Brian was being held for ransom, and now I had to worry about delivering the moola by midnight tonight or risk a blood-letting. To top it off, Malone was under fire at his office for skipping out with documents from an upcoming trial, and the Big Cheese at his firm was holding meetings threatening to oust him if he didn't show up with said docs pronto.

And I couldn't call the police, because the detectives assigned to Trayla Trash's homicide thought I was a liar—or at least a withholder of crucial scoop—plus, the Bad Guys had warned against involving the P.D., so I had to put my faith in my mother's boyfriend, the Navy veteran and ex-IRS agent, the fellow I'd been resenting this past month for trying to take my father's place in Cissy's life, when just the day before I'd all but vetoed the idea of Stephen taking Mother to Vegas.

Talk about irony.

Funny how plans to rescue a kidnapped boyfriend had changed everything.

Chapter 16

It seemed forever since Stephen had left
Mother's house, and my cell hadn't rung once
since Allie interrupted my lunch date with a
cold tuna fish sandwich.

I spent a good hour curled up on the window seat of
Mother's sitting room, staring out the window and doing
my best "pathetic girl" routine, my cell in my hip pocket
and the birthday card I'd found at Brian's apartment
clutched in my hands.

When Cissy had come looking for me and found me
gazing teary-eyed at Malone's scribbled words, she'd put
her hands on her hips and expelled a most disappointed
sigh, then insisted I get up off my booty and do something
useful.

"You could always help Sandy fold laundry," she suggested, "because crying isn't going to solve anything, you
realize."

Of course, she was right.

Acting like a soggy dishrag wouldn't bring Brian home, no matter how good it felt to mope for a spell.

So I took her advice, vacating the window seat to attempt something constructive.

Instead of laundry, however, I went to my old room and plunked down in front of the ancient Dell that whirred way too noisily when I turned it on.

I clicked on the ISP icon and hooked up to the Net on a dial-up modem that reminded me why God had created DSL, and I waited for the connection, tapping a foot and glancing around me, at my canopied bed, the Madame Alexander dolls seated in rows on the shelves of my bureau, and the neat line of my yellow-spined Nancy Drew books.

Mother had preserved my girlhood digs with museum-like care, keeping things precisely as I'd left them. I'm not sure if it was an indication that, somewhere in her heart, she wished she could keep me a child forever, or if there were just too many rooms in the mansion to worry about converting mine into something else. Like she needed another guest room or den?

It was somehow comforting to return to the house where I'd lived for eighteen years with my parents, until Daddy passed away and I'd gone off to art school, and realize a tiny piece of myself was still here.

Like this ancient computer, which kept giving me the hourglass—the international symbol of hurry up and wait—when I itched to play amateur detective and check out the phrases from the ransom demand, as Allie had prodded. I wasn't sure if I'd find anything of interest, but everything was worth a shot at this point.

Another few minutes and I was finally online.

I gave my knuckles a crack, pulled up Google and, for kicks, entered the dollar amount of the ransom, because $212,000 sounded odd even to my decidedly odd ears.

First, I spelled the words out, tapped my foot impatiently until relevant pages appeared, though as I scanned them, I realized they weren't really so relevant. Basically, I hit a dead end.

So I typed in the numbers—$212,000—which, after the Dell sputtered and whirred for a bit, pulled up more than 139,000 matches.

Yowza.

Who'd of thunk it?

I did an Evelyn Woods speed-read of the dozen entries that came up first and saw one common denominator, and a bizarre one to boot. All had to do with the dognapping of Paris Hilton's pooch. Apparently, the amount was precisely what the poor, jittery Chihuahua was ransomed for, before all the publicity scared the would-be bad guys and the critter was returned, unharmed.

Coincidence?

It was possible, I guessed.

Or were my boyfriend-nappers Paris Hilton fans?

Heavens to Britney! How frightening was that?

Because being enamored of the world's most infamous dilettante clearly implied a lack of common sense and a huge dose of irrationality, not to mention a high degree of celebrity worship that hinted at a lifelong subscription to the *National Enquirer*.

It could also mean whoever was involved kept up on the local dish and the doings of Dallas society, which might be how they'd known about my status as a daughter of fortune.

Hmmm, interesting supposition, and maybe less off-the-wall than it had sounded initially.

So the $212,000 might not have been as random as it seemed. Less a figure pulled out of thin air than a need to be a copycat. Or else they figured Brian was my pet, like Paris Hilton's Chihuahua?

Could it mean the kidnappers had a sense of humor? Or were they merely money-grubbing idiots?

Not wanting to get sidetracked by that clearly unsolvable riddle, I went ahead and dissected the phrasing the bad guy had used on the phone, searching for those parts I recalled verbatim.

"I won't waste a bullet" and "sharpen my knife" came to mind, though the search for those terms merely brought up link after link with gun- and knife-related pages, some that looked like online diaries that detailed violent fantasies or lyrics to songs, even a few dealing with hunting.

I tried a few variations, but still came up empty.

I didn't see anything that triggered an "ah-ha" kind of response, the way the $212,000 had.

So I went ahead and searched for "Trayla Trash," because I was curious about the woman who'd caught Malone's eye at the strip club—for whatever reason, and I was thinking of the obvious because, well, he was a heterosexual man and he wasn't blind.

I turned up half a dozen pages related to exotic dancers at strip clubs across the country, even the cast of a porn flick called *Hillbilly Ho*. As much as I itched to find out

more about Ms. Trayla's career, I was nervous about clicking onto any of the links. I didn't want to get trapped into
triple X-rated pages that wouldn't let me out.

Just for variation, I tried "Traylor Trash," but most of
those listings had to do with an Ohio garage band.

Who was Trayla Trash really? I wondered, recalling
that Lu had called her "Betsy," but said she didn't know
much more than that about her private life.

Maybe strippers didn't befriend barmaids. I wasn't up
on the chick-bonding protocol at gentlemen's clubs.

Out of curiosity, I plugged in the name of the case
Malone and Allie were working on as part of the defense team, taking several stabs at the spelling of "Oleksiy" before I found the one that triggered a handful of
links.

I hadn't asked Allie about it in detail, so I didn't realize
that Oleksiy was the dude's first name. His surname was
Petrenko, and he was a Ukrainian immigrant, a regular
Horatio Alger who'd risen from poverty to minimogul,
owning a string of dry cleaners and quietly investing in assorted other local businesses. Somewhere along the line
his partner—his brother, as it were, who'd been sleeping
with Oleksiy's wife, according to the pretrial articles—
had turned on him, ratting him out to the feds for things
like embezzlement and money laundering.

A money launderer who owned dry cleaning fran-
chises?

That was classic.

As was the brother sleeping with the wife and then turning on his sib.

How very Cain and Abel.

There was only the grainiest photo of Petrenko, and all I could discern was that he looked rather ordinary. Not tall, not short. Neither bald nor thick-haired. A middle-aged man who wouldn't draw second glances. The online pieces didn't share much personal info or name any of the witnesses who'd be testifying in court, besides the turncoat brother; though I figured Allie had more of that scoop at her fingertips.

I considered the amended witness list that Brian had taken from the file. Had someone on it wanted Malone out of the way? Had that same person killed Trayla Trash because of what she knew or had seen?

Was this Oleksiy Petrenko a patron of The Men's Club? More importantly, was he a client of Trayla's? In particular, was he the elusive boyfriend who'd promised her a ticket to something better?

Still, I couldn't figure out why Malone would want to talk to her or why doing so would get *him* into trouble.

I could understand why a rich man who was truly guilty of his alleged crimes and afraid of jail time would, perhaps, want to eliminate a player from the opposing team who intended to crucify him on the stand. But why would Oleksiy Petrenko mess with someone from his own defense team?

It simply wasn't logical.

I only wished I'd asked Brian more about the case. He might've dropped something about Oleksiy that could shed light on what was going on, if there indeed was a connection.

There was a lot I didn't know about Malone's job.

Did he like his secretary? Was the coffee good? Did the

cleaning people go through his desk drawers? Did his boss treat him like a lackey?

It was rare for him to bring up a current case with me, as he was fairly close-mouthed about anything ongoing. If he dished at all, it was mainly about successful verdicts or a hard-fought case lost.

Did that make me a crummy girlfriend?

Was I supposed to be deeply interested in every facet of his life, including the daily grind at ARGH, even if I found the legal world less than exciting?

Oh, man.

I could make myself crazy doing that, torturing myself with the "what ifs" and "wherefores."

But I had to stop.

Second-guessing my past actions wasn't going to fix things now.

About to sign off the Internet, I stopped myself and did one last search; this time for Brian Patrick Malone.

Like magic, related links appeared, and I scanned each one, seeing mostly attorney directories, a listing on ARGH's Web site, and a few mentions of old cases in the archives of the local papers, as one would expect.

What I didn't count on finding was a link to the Dallas Zoo, where Brian was a "zoo parent" to a Bengal tiger. He'd also sponsored several fund-raising efforts by MADD, and had participated in the last Susan Komen run.

He hadn't he told me any of that.

It was good stuff, for Pete's sake. It would've made me think all the more of him. Maybe it was just that he didn't like to brag.

Or, perhaps, he needed to keep a few secrets.

I thought of what Allie had said after we'd gone to The Men's Club.

When you think about it, really, how well do we know anyone? Everyone has secrets. Even Malone.

I hadn't wanted to believe her then, but I realized she was right.

In the past twenty-four hours, since Brian Malone had vanished from the face of the Earth, I'd discovered more about him than in the four months we'd dated and talked and kissed and shared the sheets in my bed.

What was wrong with that picture?

There was so much more that I wanted learn about him, about his family, his cases, and I was scared witless that I might not have that chance.

Frustrated tears welled against my lashes, and I brushed my sleeve across my eyes to dry them.

I would not—could not—fall part.

The last thing Brian needed was a wimpy girlfriend.

He was counting on me, and I wouldn't let him down.

I shut off the computer, picked up my still-silent cell phone, and left the familiar confines of my childhood bedroom where the gown intended for my debut still hung in the closet: still pristine white, never worn.

As I headed down the stairs, I heard the click of the front door unlatching. I saw Stephen enter as I descended quickly to the foyer.

He carried a fat black bag, which he deposited carefully against the wall as he turned to shut the door behind him.

When he saw me standing and watching him, he nodded grimly and said, "We're all set, Andy. Let's sit down, so I can tell you what I've done."

Mother emerged from the hallway that led to the kitchen, her hands clasped and worry wrinkling her normally smooth brow.

"Is everything all right?"

Stephen reached for her and took her hand between his. "I've got it under control, Cissy, I promise."

She looked up at him and smiled, and I could see that she bought every word he'd said.

I wanted to believe as well. Only trust wasn't exactly my strong suit.

"I need to talk to you both," Stephen said, and jerked his chin in my direction.

"Shall we go to the den?" my mother suggested.

"Let's get this over with," I said, not quite up to polite. The kidnappers could call again at any moment, and I wanted to be as prepared as I could get.

Without another word, Stephen retrieved the satchel he'd set down by the door. It was the size of a bowling bag, though it didn't look nearly as heavy.

"What's in there?" My mother eyed the thing suspiciously, though I figured I knew what it held.

Two hundred twelve thousand dollars. Cash. Or maybe lots of bundles of plain paper with real hundreds banded on top, like in the movies. For Brian's sake, I hoped it was the real thing. I didn't want to mess up and have to live with what happened.

"I'll show you after we sit down and chat," Stephen assured us, and we headed back to the room where we'd previously gathered.

I glanced at the clock on the mantel as I settled on the sofa, the same spot I'd taken before.

It was just past four o'clock.

My mother came up behind me, setting her hands on my shoulders, and I felt grateful for her touch.

I palmed my cell, willing it to ring, hoping I would do the right thing when it did. I didn't want to mess up.

"Andy, you with me here?"

I shifted my gaze from the mantel clock and toward Stephen. He'd set the bulging black bag on the coffee table, and his left hand rested on the zipper flap.

"Sorry," I told him. "What'd I miss?"

"The pay phone number," he said. "It's from a booth outside the IHOP on Northwest Highway, near Love Field."

"Near the airport," I murmured, thinking of all the implications, because that's where Brian's car was found, and it wasn't far from the strip club where he'd gone with Matty. "Is there any way to find out who made the call?" I asked, realizing it was a stretch even as I said it. "I have the time of the call on my cell."

Stephen shook his head. "I drove out there myself, Andy, after I located the number in the reverse directory. But there's no security camera outside the restaurant that faces the pay phone area. The lighting's bad besides, and there isn't a window in the restaurant that gives a clear shot to the phone. I'm sorry."

"Thanks for trying," I said, and he nodded.

"Listen, honey . . ."

Whoa, that got my attention, as Stephen had never called me "honey" before, and it reminded me of my dad, the way he used "pumpkin" when he'd address me.

". . . I want you to know you're not alone in this. I'll be there, every step of the way, keeping an eye on you."

Every step of the way?

But the kidnappers wanted me alone!

Did he want to jeopardize everything?

I started to protest, and he must've read the panic in my face, as he quickly got out, "Andy, breathe easy. I'll stay out of sight. No one will know I'm there. Trust me."

There he went with that "trust" thing again.

"Listen to him, Andrea," my mother said and squeezed my shoulders.

It was hard to do, but I gulped down my reluctance. "Don't let them see you, Stephen, please."

"I'll be careful, honey, don't worry."

I nodded, but I worried just the same.

"So what's in the bag?" Cissy asked without further ado, and Stephen slowly began to unzip it. When he was done, he tipped the gaping belly toward us

There they were, in black and white . . . and green.

Bundles of bills bound with paper wrappers.

And lots of them, from the looks of things.

I leaned toward the coffee table so I could peer deeper into the bag. "Is it all there? Everything?"

"Two hundred twelve thousand, yes," he said. "Go ahead. Touch it, Andy. Tell me how it looks."

I set my cell in my lap and cautiously reached forward

to dig into the bag's gaping middle. I withdrew a firm stack of hundreds, sniffed them, and riffled the bills with my thumb like a deck of cards.

Yep. They looked like crisp Benjamins, only not the new kind with the bigger middle. The older style, but I guessed that was all right.

"Do they feel okay?" Stephen asked.

What an odd question.

Mostly to humor him, I gave the bills a squeeze before I put the bundle back. "Yeah, they feel just fine."

"How do they look to you?"

That was weird question number two.

"Why? Are they not real?" I asked and squinted at Mother's beau, wondering what his question implied.

Were they fakes? Funny money? Forgeries?

If they were, they were good, to my layman's eyes, anyway.

Stephen leaned elbows on knees, gazing at the money bag. "Yes, Andy, they're counterfeit. I have a good friend who was a Treasury agent for thirty-five years. A couple times, he came across fake bills he didn't have the heart to destroy. They were works of art to him, and he saved a few for posterity."

And some people merely pilfered office pencils.

"They're just on loan for tonight," Stephen explained. "I told him I'd have them back by morning."

Unless something went wrong, I thought and swallowed hard.

"Dan gave me a couple dye packs for the topmost bundles," Stephen continued, while I listened. "Normally, the device activates when a robber passes through the electromagnetic field set up in a bank's doorway. But these"—he proffered two of the wrapped packs of bills, holding one in each hand—"are activated by a radio transmitter. I'll give the device to you. You can turn it on when you transfer the money. The dye packs will mark the money and the bad guys."

He returned the bundles to the bag, and when I didn't say anything, he looked straight at me.

"You worried, Andy?"

Yeah, I was worried, all right.

"I'm not sure about this, Stephen," I said, thinking I should've gotten the money myself—real money—because what if we weren't dealing with amateurs, as we supposed? What if they were pros and knew a bad bill when they saw it? "What if they realize we're tricking them?"

"They won't," he said, like it was as simple as that.

"How can you be sure?"

"I just am."

I searched his eyes and his sober expression, looking for cracks, for any sign that he felt doubt. My own mind was whirring with possible trip-ups:

What if the dye packs went off too soon? What if they didn't go off at all? What if they didn't give up Malone, even when they had the money in hand? What would happen then? Would I have cost Brian his life, because I'd tried to outsmart his captors?

I wet my lips, telling myself that I had to trust Stephen, because my only other choice was to go to the police, and *that* I couldn't do.

"We don't know who they are, Andy," Mother's beau went on, doing his damnedest to convince me. "We don't know that they really have Brian, do we? We've got to outsmart them, and we will."

"You're right," I told him, letting out a held breath. "I just want Brian back safe."

Cissy patted my arm, and I closed my eyes for an instant, telling myself it would all be okay. That, by morning, Malone would be home and the fake bills returned to Stephen's pal, the former Treasury agent.

All would be right with the world.

When I opened my eyes again, Stephen was removing what looked like a small black box from his jacket pocket.

I was almost afraid to ask.

So Mother did it for me. "What on earth is that?"

"It's a GPS tracker." Stephen lifted the thing, as if weighing it. "I got it for my new truck as an antitheft device. Ordered it off the Net. It uses Google mapping."

"Dear Lord, I don't even know what that means," my mother said.

But I did.

Everyone and their dog used GPS these days, mostly to trace vehicles. It was legal, so long as the person in the automobile being tracked was aware of it.

"You want to track my Jeep," I said.

"Sort of," Stephen replied mysteriously. I watched him slip the black box into the bag with the money, shoving it down the side, toward the bottom. "I want to track the bag, which will be with you until you hand it over to the kidnappers. Then I want to track *them*."

"My my," Cissy breathed. "The things they invent."

Stephen cracked a smile. "I've got my laptop in my car,

so I'll know where you are. You aren't in this alone, you know."

I stared at the satchel. Goose bumps rose over my arms. This was really going down, wasn't it?

The zipper whirred as Stephen closed the bag and slapped its side. "All right, then. We're all set on this end. Now we just have to wait for the next damned call."

"Did they mention when they'd phone back, sweetie?" my mother said, and I shook my head. "You imagine they'll try before or after dinner?"

Excuse me? It wasn't like kidnappers had manners.

"For Pete's sake, I don't know when they'll call, Mother," I said, unable to keep from sounding testy. Hell, I *felt* testy.

"I think someone needs a nap," Cissy drawled.

A nap? Like I'd sleep a wink before this ordeal was through.

I nearly said something snippy back, when, right on cue, my cell rang from my lap, the familiar idiotic music playing in aborted bursts.

I took a deep breath, thinking, *Ding dong, kidnappers calling.*

"Pick it up, Andy," Stephen said, as if I needed a nudge.

I grabbed the phone and flipped it wide-open, pressing it hard to my ear and answering with a shaky, "Hello? This is Andy Kendricks."

"Listen and listen good, because I'll only say this once," the mumbling voice instructed, and Mother hastily shoved a pen and pad of paper at me. "Here's what you do if you want to see your boyfriend alive again."

I whispered, "I'm listening."

The barely audible voice told me where to go and when, and reminded me that if I didn't show, if I didn't do exactly what I was told, or if there were any signs of police involvement, Brian was a goner.

Then it was over.

The phone went silent.

And my heart went, *Gulp*.

Chapter 17

The ransom drop activities wouldn't begin until 10:45 P.M.

I was to sit at the bar at a Highland Park restaurant called Patrizio, right before closing as it were, and wait for their call.

They gave me the starting point, but that was all. They planned to direct me from one place to another, and I'd have no idea where I was headed next until they phoned after I'd arrived at each successive spot.

It gave me flashbacks to childhood scavenger hunts, having to run around the neighborhood accumulating goodies on a list until you had them all. The first one back with all their items won a prize.

If I did my part right, I would "win" back Brian.

Who did these people think they were? Because I was thinking they had a thing for Jerry Bruckheimer action movies, where car chases were more important than plot.

Stephen said the setup was done to make sure I wasn't followed; so it worried me all the more that I knew he'd be tailing me, keeping track on the GPS.

What if they spotted him?

Would they call the whole thing off? Decide Malone wasn't worth the trouble and dispose of him, like they had Trayla Trash?

Stephen swore up and down that he'd keep a ways back, maintaining visual contact but relying on the GPS to know the direction I was headed. That way, he assured me, he wouldn't have to ride too close on my bumper.

Trust, trust, trust.

One of these days I'd get it down pat.

It was just so danged hard for me, perhaps having to do with my being an only child. I was used to counting on myself, getting everything done solo. No one had ever accused me of being a team player.

Even in school, I'd taken over group projects, never willing to sit back and let the chips fall where they may. I wasn't all-fired certain I was much good at sharing, either.

But this evening I had to play by the rules, both Stephen's and the kidnappers'. I wanted to save Malone without risking my own neck, kind of like being between a rock and an impossible place.

If all went well, I would end up at the final drop spot at midnight.

According to Mr. Mumbles, they'd release Malone as soon as they had the bag in hand and had eyeballed the contents to be sure I wasn't screwing them over.

Lovely.

Who was I to protest? I had nothing else, no other option. Malone hadn't called again, so how could I not accept that these people were keeping him under lock and key? I still had no inkling how the Paris Hilton dognapping ransom connected with the Oleksiy case, and I had pretty much convinced myself it didn't matter at this point.

My only focus was Brian.

I couldn't even allow myself to dwell on what would happen once he'd been freed, because it was nearly as frightening to think of him trying to explain to the cops that he had nothing to do with Trayla's murder.

Despite my firm conviction that just because she was found in his car trunk and one of his Calloways had been used as the murder weapon didn't mean he'd done it, convincing the police was something else entirely.

So would I be releasing him from one prison only to send him to another?

Dang.

This whole thing sucked.

Maybe we could run away, to Brazil or someplace they didn't have extradition. Only who'd take care of my mother if I slipped away in the dark of night?

Stephen?

Yeah, right.

He might be ex-Navy and ex-IRS, but he had no earthly idea what he was getting into with Cissy Blevins Kendricks. She was about the most high maintenance individual God had ever designed and built. Not only had He broken the mold after He'd made her, but He'd doubtless run up a hefty tab to outfit and shod her properly, not to mention the hair and makeup. *Ca-ching!*

How could I disappear with Malone and leave poor Stephen as Mother's only crutch and still live with myself?

I couldn't.

Okay, so Malone would have to face the music eventually; though I was sure once he told the truth about what had happened—whatever that was—he would set the record straight. He could explain that he was tied up and chained to a radiator while someone borrowed his Acura to trash poor Trayla.

I had to stop being Debbie Downer.

Everything would be all right. It would be over soon.

My head would explode if I let myself think otherwise.

I decided to go home for a few hours and reconnoiter back at Cissy's house before beginning my ransom run. Patrizio wasn't far from there, and Stephen had a few things to go over with me first; so I promised them both I'd return by ten o'clock.

I couldn't help but wonder if there was a reason the bad guys had picked that spot.

I'd gone with Malone to Patrizio a couple weeks ago, strangely enough. I wondered if whoever it was had been watching us then, already plotting to snatch my boyfriend, or if Malone had mentioned the place to them as somehow meaningful to us, to send me a message—though I figured I was trying to pull import from thin air at this point.

Still, what type of kidnappers would start a ransom drop at Patrizio, since it seemed a little upscale for lowlifes? More like the kind of spot lowlifes dreamed of going to rub elbows with the prettified crowd. Besides, it closed at eleven on Monday night, or was that the point? To make sure I was there in time and that I didn't linger, attracting unwanted attention.

Hmm.

I wondered if I were allowed to order a medicinal margarita at the Patrizio bar while I killed time waiting for further instructions.

Or was that not kosher, per the Kidnappers Handbook?

Mother seemed anxious about my leaving. She offered to feed me dinner, but I wasn't hungry. What she really wanted, I supposed, was to keep me in arm's reach; so much so, in fact, that she'd dispatched Sandy and Stephen to retrieve my Jeep and bring it around. She'd hoped that might encourage me to stay put, but I wanted some time alone. So that's what I did.

The sun setting to the west, the sky purple above me, I drove home in silence, no radio or CD playing, just my thoughts as company. And I had plenty of them to spare. I kept thinking of all the people in the cars that passed mine and wondering what their lives were like, if the most they were worried about was where to eat tonight or what color to paint the living room or if the babysitter would show up on time.

Were any worried about the life of a loved one? Did a single one of them have to contemplate driving around Dallas in the dark, running down clues from a list of nightspots, all in hopes that counterfeit money in a bag rigged with GPS and dye packs would serve their purpose and set a man free?

I would have guessed the answer was no, although I couldn't say for sure in this day and age when crazy things happened all the time. All you had to do was turn on the nightly news and watch for a few minutes in order to learn about one atrocity after another. Like a kid taking a gun to day care in his knapsack and shooting another kid, or a defenseless animal being tortured. How about soldiers dying overseas? Or earthquakes, tsunamis, and hurricanes causing massive destruction?

That stuff usually made me feel fortunate, realizing how relatively untouched my life had been with regard to tragedy.

Until something like this happened, and it reinforced that bad stuff could happen to anybody.

Any trace of the sun was long gone by the time I made it to North Dallas and turned off Preston Road into my cozy enclave of town houses and condos. A flock of geese had wandered over from the lake of the nearby country club, and they waddled across my parking lot, squawking and pecking at each other, oblivious to the fact that my Jeep had to idle until they'd safely passed through its headlights.

Were that I was a goose, I mused.

All I'd have to worry about was flapping my wings to head south for the winter and avoiding cars and hunters' bullets.

That sounded so nice.

As I angled the Jeep into a spot near my front door, I saw nothing amiss, no media vans lurking, no unmarked police cars containing anyone remotely resembling Starsky and Hutch.

Home free.

Or so I thought.

Until I stepped out onto the sidewalk, and I heard a car

door slam followed by the staccato rush of high heels on the pavement behind me.

I turned as the noise got closer, the glow of my porch lamp illuminating a specter so terrifying I was tempted to run and hide.

Attila the Blonde.

Live and in the flesh.

Well, okay, not flesh exactly. More like an Ann Taylor suit.

How could I have missed her shiny red Beemer, for Pete's sake?

I blamed it on too many distractions.

"Allie, what do you want?" Friendly, I wasn't. I didn't even wait for her answer, merely marched up the porch steps and shoved my key in the dead bolt.

"What do *I* want? Let's just say you'll definitely want to hear what I've found out, Ms. Snippy," she announced and trotted after me, right into the condo.

"Were you waiting long?"

"Not more than five minutes. I was gonna call you if you didn't show any sooner. I figured you had to come home sometime."

"You want a beer?" I asked and dropped bag and keys on the kitchen table. I flipped on lights and headed for the refrigerator to snag one of Malone's bottled brews. I didn't drink often, but figured it was as good a time as any for a snort.

Allie declined, so I popped one open and sat down in a chair, taking a long, hard swallow as she set her briefcase between us, snapped the lid up and withdrew papers, which she shoved across the table.

"Take a look," she said, tapping a finger on the topmost sheet. "Tell me, Andy, what do you see?"

I set my beer aside and leaned forward to scrutinize the page, which looked exactly like a column of names. The letterhead at the top told me even more. "It's the prosecution's addendum to your witness list for the Oleksiy case, right?"

"Right as rain," she quipped. "But did you notice the one I've highlighted?"

I glanced down again. "Elizabeth Wren," I read aloud, then looked up at Allie. "Am I supposed to know who that is? Is she famous or something?"

"Infamous is more like it." She folded her arms on the table and smiled smugly.

Let me tell you, there's little more annoying than a smug blonde in a size two suit. If she'd been a dry erase board, I would've wiped the smirk right off her face.

"Here's the dope," Allie McSqueal explained. "Brian's secretary said he'd mentioned a meeting with Elizabeth Wren sometime on Friday afternoon, though I was too busy with a depo to come along. Guess he figured he'd start tackling the add-ons without me and impress Old Abe with his get-up-and-go, the brown-nosing bastard."

So Brian had initiative? What did that prove?

"I don't follow." I had a feeling Allie liked keeping me in the dark, in the way that mystery novels waited until the very end to reveal the denouement. "Would you spit it out, please, because I haven't got all day. I have a ransom drop to make tonight, and I haven't even had a shower, so make it snappy."

She made a "tsk-tsk" noise that grated on my last nerve.

"My God, Kendricks, but you're impatient. If you'd just sit still and listen, I think I may be able to connect the dots between Brian's vanishing act, Trayla's murder, and the witness list."

Why did her very tone of voice make me want to reach across the table and smack her? But I didn't. Because I wanted to hear what she'd dug up.

I yearned to take another deep swig of beer but resisted, planting clasped hands in my lap and paying attention.

"That's better," she said, like a schoolmarm who's bribed an unruly student into behaving. "Apparently before Brian left on Friday he had a brief conversation with his secretary, reminding her that he was off to vet a witness—"

"You already told me that," I interrupted.

"Only he didn't call her 'Elizabeth' that time. He called her 'Betsy.'" She stared at me, as if awaiting some reaction. "Don't you get it? Betsy's short for Elizabeth." She sighed. "C'mon, Kendricks, think! When we went to the strip club, remember what Lu said Trayla's real name was?"

"Um, give me a sec." I'd been a wreck, frantic about Malone, hardly able to concentrate on much else. So I scoured my gray matter, tapping my chin, until I coughed up, "Betsy."

"Yes, of course, it's Betsy!" she fairly screamed at me. "Can't you see the obvious?"

Geez, Louise, but the woman was high-strung.

I cleared my throat and asked, "What's this all about, Allie?" I fervently hoped she wasn't having some kind of nervous breakdown. If so, I figured a Hazmat suit would be in order. "Lots of woman named Elizabeth are called Betsy. What makes you think the Elizabeth Wren on your witness list is Trayla Trash?"

"Oh, it's no guess," she said, coy as ever, and pushed several additional pieces of paper at me. "Take a gander at *that,* Ms. Cynic."

I dropped my gaze to the pages and nearly swallowed my tongue when I realized what they were.

Mug shots and a rap sheet for one Elizabeth "Betsy" Wren, aka Betsy Bangher, Tawni Kitten . . . and, ta-da, Trayla Trash.

I blinked like an idiot.

Much as it pained me, I had to give Allie credit for turning over enough rocks to find this big-ass worm.

She'd strung the dots together like Christmas lights.

"Wow, but Trayla was a busy girl," I murmured, noting misdemeanor charges for solicitation, public intoxication, and forgery.

The murdered stripper had hardly been an upstanding citizen, had she?

And playing on the wrong side of the law could tend to get a person burned, or worse.

I gazed at the mug shots, seeing a disheveled blonde who looked older than her recorded age but still exuded an Angelina Jolie pouty-lipped sexuality that burst forth from the Xeroxed pages. Her hair was more a tangled rat's nest than the funky flip I remembered from the photograph stuck to her dressing room mirror.

She looked like a gun moll, a modern-day Jean Harlow from that old *Hell's Angels* flick. Not a chick to be messed with.

Though I envisioned her as once having been a nice girl from Peoria who'd come to Big D with dreams of finding herself a Bobby Ewing to call her own.

Instead, she'd ended up stripped bare and dead in the trunk of Malone's illegally parked Acura.

"When I figured Betsy could be Trayla, I called Robby . . . er, my contact at the DPD," Allie told me. "Although he wouldn't confirm the two were one and the same. Still, he didn't deny it either. He said they're still trying to contact next of kin and aren't releasing the victim's name until they do."

"But they *are* the same person," I said, staring at the rap sheet which stated exactly that in no uncertain terms. "This means something, I know it."

"Don't hyperventilate yet, Kendricks, because there's more." Allie's cheeks flushed and her eyes crackled with unsuppressed glee. "I also confirmed that our Betsy moved into a Turtle Creek high rise six months ago, only whoever was providing her rent cut her off a few weeks back. The landlord had been paid in cash by messenger, so he never saw Betsy's sugar daddy. When the jig was up, the landlord was instructed by phone not to let Little Miss Wren back in, for fear she'd steal something that wasn't hers."

Allie barely paused for breath before she went on, "Then, lo and behold, just last week, the girl turns up on the prosecution's list of new witnesses who'll testify against Oleksiy at the trial. What does that say to you, Nancy Drew?"

My heart sang with hope.

Excitement shot up my spine, and I sat up straighter. "It could be that her sugar daddy was Oleksiy Petrenko."

"Bingo." Allie nodded. "My theory precisely."

"He dumps her, and she decides to get him back by testifying against him?" I suggested, because that's sure what it sounded like.

"Won't be the first time that's happened," she said and settled back into her chair. "Hell hath no fury like a woman scorned."

Or a stripper whose sugar daddy has cut off her rent?

Oh, oh—I wanted to shout, as new theories popped into my head.

Like, what if Trayla was at The Men's Club on Saturday night, and Brian saw her, after having met with her earlier that day regarding the Oleksiy case, albeit when she was Elizabeth Wren? No wonder he'd followed her backstage. Had he realized one of the prosecution's new key witnesses was a stripper, working the stage the very night he'd taken Matty for one last wild ride? Had it freaked him out to see her there?

What if his getting snatched wasn't premeditated, but a matter of bad timing?

What if Oleksiy Petrenko, the money laundering dry cleaner, had sent some goons to pick up Trayla and take care of her, only to find Malone in the way?

I brought that very idea up with Allie, only to have her shoot me down none too graciously.

"I'd agree with you, Kendricks, except for one thing."

"What?"

"The ransom," she said. "It makes no sense."

"Since when does kidnapping make sense, Allie?" I angrily picked at the label on my Sam Adams, wondering what exactly she was getting at; hating that she was raining on my parade when we seemed so close to . . . *something*.

Her shiny gold hair shimmied on either side of her face as she scooted forward in her seat. "Why on God's green earth would Oleksiy Petrenko call to ask you for money? The guy has tens of millions of his own, maybe hundreds of millions if you count his offshore accounts."

"Okay, you're right." She had me there, because I'd assume a money launderer probably had plenty of the green stuff at his disposal. "But even you said the ransom demand sounded too bizarre to be real. Maybe it's a distraction, just to throw me off."

"To throw *you* off?" She snorted. "No disrespect, Kendricks, but who cares about you in the scheme of things? Oleksiy has much bigger fish to fry. He's going on trial soon, and the prosecution's got his own brother testifying against him, not to mention threats to put good ol' Mrs. Petrenko on the stand, if she gets back before the trial."

"Gets back from where?"

Allie shrugged. "The woman slept with her husband's brother. Who can blame her for seeking refuge once the shit hit the fan?" She released a slow breath. "We're gonna have to work like hell to get him off as it is, so it's better for our side if Mrs. Petrenko doesn't come back to testify. Having his brother on the stand is gonna be bad enough. If Oleksiy was sleeping with Trayla and she knew anything about his business—" Allie stopped, as if catching herself saying too much. "Anyway, I can only imagine how he'd want her out of the picture."

Instead of making me feel better, she was doing the opposite.

"You think he wanted Brian out of the picture, too?" I asked, despite my dry mouth. "Only he's on Oleksiy's side, so that makes no sense."

Her Blondeness tapped a finger on the table. "I figure Malone saw something he shouldn't have, and Oleksiy had no choice but to make our boy disappear."

"So he had him kidnapped?"

"That's the part that doesn't fit," Allie insisted. "Even if Oleksiy had his goons grab Malone, why would he call you and ask for a ransom? That's just plain stupid."

"Gee, thanks." I glared at her. "That makes me feel so much better."

Rather like a kick in the ribs.

"I'm not finished, Kendricks."

"Oh, yeah, you are," I cut her off, pushing her papers back across the table. "I've heard enough gloom and doom. I can't take much more of it."

Not with such a long night stretching ahead of me.

I wanted a hot shower, not more conjecture time with Allie. She'd depressed the hell out of me already.

"I'll walk you out," I said, though it was about ten easy paces to the door. I started to rise, but was stopped by her sharp tone.

"Not so fast, Ms. Cotillion," she said, jerking her chin to indicate I should sit down again.

I did.

"There's something about the ransom that I figure you'll want to know." She didn't meet my eyes, merely gathered up Trayla's rather lengthy rap sheet and stashed it back in her briefcase.

She then removed a single page and set it on the table.

This time, she looked dead at me. "So, do you want to hear what else I know, or would you like me to leave?"

The girl was clearly sadistic.

"I'm listening," I said, even though it was the last thing I wanted to do, well behind kicking her out and finishing my beer in peace.

"The ransom demand"—she slid the paper toward me—"it comes from a movie."

"No, you're wrong," I shot back. "I did some checking online, and the amount's tied to Paris Hilton's kidnapped pooch." At her raised brows, I explained, "It's what the dognappers demanded for the return of her Chihuahua. Happened last spring. It was all over the tabloids."

Allie's brow creased. "Kendricks, I don't know what you've been smoking, and I won't ask, but I'm not talking about the money. I'm talking about the pitch." Since I still ignored the page in front of her, she picked it up, cleared her throat, and read: " 'Pay me my money . . . or you're gonna find pieces of your little boy all over New York. I'm not gonna waste a bullet. I'm just gonna sharpen my knife.' "

My God.

That *was* it.

Well, sort of.

What little boy?

Wait a minute.

The mumbling bad guy had said "New Dallas," which had puzzled me at first, but I'd figured he was just nervous, being that he demanded over two hundred grand from a total stranger and threatened to kill someone.

"Okay, now I'm totally confused," I admitted, my head

on sensory overload, the rest of me so exhausted I felt like a zombie whose brain had been sucked out. "Where'd you get that? It's almost the same, but not quite."

"From a film," she reiterated. "Not coincidentally, Ron Howard's *Ransom*, which starred Mel Gibson before he lost his hairline and found religion. It sounded familiar, so I did a little checking on that IMDB Web site. I looked in their memorable quotes section, and there it was. Here, read it yourself."

She pushed the paper in my direction, and I swung it around to see a printout of the quote from the Web site.

I read the words a dozen times, until my eyes blurred.

This was unbelievable.

What kind of kidnappers used a ransom straight out of, well, *Ransom*? Or made a monetary demand that equaled the cash paid for the safe return of Paris Hilton's pooch?

"Someone's yanking your chain, Kendricks," Allie said, drawing me out of my muddled fog. "This can't be for real. It has to be a hoax. None of the pieces fit."

But it was real enough to me. I'd been the one on the tail end of the phone calls, listening fearfully as Mr. Mumbles gave me ultimatums that involved my boyfriend's life or death. And I can say for damned sure that the alleged Malonenapper sounded entirely serious.

So how I could I brush it off?

Maybe Allie's heart was made of stone, but mine wasn't.

It was more like Play-Doh

"You can't go through with it," she said, flat out, like she was the boss of me. "It feels off, Kendricks. Someone's taking advantage of you. Brian's name has been all

over the news. Even that Channel 8 reporter who interviewed your neighbor managed to link you to him. The
cops, too. By now, every media outlet in Dallas knows
you're the girlfriend of the dude whose car was found
parked at Love Field with a very dead stripper in his trunk.
Your so-called kidnappers could be anyone, pretending to
have Malone so they can make a quick buck."

Then again, sometimes a cigar was just a cigar.

"But what if it's real?" I whispered.

"You can't do it," the Blond Avenger repeated, like I
hadn't heard her the first time.

I set my hands in my lap, curled my fingers to fists.

I looked her dead in the eye. "Oh, yes, I can," I said.
"And I will."

The plan was already in motion. Stephen had done all
the heavy lifting, and we were loaded for bear. There was
no way I would ever back out at this point, even if Allie
was on the nose about the kidnappers being nothing more
than film-quoting, tabloid-reading bloodsuckers who
wanted to make a buck off my misfortune.

If there was any chance they had Malone, I wouldn't
risk it.

"I'm going," I said again, staring her down.

She stared right back. "Then I'm going, too."

"The hell you are."

"The hell I'm not."

I rose from my chair, palms flush on the table. I was too
tired to argue. "Go home, Allie. I've got things to do."

Her mouth fell open, and I readied myself for a barrage
of words befitting a defense attorney on the rise at the
hottest firm in town. Only she ended up pressing her lips

closed. She quietly gathered up the loose paper, stuffed it in her attaché, snapped the locks closed, and stood.

She'd already taken several steps toward the door when she hesitated.

"I want to find Brian as much as you do, you know," she said over her shoulder. "But I think you're barking up the wrong tree with this ransom thing. You'll just be wasting precious time."

The starch had gone out of my voice, so it was soft as I answered, "But what if I don't go through with it, Allie, and it is real and you're wrong?"

She sighed and turned to give me one last glance. "Do what you have to do," she said. "And I'll do what I have to do."

I nodded.

Well, all right then.

She opened the door and stepped out.

I followed behind, standing in the doorway and watching as she descended the front steps and strode across the lawn in her stiletto heels.

The sun had set sometime since I'd returned home, and the sky was already slipping from afternoon blue into a chilly shade of dark.

I shut the door as I heard Allie's Beemer start up.

I chewed on my lower lip, my stomach tied in king-sized knots, as I checked the mantel clock.

It was already a little past eight.

A couple hours to kill before I started off on what Allie thought was a wild goose chase. I needed a shower first, then I'd go through my closet to try to find something appropriate to wear to a ransom drop.

I'm not sure what my couture-loving mother would have recommended—Escada camouflage and pearls?—but I was thinking basic black, and maybe my pink high-top sneakers for luck.

I could use all the help I could get.

Chapter 18

 I was back at my mother's house by ten o' clock, my nerves close to shot, nothing more in my belly than half a beer and a bare-naked Brainy Bagel.

After I rang the bell, Mother dragged me to the den to catch the nightly news, as every station was doing updates on the mysterious beating death of Trayla Trash, aka Elizabeth "Betsy" Wren. She didn't stick around to watch, murmuring something about having Sandy pack a sandwich and thermos of coffee for Stephen.

How ultracalm and Donna Reed of her.

I frantically flipped around to three different stations, all of them broadcasting Trayla's real name and occupation. I guessed the cops had notified her next of kin, because her identity was clearly no longer a secret, not with the media blasting it across Dallas, Fort Worth, and everywhere in between.

On Channel 2, I spotted Lu McCarthy, the barmaid, with a microphone shoved in her face, the camera lights causing her to blink excessively as she talked about her dear friend, the deceased, and how close they'd been. A caption above her head read LIVE in bold red letters.

I wrinkled my forehead, surprised that Lu would want her mug on the news. She hadn't seemed the attention seeking type to me. If anything, I'd gotten a "leave me out of this" vibe from her; but she was probably no different from ninety percent of the population, who'd gladly give up their privacy for fifteen seconds of fame.

"I wish I'd known she was in trouble, but she must've kept it from me," the barmaid was saying. "The last time I saw her, she seemed okay. She was such a good girl, really, no matter how tough she acted. In some ways, she was almost like a sister to me." Lu finished by swiping a lone tear from her cheek.

Oh, please.

Like a sister, huh?

Just a wee exaggeration, eh?

Lu hadn't seemed to know much more about Trayla than her nickname of "Betsy," which hardly constituted "close." And what a big fat lie about Trayla "seeming okay" the last time she saw her, when Lu had admitted to Allie and me that she'd glimpsed her stripper pal leaving through the rear door of the club in only her robe.

Did that constitute "okay" in her book?

Unless—*oh, damn*—unless she'd been throwing Allie and me a pack of lies, holding back from us, figuring to protect either Trayla or herself.

I was having a hard time sorting truth from fiction

these days, considering how mixed up things had gotten.

Instead of dwelling on what secrets Lu McCarthy could be keeping, I changed the channel, and found myself further distracted.

Good Lord, could it be?

I squinted at Mother's plasma TV.

Oh, my.

I stared ahead and frowned at the face that filled the screen.

Lu wasn't the only one talking smack on the boob tube. Mother's snitch and my next door neighbor, Penny George, appeared on Channel 11, telling the world how she lived above the girlfriend of the "fugitive" the police were looking for in connection to the crime. She noted that "he appeared to be a nice enough boy, though hardly of great moral fortitude."

Hello?

Because he stayed over at my place when we weren't legally bound to love, honor, and bail out of jail? I thought, shaking my head.

So Malone had never killed a man, had never robbed, maimed, mutilated, carjacked, shoplifted, or kicked a dog, so far as I was aware—and he couldn't even stomp a spider, per Allie McSqueal—yet his moral fiber was in question because he spent an occasional night with his girlfriend of four months?

Call the Guardians of Good Behavior and make a citizen's arrest!

For Pete's sake.

I could hardly sit still when I saw Brian's picture on the screen, an unsmiling black and white photo from the Bar

Association directory that made him look like he had his boxers in an uncomfortable twist.

Poor, poor Malone.

He'd still have hell to face once I got him out of whatever hell he was in now. That was hardly fair.

I felt my mother's hands on my shoulders, and I looked up into her worried face, her expression a sad reflection of my own.

"You about ready, pumpkin? Stephen wants to go over a few things with you," she said, and I nodded.

I shut off the remote and made sure my cell was still in its case on my belt. I didn't like wearing the thing, but I figured it'd be awfully handy tonight. I had my driver's license and some cash tucked into my back pocket.

My mother leading the way, I shuffled behind her toward the foyer, where Stephen stood with the black bag full of dye-packed counterfeit cash as well as a shoulder bag that likely carried his laptop.

For ten minutes, he went over my instructions, step by step, having me repeat them so he was sure we were on the same page.

I took a quick bathroom break, splashed my face and stared at myself in the mirror long enough to repeat a few times, "You can do this, Andy."

It couldn't be worse than all those debutante teas my mother had forced me to attend before I'd put the kibosh on the whole silly "coming out" thing.

Besides, tonight's outcome would be much more gratifying than having Cissy weep with disappointment, deeming me a lost cause (well, lost to *her* cause) and a social misfit like my father.

I don't know if she'd realized that I'd taken her comparisons to Daddy as the highest of compliments. Stanley Kendricks had remained true to himself, despite his wealth and standing, and I'd hardly been his only admirer.

How I wished he were with me now, telling me what to do and assuring me everything would be fine.

I sincerely hoped he was watching over me somehow.

The name Andrea meant courage, I reminded myself. My father had picked it for a reason, and I wouldn't prove him wrong.

I made sure my cell was on before I left the house after a hug from Sandy and a warning from my mother to be careful and not drive too fast.

I felt like I was leaving for my first day at school, rather than heading off into the night with a bagful of cash to recover my snatched boyfriend.

Stephen assured my mother that he'd keep close tabs on me, reminding her of the GPS in the satchel and the Google map on his laptop with its satellite link.

I noticed he'd driven a dark-colored Volvo this evening, instead of the shiny pickup truck. I wondered if the sedan belonged to him or if he'd borrowed it for the festivities. No matter, it wouldn't stand out in a crowd.

Stephen double-checked that I had his cell number in my digital address book—I did—then he set the money bag in the backseat of the Jeep, patted my arm and said, "I'm right behind you, Andy."

I took a deep breath and climbed into my Wrangler.

It was 10:35 when I drove away from my mother's house, traveling toward Highland Park Village, not far

away, and home to some of Cissy's favorite stores, like
Chanel, Escada, and St. John, to name a few.

Within five minutes, I'd arrived at the shopping center
and found a parking spot between a pair of polished Mercedes in front of Café Pacific, catty-corner from Patrizio.
As I hopped out of the Jeep, I was nearly bowled over by a
white-haired woman in mink and a gent in a three-piece
suit, angling across the lot toward a silver Jaguar.

I caught my breath, looked right and left for oncoming
traffic—pedestrians and cars—then hurriedly crossed the
asphalt path toward the restaurant.

Patrizio was tucked back in a corner, strands of soft
white lights twinkling above the outside patio. With only
twenty minutes until closing, patrons exiting the Italian
eatery waited curbside for busy valets to bring their cars
around: a steady stream of Porsches, hip BMW roadsters,
and even a striped Lamborghini.

I spotted a few vaguely familiar faces, girls I'd gone to
school with all those years ago; now grown women with
husbands, kids, and volunteer work.

Ah, would that I were them, wearing pearls and cashmere
twin sets! I would've made Cissy the happiest mummy in
the world.

Instead, I'd carved my own path, which didn't include
expensive foreign cars, cashmere, or a husband. I drove a
Jeep Wrangler, wore secondhand clothing from vintage
shops, and dated a man who'd disappeared from a strip
club. Though I guess you could call most of the Web design
work I did for nonprofits—largely pro bono—volunteer
work of sorts. Still, I'd wager my former schoolmates had
never done a ransom drop.

And I was dead sure they'd never donned pink Converse high-tops, either, with or without socks.

Before I went inside, I glanced back to the parking lot, looking for Stephen's dark Volvo and not finding it.

I told myself he was out there, just doing what he'd promised, staying out of sight.

Beneath my T-shirt and jacket, my armpits felt damp. I wiped my hands on the front of my jeans then slipped my cell from the case that dangled from my belt. From here on out, I'd hold it.

Heart thumping, I maneuvered through the departing crowd, entering the restaurant with its creamy walls topped by elegant molding, lit brilliantly by lavish fixtures. I sidled my way to the bar area, raised above the dining room, the two separated by a wooden railing topped with glass.

The wood floor beneath my sneakers was mostly smothered beneath an Oriental rug. Plenty of young couples still lingered, smoking and sipping pretty-colored cocktails, most in the uniform du jour: guys in untucked striped shirts and blazers, cuffs casually turned up; girls in hipster jeans, barely-there tops, and stiletto heels, straight blond hair falling past shoulders and cell phones glued to ears.

I found a deserted spot at the bar and took it, setting my cell right in front of me. The bartender, dapper in crisp white shirt and black bow tie, did the usual, "What'll it be?" and I ordered tonic water and lime. Then I swiveled to glance around me.

Even at fifteen minutes before closing, stools were at a premium, though I noticed, down below, that diners were beginning to clear out, leaving busboys cleaning up empty tables. The couple in the coveted spot near the fireplace didn't appear any too eager to go, and I remembered how cozy it had been when Malone and I sat there, holding hands atop the table, gabbing about nothing in particular while he finished his espresso.

It seemed like a lifetime ago.

It made me realize how many such moments I'd taken for granted, just assuming I'd have time for more tomorrow and the next day.

If I ever did that again, may a wet noodle descend from the sky and smack me flush across the face.

"Here you go."

I spun around on the stool at the bartender's voice, dug into my back pocket for cash for my tonic and a tip. I took a sip and stared at my cell phone, feeling another attack of nerves as I noted the time.

Ten-Fifty.

What the heck were those kidnappers waiting for?

Where they here? I wondered. *Had I done anything wrong? Parked in an unapproved spot? Arrived a minute too late? Where they watching me?*

The hair prickled at my nape, and I hunched over my drink and the phone, willing it to ring.

The bartender did a final call at the bar, and I heard the musical notes of a phone going off somewhere near me.

Like a copycat, mine went off, too.

I snatched it up and leaned hard over the bar, using my free hand to cover my other ear.

"You're at Patrizio?" the mumbling voice asked.

"Yes, I'm here."

Didn't they know that? Wasn't someone keeping tabs

on me? The digits displayed appeared to be the same number as the pay phone used earlier. Did that mean there were two of them? One traipsing around on my heels and another back at Kidnapper HQ (i.e., the Northwest Highway IHOP's phone booth)?

"Of course you're there. Good girl," the barely audible voice said. "Now, get to the Time Out Tavern in fifteen minutes. And you'd better be alone."

"When will I see Brian?" I whispered.

The line went dead.

Well, crud.

Cell phone in hand, I cut through the last of the stragglers ultimately abandoning bar stools before Patrizio locked its doors for the night. I emerged into the crisp night air, unimpressed by the twinkles of lights, the fancy cars, or even the stars blinking bright against the cloudless night sky.

I rushed across the parking lot, nearly getting myself run over by a metallic blue Hummer whose driver leaned out the window to yell, "Watch out, you stupid chick!"

By the time I got to my Jeep, my breaths came in a rush; but I hadn't a spare second to rest. I hurriedly unlocked the door and jumped in, cranked the ignition and shifted into gear. It was all I could do not to smack the bumpers of the vehicles ahead of me, each seeming to move at a snail's pace as they exited Highland Park Village.

Despite Mother's warning to drive safely, I hauled ass to Lovers Lane, where the Time Out Tavern sat in a tiny strip mall beside the London Market Antiques Store.

I used to hang out there some during high school, when I was too young to drink but didn't care and had a fake ID should I get carded. My friends and I used to sit at the picnic table near the door and play quarters, squealing like idiots whether we hit or missed.

In normal circumstances, I'd have been happy to make a return trip to the place. I associated good memories with it.

But nothing about this night was good.

As I took a fast corner, racing through the tail end of a yellow light, I glanced in my rearview and saw a flash of red rip through the intersection behind me.

I didn't think much of it until I pulled off Lovers Lane, sliding the Jeep into an empty parking space in front of the antiques shop.

When I looked into the mirror again as I cut the engine, I noticed the red car taking a slow pass by where I sat. Beneath the street lamp the driver's pale hair glowed for an instant, and I recognized the BMW Roadster that belonged to Allie.

Anger flooded my veins, rushed heat to my face, and I cursed her as I unclipped my seat belt and scrambled out after locking the duffel inside. I wondered what the hell she was up to; thinking she must've been following me since I left home. How else would she know where I'd gone? I certainly hadn't told her.

I hesitated only a second, watching for her car to U-turn somewhere down the road and turn back. But I only saw taillights.

Please, don't screw this up, I prayed, rusty at it as I was. I pulled my jacket tighter around me as I hurried toward the entrance, beneath the white awning, hoping Allie stayed as invisible as Stephen.

What was this? A parade?

All I needed was for Cissy to tail me in her Lexus.

Not funny, I told myself as I swallowed hard and went in.

It was like stepping into a shoe box.

The interior looked just as I remembered; the walls crammed with sports memorabilia. Worn-out sneakers and hockey skates dangled from the ceiling, along with grimy old towels that doubtless reeked of putrefied sweat. Scattered around the tiny space were TV screens silently flashing some sporting event or another. A jukebox playing an old Van Halen tune served as the backdrop for the sharp click of balls from the minipool table.

Everything inside the Time Out Tavern appeared to have seen better days, but it was a comfortable spot to have a Shiners Blond and hang with pals. Malone and I even dropped in on occasion, though hardly enough to be regulars.

The clientele was diametrically opposite the posers who'd crowded the bar at Patrizio. I glanced around at the grizzled-looking dudes in baseball caps and ponytailed women sucking hard on their Marlboros, and I realized that prettified singles putting on airs and pretensions weren't a problem here.

A few heads turned to check me out as I stood up front, solo, and I wondered if my friendly kidnapper was in the room, making sure I acted like a good girl and didn't share a beer with a cop.

I wasn't sure if I was supposed to really do anything. Should I order tonic water that I wouldn't drink, like at my previous stop?

Should I loll around and not order anything, so I stood out like a sore thumb and gave the impression I was out to score drugs or sex?

Honestly, my Little Miss Manners classes hadn't prepared me for anything like this, nor had all the lectures on
social graces my mother had given me through the years
(which hadn't seemed to stick too well).

I finally decided it was best not to stand near the door,
looking unsure of myself, so I headed over to the bar and
slid up on a stool.

Not wanting to be any more conspicuous than I was—a
lone woman in black with pink high-tops, clutching her
cell—I ordered a beer. A pair of whiskered and not-so-
gently creased men halfway down the bar shot me grins
that were a mite too friendly for my taste.

Did they think I was a badly dressed hooker? I wondered.
Or just a desperate chick sorely in need of male attention?

I tried to give them discouraging frowns in return and
leaned toward my left, where a middle-aged female in
leopard print played some kind of videogame while she
alternately inhaled her cigarette, took tequila shots, and
mumbled, "Well, shit."

Obviously, Cissy's doppelganger.

Ha ha.

A nervous smile touched my lips, but quickly faded. I
had my hand on my cell, willing it to ring. With the other,
I fingered the neck of my Shiners before I began my bad
habit of picking off the label.

I felt the sudden puff of breath against my hair before I
heard a voice rumble, "Hey, pretty lady, can I buy you a
drink? You all by yerself? What a shame."

A scruffy-looking fellow with an unshaven jaw and
brown chunks of hair hanging over his eyes planted a
palm on my right and greeted me with a full-on leer.

"No, I'm not alone," I shot back, and the dude glanced at Leopard-Print Smoking Lady on my other side. I realized where *that* was going, and I shook my head. "I'm not actually *with* anyone, but I'm waiting on a call from"— how best to put it?—"someone close to my boyfriend."

Scruffy Dude squinted. "So I can't buy you a drink?"

"No." Besides, I already had a full Shiners plunked squarely in front of me, and I wouldn't even have time to drink that. I squinted back at him, wondering suddenly if he wasn't part of the kidnapping posse, making sure I was flying solo. Though I think he mistook my narrowing my eyes on him as a sign of interest.

"Maybe I could meet you later?" He bent nearer so I could smell the tobacco and beer on his breath, not to mention the manly-man scent of one-hundred-percent perspiration. "I've got a six-pack on ice in the cab of my Silverado, right in the parking lot."

I'll meet you when hell freezes over, cowboy, I wanted to say, deciding he was just a loser out looking for love in all the wrong places—well, at least on the wrong bar stool— but I didn't get the chance to open my mouth.

My cell chimed its silly musical ring at just that moment, and I elbowed the guy in the gut—for which, ungraciously, I did not apologize—as I snapped the phone to my ear.

"Yes?" I said and hunched down over the bar with palm pressed to my other ear, trying to hear, ignoring all else around me.

"The IHOP on Northwest Highway, on the way to the airport. It's your final destination. Be a good girl and drop it behind the Dumpster in back. You got that?"

Wait a dad-blamed minute.

Was that where the mumbling kidnapper had been phoning me from all along? So he could've directed me there in the first place, instead of jerking me around?

Grrr.

I was far less sure at this point that anyone from Team Bad Guy had been watching me. They'd probably strung me along all this time, merely to keep me in line and make sure I behaved.

A tactic surely Cissy would envy.

"Did you hear me?" The muffled voice sounded impatient, and I detected the vague buzz of white noise in the background. It sounded like traffic.

"Loud and clear," I said.

"And come alone," the bad guy reminded me, as if I'd forget something like that, "or he's chopped liver."

"I'm alone, for Pete's sake," I snapped into the phone, but the line had already gone dead.

I dug in my back pocket, tossed ten bucks on the bar, and ran out of there faster than Carl Lewis in his prime.

When I climbed in the Jeep, the clock on the dash showed eleven-twenty.

I hadn't been playing this ransom game for an hour yet, and it felt like an eternity.

I put the Wrangler in gear and took off in a screech of brakes.

My cell rang again, not long after I'd reached Northwest Highway, heading west. If it was the kidnappers, changing plans, I was going to throw up.

But it wasn't.

It was only Stephen.

"You all right, kiddo?" he asked, and I quickly told him where I was going and that I'd be dropping the bagful of his old pal's fake *dinero*.

"I've got your back," he reminded me, "though I don't think I'm the only one tailing you, Andy. There's a red BMW Roadster that's been behind you for a while."

"Allie Price," I hissed. It had to be. I wasn't about to believe the kidnappers drove the same kind of car as Brian's ex-girl. That would've been one coincidence too many. "The red car belongs to Malone's colleague," I told him. "I told her to stay out of this, but she can't."

"Well, er, neither could your mother, apparently," Stephen said, though he sounded reluctant to have dropped that particular bomb.

"What does that mean?" I did my best to keep from yelling, but I felt close to exploding. It was all I could do to keep the Jeep on the road and talk at once.

"Now don't get upset, Andy, but I do believe she's following me, following you. I spotted her beige-colored Lexus with the tinted windows."

My mother had joined my ransom drop parade?

Was he kidding me?

"You have to make them stop, Stephen," I said, feeling a rush of sheer panic. "What if someone sees?"

Namely, the kidnappers.

If Stephen had noticed I had a red Beemer and a champagne-hued Lexus on my tail, wouldn't Malone's captors, who'd arranged this whole run-about-town so they could make sure I hadn't called the police?

Could Cissy and Allie have spoiled everything already?

"Oh, God," I moaned, trying to keep my eyes clear and on the road, when I wanted to pull over and weep.

"Just stay cool," he told me in that unwavering way of his. "If they suspected anything, they would've called off the drop by now. I have a feeling this whole setup was more of a scare tactic than anything, which adds to my suspicion that these folks aren't pros."

Aren't pros?

What did that mean?

Amateur kidnappers?

Well, *that* was reassuring.

"Just continue to follow their instructions, Andy, and we'll go from there," Stephen said. "We'll pin 'em down with the GPS, find out where they live. Then, once we've got Brian safely home, we'll call the police."

"Okay." That sounded great to me.

"Good girl," he remarked before he hung up, and I shakily set my cell in my lap, returning both hands to the steering wheel.

Good girl.

There it was again.

I scrunched up my forehead, overwhelmed by a sense of déjà vu.

Those were the very words the kidnappers had used, and not just in this last phone call. I forced my mind back to what they'd said earlier and tried to figure out why the phrase nagged at me.

Be a good little girl, and he won't get hurt, okay?

Be a good girl and drop it behind the Dumpster in back. Got it?

As hard as I tried, though, I couldn't nail down the connection.

If I hadn't been so distracted by the satchel full of counterfeit money sitting on my backseat or the thought of rolling along Northwest Highway with a caravan behind me, I might've been able to retrieve that lost information more quickly. It'd be one of those things that popped into my head in the middle of the night or during an unrelated conversation, one of those "Eureka!" moments that's so annoying, because it's always on a time delay.

I fixed my eyes on the road, watching the same landmarks pass that I'd seen out the window the night before, en route to The Men's Club with Allie.

The Walgreens, the Jack Daniel's billboard, the Family Dollar store, the Jaguar dealership, and the Best Western.

And then the edifice I'd been seeking appeared on my left.

Violà!

The International House o' Pancakes.

Complete with blue roof and grimy whitewashed walls.

My pulse cranked into overdrive, and I prayed my mother and Allie would be smart enough not to pull in right behind me, even though it was late and the place looked damned near vacant. Surely, whoever was waiting for me to dump the cash would have some kind of surveillance in place.

For all I knew, the bad guys were inside, peering out a window, or slouched down in one of the three other cars in the lot. Regardless, I felt eyes on me as I searched for the best place to stop. In the process, I spotted the pay phone, from which Señor Kidnapper had made all the calls to my cell.

So what next? How was I supposed to do this?

I gnawed the inside of my cheek, fearing I'd make a fatal misstep.

If anything I did triggered an adverse reaction, I would fail and Malone would be left at the mercy of the knife-wielding nut balls who quoted movie lines and worshipped Paris Hilton.

I couldn't let myself consider that or I'd panic. I was on the verge of hyperventilating already.

The only thought that filled my mind as I slowly angled around the IHOP's nearly vacant parking area was: *Where's the Dumpster?*

I peered ahead and spotted a hulking shape behind the building, where a light had gone out, leaving the rear in shadows.

Great.

The thud of my heart filled my ears as I drove the Jeep closer and closer to the giant bin. I wasn't sure if I was supposed to cut the headlamps when I parked, figuring if I did, I wouldn't be able to see a thing.

I left the lights on and the Jeep running, tugging the satchel from the backseat into my lap.

As I gripped the handles and prepared to get out, worries flooded my brain. What if the dye packs went off too soon? What if the Bad Dudes realized the bills were fakes? What if they ditched the sack with the GPS before we found them? What if nothing went wrong, yet they decided not to let Malone go?

What if Brian turned up as dead as Trayla Trash, aka Betty Wren?

What would I do then?

Stop it, Andy, I told myself, as it did me no good to keep wondering "what if " when I had a mission to accomplish.

I looked around as I slid out of the Jeep, but didn't see a soul. Beyond the noise of my pulse, I could discern the whoosh of cars driving past the restaurant on the busy road that led to the airport.

The stench of garbage hit me smack in the face as I approached the Dumpster, my sneakers shuffling on asphalt, and I wondered where the best place was to leave the bag. Mr. Mumbles hadn't told me anything specific, such as "toss it in the bin" or leave it next to the empty syrup carton.

I didn't want to set it in plain sight of the IHOP, where an employee or patron could spot it. I hadn't gone through all this trouble just to have some stranger take the booby-trapped loot.

I meant *a nonkidnapping stranger,* of course.

So I tucked the bag around the back of the smelly green receptacle; hidden from prying eyes but surely locatable if one were looking for it.

As I rose from my crouch, I felt motion behind me.

I turned in time to catch sight of a figure in black . . . tried to look at the face but saw only as far up as his neck, as an arm came around my chest and another pressed a cloth hard to my face. I threw up my hands, swinging at him, but mostly hitting air.

I inhaled the most awful smell, something like paint

thinner, before I stopped fighting. I vaguely felt my eyes roll up into my head, and the rest of me went limp.

After that . . .

Zilch.

Chapter 19

 I smelled Joy.

And I don't mean happiness or pleasure. The way my head throbbed, I felt a whole lot less than ecstatic.

The Joy I inhaled was French perfume.

My mother's scent.

"Wake up, pumpkin. Please, wake up for Mummy."

When I could finally force my eyelids apart, it was Cissy's face I blearily focused on, hovering so near above my own it was hard to differentiate between the tip of her nose and the tip of mine.

"Andrea, thank goodness! Darling, can you hear me? Are you all right?" Her normally smooth as silk drawl ran over itself, fast as the staccato clip of a carpetbagger. "Did you fall? Is anything broken? Should I call an ambulance?"

I managed to squeak out, "Nothing broken."

At least I didn't think so.

"Up," I croaked and felt hands at my back, helping lift my shoulders from the ground, and I heard Stephen's voice, saying, "That's right, sit up, good girl."

Good girl.

Hell's bells, there it was again.

Good girl, good girl, good girl, good girl.

I shut my eyes as my thoughts came unscrambled, as if my unconscious mind had been waiting for just the right moment to connect all the dots.

In this case, post-knockout.

Like clouds abruptly breaking after a storm, allowing shafts of sunlight through, I recalled clear as day where I'd heard those words before, besides my one-sided conversations with the mumbling kidnapper.

I'd seen them uttered on the television at Mother's.

During the news segment about Trayla's murder.

I could hear them spoken as vividly as I remembered the face of the woman from whose mouth they had emanated.

She was such a good girl, really, no matter how tough she acted. In some ways, she was like a sister to me.

The brunette barmaid at The Men's Club.

Lu McCarthy.

"Andy, how many fingers am I holding up?" Cissy asked, and I obediently shifted my attention to the pink-painted fingernails and the glittering diamonds settled below her knuckles; but something more important than her fingers flashed before my eyes.

The man in black.

The dude who'd killed at least a couple of my brain

cells with that turpentine-soaked rag he'd held on me.

I'd seen his skin above the collar of his T-shirt.

There were wingtips drawn on his skin, wrapped around his neck.

The black ink of a tattoo.

One that struck a familiar chord.

It was exactly like the design I'd noticed on Cricket, the burly bartender with the girlie voice, whom Lu had been talking to when Allie and I had dropped into the strip club to ask some questions.

Cricket had mentioned that Brian reminded him of John Cusack in *Say Anything* and Matt Damon in *Good Will Hunting*, which told me that he'd seen Brian that night and could describe the pink shirt he'd been wearing. It also implied he had a thing for celebrity, like someone who'd steal lines from *Ransom* and who'd demand the precise amount that Paris Hilton paid for the return of her stolen puppy.

Lu and Cricket.

Aka the Boob Bar Bonnie and Clyde.

It fit like the kid gloves Mother forced upon me when I was a child at my first afternoon tea.

I'd given them my business card with my cell number, had told them I'd pay good money for any information that would help me locate Brian. They must've figured out who I was—maybe even Googled my name, as Stephen had suggested—and decided I was their ticket out of Stripper Land.

If I was so desperate to find Malone that I'd hit The Men's Club to chat with anyone who'd listen, they had to figure I'd be willing to pay big bucks to get him back in one piece . . . even if they didn't actually have him. Because how could I have known they were pulling my leg?

I couldn't.

I'd been an easy mark, willing to jump at whatever carrot was dangled before me.

So who really had Malone, if not the two of them?

Damn, damn, damn.

Think, Andy. Think.

Something else filtered through my aching brain, a comment of Allie's.

I figure Malone saw something he shouldn't have, and Oleksiy had no choice but to make our boy disappear.

Allie had been right all along.

The kidnapping was bogus.

If I hadn't believed it before, I did now, in every way that mattered. I'd been naïve, ignoring any niggling doubts, like Stephen's questions about proof, because the ransom demand had allowed me to fixate on something tangible that connected me to Brian and made me feel like I had some power to get him back.

Lu and Cricket hadn't cared that I was frantic about my disappearing beau.

They'd just wanted my money.

The greedy bastards.

It almost made me laugh to think the pile of bills in the satchel was as bogus as their threats to hurt Brian.

I wondered if either of them had any inkling where Malone was, or who'd grabbed him and Trayla as they'd left through the back door of The Men's Club?

What had Lu really seen that night? She'd said Trayla had fled in just her robe, without finishing her set. What else had she glimpsed? Someone with her besides Brian? One of Oleksiy's armed goons?

Maybe Lu had been too scared to spill the truth.

Could be why she'd let them interview her on TV. She wanted to make it clear to Oleksiy and his people that, regardless of her connection to Trayla, she wasn't about to play ratfink.

I wish I'd known she was in trouble, but she must've kept it from me. The last time I saw her, she seemed okay.

That was bull, I realized.

Lu had been doing what frightened folks had done for centuries: covering her ass. I had a pretty strong sense that Trayla had confided in her, maybe even discussed Oleksiy. I had to find out what Lu really knew.

I gritted my teeth, wanting so badly to squeeze the truth out of Lu McCarthy and her pal Cricket. If they didn't crack, I'd turn them into the cops for committing fraud and feigning a boyfriend-napping.

It feels off, Kendricks. Someone's taking advantage of you. Brian's name has been all over the news. Even that Channel 8 reporter who interviewed your neighbor managed to link you to him. The cops, too. By now, every media outlet in Dallas knows you're the girlfriend of the dude whose car was found parked at Love Field with a very dead stripper in his trunk. Your so-called kidnappers could be anyone, pretending to have Malone so they can make a quick buck.

If I hadn't bought Allie's spiel before, I did now.

Brian's vanishing act wasn't a kidnapping, not in the way I'd been imagining.

It had everything to do with the prosecution's witness

list for the Oleksiy Petrenko trial, as Allie had suspected. I figured the money launderer had ordered his boys to snatch Trayla to keep her quiet; only Malone had gotten in the way. If Brian had seen them kill Trayla, it certainly explained why they'd used his car to take her to the airport and why they'd left it there in a no parking zone for the cops to stumble upon eventually.

Was Petrenko unsure of what to do with him? After all, Malone was part of his defense team. Did that matter? Did Oleksiy care a fig, even about his own attorneys?

I had to believe he hadn't harmed Malone yet, at least not fatally. Something told me that Petrenko would hold onto Brian, maybe until after the trial, because the cops would surely put two and two together if they found his body so soon after Trayla's.

Wouldn't they?

"This stinks," I said, not realizing I'd muttered aloud until I heard my mother say, "Stephen, let's get her away from this trash receptacle. She should be breathing fresh air, not the smell of refuse."

"Will do, Cis."

I hadn't realized Stephen had gone anywhere until he appeared from behind me, which meant from behind the Dumpster, as I realized I was lying just to the side of the hulking garbage bin.

A vague light from the eaves of the IHOP flickered in my eyes as I tried to take in a deep breath. Maybe it was a blessing that my sinuses were still numbed from whiffing paint thinner, as I could barely differentiate the "smell of refuse" from Mother's perfume.

"Help me up, please," I said as Stephen reached beneath my arms to get a grip. "I want to stand."

There was a slight slur in my voice still, and I could taste the gauzy dryness of my mouth; but I felt more clearheaded by the minute, absolutely positively certain of who the GPS would lead us to and wanting to strangle the culprits with my bare hands.

"Geez, Kendricks, you scared the crap out of us."

As Stephen assisted me from the ground to my feet, I realized he and Cissy weren't the only ones who'd dropped by the Dumpster to retrieve me.

The Blond Menace had shown up as well.

Hail, hail, the gang's all here, I thought as I swallowed hard to rinse the taste of the paint thinner from my mouth.

"What the heck happened to you?" Allie grilled me like a witness on the stand. "I wasn't but a minute behind you—"

"As was I," my mother butted in, not to be left out.

Allie cleared her throat. "When I pulled into the parking lot, I saw your car with its lights on, then I spot you flat on your back. What did you do? Run into something?"

What did I do?

"Thanks, all of you," I muttered, hearing gravel in my voice, "for your concern and for thinking I couldn't handle this without a host of Chuck Norris wannabes pretending to be Texas Rangers."

"You know Chuck wasn't really a Ranger, don't you, Kendricks?" said the ever-helpful Allie. "He just played one on TV."

If I were *really* Chuck Norris, I would've given her a high-karate kick and knocked out all her teeth.

"How long was I out?" I asked and looked straight at Stephen, clearly the only sane member of my posse.

"A minute, maybe a little longer than that. I got here pretty quick after you did, Andy, but not fast enough to see who grabbed you," he said, keeping a steady grip on my shoulder as I wobbled a bit until I found my sea legs.

"It doesn't matter," I told him, doing the best I could to ignore the ache in my head. "I think I know who's responsible."

"For kidnapping Mr. Malone?" my mother asked, slipping her hands into the pockets of a black silk jacket. I noticed she wore matching silk pants, even a black silk camisole and black pearls.

Ah, yes, the perfect attire for a society maven engaged in nefarious activities. She could write a book on what the well-bred woman should wear to an intimate little kidnapping.

"No," I corrected her. "I mean, who's behind this whole charade, because it was all about money, not about Brian. The bag is gone, Stephen, isn't it?"

He nodded, his mouth set grimly. "I'm still tracking the GPS, Andy. We'll catch 'em."

"I know we will," I told him, as I had a good idea where the money trail would end, even without the fancy GPS equipment.

"You called it a charade, Kendricks," Allie the Observant remarked, giving me a "told you so" smirk. "So you believe me, that the ransom demand isn't connected with Malone going MIA?"

Much as I despised having to say it, I coughed up a "Yeah, I believe you."

Even through the dark, her smile gleamed.

I took a few slow steps toward my Jeep, which had seemed so close to the Dumpster when I'd parked but suddenly appeared a million miles away.

"I don't think you should drive in your condition, Andrea," my mother stated, and I paused, looking over my shoulder at the three of them, thankful to see only one of each. No double vision. Maybe all the furniture stripping I'd done in the past, rescuing old pieces from flea markets, had helped my tolerance to the turpentine.

"What's my condition?" I said, wanting to laugh. "That I'm an imbecile for buying the ransom plot? That I'm a dope for not involving the police? Or that I'm about the worst judge of character ever? Take your pick."

That left them dumbfounded, which should've tickled me.

Instead I felt queasy.

"Why don't you ride with me, Andy," Stephen suggested. "I've got the laptop with the GPS tracking map. We'll see where it leads."

I'd wager it would point us right up the street.

To the strip club.

I jerked my chin at Mother and Allie. "Tell them to go home, would you, Stephen? I don't want them getting more involved than they are already."

My mother's beau had the gall to laugh, and I watched the play of shadow across his weathered face, his expression softening. "Oh, sweet girl, I don't know Ms. Price well enough to order her about"—he gestured at Mother—"and I wouldn't even try telling Cissy where to go. I'm much too fond of the family jewels."

"Smart man," my mother drawled, winking at him, the exchange between them enough to make me nauseous, if the turpentine hadn't done the trick already.

"Let's go," I said, figuring we'd stood around long enough.

It was time to shake down Lu and Cricket. I was through being a patsy.

I just hoped that I wasn't too late.

Chapter 20

 As I suspected, the blipping red light on Stephen's laptop showed the GPS chip had stopped moving a mere smidge farther up Northwest Highway.

A small hop, skip, and a jump away from the IHOP, as it were.

How convenient, I mused, *for us and for the lying pair who'd been pulling my leg—and stringing along my hopes—for the last twelve hours, the jerks.*

In the few minutes it took to get to our target location, I filled Stephen in on every epiphany I'd had about this whole thing since I'd awakened from my turpentine-induced stupor: who I believed was behind the kidnapping stunt, as well as what I'd learned from Allie, and how it all fell together to point toward Oleksiy Petrenko as the real Malone-snatcher.

From the grim look on Stephen's face, he didn't

exactly like thinking a good old-fashioned mobster was involved.

Not that it made me feel any too warm and fuzzy either.

As Stephen guided the black Volvo sedan toward the pink stucco building with its ornamental lions and deceptively elegant sign, I composed a million different scenarios in my head, everything I wanted to say to Lu and Cricket, all of it as violent as a Bruce Willis movie.

I was ready to jump out of the moving car as Stephen pulled up to the valet in front of The Men's Club. This time, I didn't smile back at the pimple-faced fellow in the white shirt who took Stephen's keys, the very same dude who'd parked my Jeep when Allie and I had come the night before.

As soon as the locks popped up, I scrambled out of the Volvo, pausing to suck in a deep breath and square my shoulders. Then I took the steps, one by one, slow and steady, my eyes narrowed on the doors; my heart set on doing battle.

Stephen caught me from behind, taking hold of my shoulder. I didn't want to stop, but I did. I even turned around and gave him a chance to speak his piece.

"Maybe it's time we got the police involved in this, Andy," he said, blue eyes so damned earnest beneath the hank of faded ginger-colored hair rumpled across his brow. "I don't know that it's a good idea to just march in there and confront anyone. We should exercise caution."

I didn't care about caution. I wanted to kick some barmaid butt, and how.

"Give me fifteen minutes, Stephen," I pleaded, glancing back at the driveway and noting a red Roadster disgorging a blond driver, while a pale Lexus with tinted windows sat patiently behind, awaiting its turn with the valet. "You keep my mother and Allie out here, so they don't screw things up. Or see anything that would burn the back of Cissy's eyeballs."

"Is that all?" Stephen smiled tightly, and I realized that was no small task.

But I didn't want my mother setting foot inside this place.

I was sure she'd have a heart attack were she to catch the goings-on beneath the chandeliers and red velvet drapes. I could already envision her pulling near-naked women off the laps of drooling men and throwing her silk jacket over the bare-breasted stripper onstage.

Like that wouldn't cause a stink.

Allie was starting up the steps just as Stephen released me. "All right, Andy." He relented. "You go in alone. But if you're not back in fifteen minutes flat, I'll ring your cell. And if you don't answer, I'm coming in, and I'm bringing the cavalry."

"Okay," I said, because it sounded more than fair. Though there was one little thing I would need from him, and I told him what it was. He didn't look any too happy about my request; but he did as I asked, and I pocketed the item in question.

I murmured "Thank you" as I pulled away from him and slipped through the front doors. I thought I heard Allie howling, "Hey, Kendricks!" from somewhere behind me, but I didn't hesitate. I didn't want a sidekick this go-round.

A different hostess was taking covers this evening, a dark-skinned girl with close-cropped hair and very shiny makeup. She didn't try to make conversation, and neither did I, even as I handed over the last of the cash from my back pocket.

I locked eyes briefly with the bouncer who had previously studied Malone's photo and dismissed it; then he glanced away, dismissing me, his expression bored. Not like someone who'd been involved in a kidnapping scam with the tattooed bartender and duplicitous barmaid.

As I reached for the doors leading into the club itself, I paused to take a deep breath—still smelling paint thinner in my nose—before pushing my way into the Wonderful World of Stripdom.

At this point, nothing surprised me, not the green and blue laser lights shooting through the dark or the sea of endless boobs or the ongoing lap dances being performed right in the middle of the room.

Maybe that's what happened if you worked here. You just got used to it, stopped seeing the decadence and nakedness, ceased to smell the cologne and perfume, and ignored the pounding of the overloud music in your head.

Thank God, I'd never get the chance.

I strode straight up to the bar on the right-hand side of the stage, planted my palms on the counter and caught my wild-eyed appearance in the mirror. If I'd had the chest for it and fewer layers on, I could've passed for an angry stripper whose G-string had cut off her circulation.

"Can I get you something, honey?"

I frowned at the unfamiliar skinny dude with glasses who'd had the gall to ask such a question. Of course, he could get me something. Like, um, how about a man with a funny name for starters?

"Cricket," I told him.

He squinted at me. "You mean a Grasshopper?" he said over the noise of Shania Twain wailing, "Man, I feel like a woman!"

"No, I'm looking for Cricket, the other bartender. The one who was here last night before ten," I practically barked at him. "And where's Lu McCarthy?" I added, because I knew she was working tonight, as the reporter on the six o'clock news had interviewed her from here and the shot was live. She had to be around somewhere.

He swung a white bar towel over his shoulder. "You a friend of theirs? You don't look like their type."

"Well, no and yes. I'm sort of an acquaintance who loaned them money, and I want it back," I said, because it was hardly a lie. They owed me a bowling bag full of it.

He cracked a grin. "Oh, shit, honey, you should've never loaned the likes of them cash. You'll never see a dime. Those two would pick your pocket if you turned your back on 'em."

"Wish I'd known that before," I replied, thinking that I sucked big-time in the first impressions department. I gave folks the benefit of the doubt, when I probably should just figure everyone was out to get me until they proved otherwise.

Or would that make me paranoid?

"I've got no allegiance to either one of 'em, sweet cakes, so you can break their knees for all I care." He jerked his chin in the direction of the stage, and I knew he meant the doors beyond it. "Lu's in back, on a break. I saw Cricket pop in a few minutes ago and head for the back. Looked like he had a bag packed."

Oh, yeah, he had a bag packed, all right. And I knew precisely what was in it.

"I'll bet he did."

"Maybe he's gonna take a trip."

"I do believe you may be right about that," I said.

It'd be a one-way ticket to the pokey, if I had anything to do with it.

"Good ol' Crick let it slip earlier that he was coming into some dough, an inheritance or something. Said he wanted me to cover for him if he took off for a while. Can't imagine who'd leave him squat. Unless one of his, um, buddies from his motorcycle club from Brokeback Mountain went boots up."

So Cricket had invented a cover story for the money?

How very enlightening.

I felt my innards tighten, like spaghetti that's cooked too long and sticks together in a big clump.

"Thanks for your help," I told him, and if I'd had any bills left in my back pocket, I would've tipped him large, because he could easily have made it hard for me, or called Security because I smelled like trouble, or rather, reeked like the Dumpster behind the neighboring IHOP.

I skirted the stage where the dancer was engaged in such heavy shimmying I wanted to shout, "Shake it, don't break it!" But I restrained myself and ducked into the same door through which Lu had led Allie and me once before.

I sidestepped a pair of heavily made-up women who lounged in the hallway, wearing nothing but the highest of heels, the skimpiest of thongs, and the tiniest sparkly pasties.

Though my gait wasn't quite as steady as it usually was—thanks to the whiff of solvents—I was feeling extremely sure-footed, and the flood of adrenaline shooting through my veins propelled me forward; straight back toward the room where Lu had taken me the day before.

I had a feeling that's where she and Cricket would be examining their loot. I couldn't imagine Lu letting him take the cash anywhere without giving her a gander first, and that seemed the perfect spot. Empty and with a door that locked. Being near the rear exit surely didn't hurt. If Cricket had had an ounce of brain cells, he would've slipped in that way instead of parading through the club with the bag in hand, although it sounded like he'd been bragging about the money already.

I figured he'd end up on one of those "Stupid Criminal" Web sites someday after passing a robbery note to a bank teller on the back of his business card.

Genius.

The noise of the pulsating music dimmed the farther I walked, until I was there, outside Trayla's old dressing room with the handmade star on the door.

I put my palms on the surface, leaned my ear against the wood and heard mumbled voices, unmistakably those of a man and a woman. When I heard a burst of laughter, it was all I could do not to rush in kicking and screaming.

But I couldn't.

I had to do this right.

Emotion bubbled inside me, anger like I hadn't felt since I can't remember when, and I stood back for a moment, gritting my teeth and getting ahold of myself.

Then I reached for the knob and twisted.

The door didn't budge.

I gnawed the inside of my cheek, wondering what to do next, how best to approach this. But that hesitation was short-lived.

I snapped.

I was mad as hell and I wasn't gonna take it anymore!

With both fists, I started beating on the door.

"Lu and Cricket! I know you're in there," I shouted, my forehead pressed against the wood. "It's Andrea Kendricks, you lousy frauds. Let me in, or I'll have the cops on your tail in five seconds flat. You got that?"

I turned around, breathing heavily, glancing right and left to see if anyone had heard my raised voice; but I didn't spot any concerned parties racing in my direction. I was about to bang again when the door pulled in, and I fell inside with it.

As I scrambled to stay upright, I heard the door click closed behind me, and I glanced back to see Lu in her red corset and black thigh-high boots leaning against it. She didn't appear any too pleased to see me there.

The feeling was mutual.

"What the *hell* are you doing? You shouldn't be here," she hissed.

"Is that so? Well, you know, I decided if I wanted to hunt a couple rats, I had to drop in on the nest. You counted your blood money yet?" I asked, and my gaze ping-ponged from her to Cricket, who sat on the floor with the satchel between his legs.

He was all in black, and I realized such a color scheme was perfectly suited to both picking up a ransom drop and bartending.

How convenient.

He didn't seem angry, not like Lu. Instead, beneath his cue-ball skull, his tough-guy features crumpled, and, resembling a recalcitrant puppy more than a Hell's Angel, he cast his eyes down, staring sadly at his meaty fists, each one wrapped around a pack of bills.

If I didn't know better, I'd say he looked positively remorseful.

Or maybe he'd just run out of fresh gum. I didn't know him well enough to decipher his moods.

"Two hundred twelve thousand," he said, his high-pitched voice sounding doleful. "Did you know it's a famous number?"

"Yeah, yeah"—I brushed him off with a wave—"it was the ransom demand for the Paris Hilton pooch. Oh, and nice job filching the lines from *Ransom* and using those on me. You had me scared witless."

"Mel Gibson rocked in that one," he chirped, perking up. "He was so handsome before he let himself go to pot and made *The Passion*. Although the dude who played Jesus? Jim Caviezal? Now, he's extremely *hot*."

I blinked at him, wondering if the guy was soft in the head, though I knew he had to have brains enough to mix margaritas and martinis. Still, how much gray matter did that take?

"Aren't they pretty?" He offered up a pack of funny money, but I didn't want to touch it; so I put my hands in my pockets, one on my cell phone and one on the sweet little device Stephen had entrusted to me. "I've never seen so much green, except when Julianne Moore's on the red carpet. She looks best in emerald. It goes well with her pale skin and red hair."

Are you kidding me?

Man, this guy was in La-La Land in more ways than one.

"Don't get too chummy with all those Benjamins," I said, restraining myself mightily, taking in the tiny dressing room I'd visited so recently. It looked just the same, down to the snapshot stuck to the mirror and the gooey puddle of makeup. "Hope I don't break your hearts when I say you won't be keeping a penny. You'll be lucky to stay out of jail, and you won't"—I faced Lu again, fingering her as the ringleader, as Cricket didn't seem to have the balls—"not unless you tell me everything about Oleksiy Petrenko and Trayla."

"How did you—" she started, but cut herself off. Still, her dark eyes had widened as I'd said the names, her mouth falling into an O.

"And you'd better spill all you know about where his goons might've taken Malone. I've got backup outside, ready and willing to nail your asses to the wall," I assured her, in case she thought I was stupid enough to come alone after that wild goose chase they'd led me on. "So don't play games with me, girlfriend, I'm not in the mood."

Lu stood still a moment, biting her lower lip, doing a good job of acting like she was contemplating fiercely. It looked like it hurt.

Then she took a step away from the door, nodded and said, "Okay, you win."

Well, all right then.

I puffed out my chest a little. I couldn't help it.

It was about time I had the upper hand.

We were all wedged pretty close together in Trayla's old digs, so Lu had to two-step around me to get to the vanity. Her dark-cropped hair and red-painted Clara Bow lips jumped out at me from her reflection, even in the dim lighting.

She plucked the photo from where I'd left it wedged in the mirror's frame, gazing at it as she said, "I'm sorry that I wasn't straight with you, but I wanted some of what Trayla had. I thought you were my free ride."

"Trayla's dead," I reminded her.

"I feel bad for her, but that's all." She fingered the picture, while Cricket remained on the floor, straddling the bag and fondling the money, oblivious to all else. "Trayla wasn't all that nice, ya know. She was kind of an uppity bitch."

A woman who called herself "Trayla Trash" was uppity? I guess Lu meant in a gold digger sort of way.

"She rubbed all our noses in it when she found herself a man with deep pockets," Lu went on, and I remained quiet, afraid to interrupt. "She started showing up with new clothes and fancy jewelry, bragged about some posh condo he had her stashed in down in Turtle Creek. Told us she could ask for anything and get it, and all she had to do was play the slut between the sheets." The barmaid released a throaty laugh. "Now *that* was something she could do in the dark with one hand tied behind her back. She had to be better at it than she was at pole dancing. She had two left feet, I swear."

So long as she had two breasts, I don't think any of her audience had much cared about her lack of grace.

"Was her sugar daddy Oleksiy Petrenko?" I dared to ask.

Lu's dark head bobbed up and down.

"When did things turn sour?" I figured it was about the time Petrenko realized he was going to trial. Maybe he'd even whispered more than sweet nothings in bed, and he figured she knew too much.

"She showed up here one night with a suitcase, looking like a wreck," Lu said with a sigh. "She was cryin' up a storm, acting afraid, telling me she was leaving town after she finished her set 'cuz she needed the paycheck. She figured she was okay sticking around for a few days, but no more than that, 'cuz Lexy—that's what she called him—didn't know she was working again. At least that's what she thought. Only, she didn't make it long enough to collect her check, did she?"

So Oleksiy had found her.

Couldn't be too hard tracking down a wayward stripper-girlfriend if you had the resources. Dallas was big, but not *that* big.

And I'm sure he'd been looking, ever since he realized she'd gone to the prosecution and turned on him.

"She did manage to grab some things before the landlord locked her out of her posh pad a few weeks back, just what she could squeeze into a beat-up piece of luggage she borrowed off me." The barmaid pushed the photo into my hands. "That's when I saw the painting. She hung it up in here, but it disappeared the same night she snuck out the back door with your boyfriend. I have a feeling she ran into trouble before she got clear of here."

Well, duh, that was the understatement of the year,

seeing as how she'd ended up naked and dead in the trunk of Malone's Acura.

I took the snapshot from her and stared hard at it, moving closer beneath the vanity lights to see better.

I wished I'd had a magnifying glass, because I couldn't make out much more than I had the first time. I could discern hues of deep pink and brown, a touch of green, and tiny images of people, as well as a rider on a horse.

"Did she tell you anything about the painting, Lu?"

"It came from the condo is all I know. Trayla said there were lots more of 'em, but most were too big to pinch easily." The woman crossed her arms, rubbing them. "She said he gave it to her, so it was rightfully hers. But I'm sure she stole it. She said it was worth a fortune, and that it was her ticket out. I almost got the feeling she knew something she shouldn't."

"About the painting? Or about Petrenko?"

Lu shrugged. "I don't know."

I leaned even nearer one of the lightbulbs, staring at the tiny image of the artwork and thinking I'd seen it somewhere before.

But where? And how?

It wasn't like I'd ever visited Trayla in her Turtle Creek penthouse.

There was a tiny scratching at the back of my brain, plucking bits and pieces of things I'd tucked away, and I remembered something, a conversation I'd had with Allie in my kitchen earlier in the day.

We'd been talking about Oleksiy Petrenko and money laundering, when she'd told me, *Let's just say that it's a whole different ballgame in this brave new world. With the*

Patriot Act clamping down on banks, things like gift cards and stolen art are becoming the currency of choice.

Stolen art.

Trayla's painting?

The rattling in my head intensified, shaking out another piece of information I'd stowed away.

The magazine I'd found in Brian's apartment, several pages dog-eared, including a piece about an art heist at the Isabella Stewart Gardner Museum in Boston.

I looked up from the photograph to where Lu had settled on the floor beside Cricket, chunks of banded bills clutched in her hands—in both their hands—as if they were saying good-bye, knowing I wouldn't let them have it.

"Did Trayla tell you if she thought that painting was stolen?" I asked, and Lu didn't take her dark eyes from the money as she answered.

"It was cleaned and pressed, that's what she said, which I thought was pretty odd at the time."

Cleaned and pressed.

As in "laundered"?

My mind shuffled like a deck of cards, bits that hadn't fit before sliding together to form one solid mass.

I stuck the photo in the back pocket of my jeans.

"Do you know where Oleksiy took Brian?" I took a shot in the dark.

"Maybe to his place," Lu said, still playing with the cash. "Trayla mentioned one time that he had a cellar with soundproof walls. He told her he'd kept his wife down there for a week after he found out she'd been shagging his brother."

The brother that squealed on him to the police, I recalled. And didn't Allie say the wife had taken off for parts unknown until the smoke had cleared? Sounded like a smart move, considering what I was learning about Petrenko.

"Did Trayla say where her sugar daddy lives?"

"Yeah." She sniffed. "Same area where the squeaky-voiced billionaire with the big ears camps out. You know, the one who ran for president a billion years back."

"Preston Hollow?" I suggested, assuming the squeaky-voiced billionaire with the elephant ears was Ross Perot.

"That's it. In a big mansion, Tray said. He took her there a few times, after he split with his wife. Seems he doesn't go out much. He's kind of a hermit. Has that phobia of public spaces. Tray told me he's got a couple armed thugs that hang around, and a security gate. You have to get buzzed through to make it to the door."

Oleksiy lived in Preston Hollow?

That wasn't far from Highland Park, which was Mother's neck of the woods.

Why hadn't the online articles I'd read about him mentioned that? Or maybe it wasn't public knowledge.

Could be he'd done something tricky when he'd purchased the real estate, so it wasn't even in his name.

I wonder which street he called "home"?

Although I was sure that finding out would be a piece of cake, faster and easier than Oleksiy tracking down which strip joint Trayla was shaking her bon-bons in after she'd skipped out on him with his painting.

Surely Allie knew the address of her firm's client, right?

If not, Cissy could find out in a heartbeat. Her chatty

friends were faster at gathering and sharing information than those guys from the Smoking Gun.

"Okay, I'm done here," I said aloud, and Cricket and Lu looked up in tandem.

"You're not calling the cops on us, are you?" Lu asked. "I helped you out, and you promised."

"No cops." She'd given me what I wanted, and I'd given my word. I wouldn't take it back.

"Can't we keep the money?" the tattooed bartender whined, sounding like a prepubescent boy whose voice would never change. "Just a couple of the packs?"

I sighed. "Look, why don't you hold onto those"—I indicated the ones in their hands, the topmost bundles from the stash—"and I'll take the rest of the bag. But I'll be back for those later, okay? They're just on loan."

"Yeah, yeah, come back later," Cricket said and rubbed a stack of bound bills against his cheek. "I just need to pretend for a while."

"You do that," I said, stepping forward to retrieve the satchel from the floor and zip it up. I grabbed the handles tight and headed for the door.

"I'm sorry," Lu murmured, "for all the trouble." She added grudgingly, "And thanks for not turning us in."

"No, thank you," I told them, *for putting me through hell, you ratfinks*. What comes around goes around, I reminded myself. They'd get theirs. I was counting on it.

I let myself out, pulling the door tightly closed, and then pausing briefly just outside. I slid my hand into the pocket of my jacket that held the remote control device Stephen had given me. I firmly pressed the button, sending out unseen radio waves.

I held my breath and listened for what Stephen had assured me would come soon after.

An audible *pop!*

Lu and Cricket squealed.

A puff of red smoke oozed from beneath the door.

Nothing says "screw you" like a bright red aerosol dye pack.

I smiled and started walking up the rear hallway, toward the glowing sign that said, EXIT.

Ah, revenge really was quite sweet.

The cell in my other pocket rang, and I answered.

"Andy, you all right in there?" It was Stephen.

"Fine and dandy."

"You find the money?"

I felt the weight of the bag in my hand. "It's here, only minus a few packs, Stephen, I'm sorry. But if you want those bills, we can come back for them. They'll just be a little more colorful than they were a few minutes ago," I confessed, ducking through the back door of the club, eager to get out of the place.

"Andy, you didn't?" he said, but I wasn't about to let him dwell on something like red-stained funny money, not when I felt such a rush of hope.

"I think I know where Malone is being held," I told him, "and I want to get him out. Tonight."

No more fooling around.

It was time to end this nightmare, once and for all, and I was willing to do whatever it would take.

No more Ms. Nice Girl.

Chapter 21

In mere minutes, Allie produced the address for Oleksiy Petrenko. Seriously, she pinned down that location faster than Donald Trump could spit out his trademark "You're fired," thanks to her work on the alleged money launderer's defense team.

Though it was Cissy who quickly gathered enough facts about the man's digs to do a real estate listing. Okay, sure, she got the scoop from an Ebby Halliday agent-friend of hers, Margie Fenton, whose specialty was handling up-scale homes, so a fast cell-phone call did the trick. Mother feigned interest in the property on behalf of a pal moving home from London. The CIA would do well to recruit her, if they had any sense.

From the sound of things, this Petrenko was no slouch, having scooped up a five-million-dollar-plus French tradi-tional mansion in prestigious Preston Hollow for some-thing in the mid-four-million range. *Woo doggie, what a steal!* It had eight bedrooms, 6.2 baths, surrounded by a creek and waterfalls, as well as a privacy fence.

Heck, everyone should have eight bedrooms and a waterfall in their backyard, right?

I thought of the article I'd read online that called Oleksiy a modern-day Horatio Alger, coming from Ukraine with nothing but the clothes on his back and making his fortune, but I wondered how much of what he had was due to ill-gotten gains.

And they said that crime didn't pay.

Hogwash.

We used Stephen's wireless laptop to get online and link to the Isabella Stewart Gardner Museum, or rather, to scoop on the mega-million-dollar art heist from that site in 1990, as I had a gut feeling about that bookmarked article in Malone's *Smithsonian* being tied to the painting in the photograph with Trayla.

And damned if my gut wasn't right.

It took a couple page-downs to spot it, but there it was: *La Sortie Du Pelage* by Degas, 10×16 cm. Pencil and watercolor on paper. It depicted a jockey on a horse being led toward the racetrack, people milling about. Lots of deep pinks and browns with a touch of green.

That was it.

I had no doubt it was the artwork in Trayla's pic, the one Lu said her pal had swiped from the expensive condo Petrenko had rented.

I wondered when Oleksiy had noticed it missing.

About the same time he got wind that she would testify against him?

Was the Degas still in her dressing room when Brian

had followed her backstage on Saturday? Had he seen it and recognized it from the *Smithsonian* magazine article about the museum thefts? Had he asked where she'd obtained it, knowing it was stolen?

If she'd confessed, he must've realized that his client, Oleksiy Petrenko, had a hot piece of art on his hands. That was the kind of dirt even a good laundering couldn't wash off, particularly for a man heading to trial in a few short weeks.

I had a strong sense my upstanding boyfriend had confronted Petrenko, informing him that, as an attorney, he was obligated to go to the authorities with the information about the black-market Degas.

Oh, boy, I thought, realizing how that would've gone over with a Ukrainian mobster; doubtless much the same way my couture-conscious mother would react should someone insist she wear Lycra.

It made perfect sense why Petrenko wouldn't want to let Brian go.

And why he'd gotten rid of Trayla.

They were both loose ends for Oleksiy, though he'd obviously deemed one more expendable than the other.

But he might decide Brian needed taking care of, too.

How could he risk anyone sniffing around and finding out what Malone had doubtless learned? I imagined Petrenko was already making plans to dispose of my boyfriend soon.

Which is why my posse and I had to quickly cook up a plan to liberate my dude, and we didn't have a moment to waste.

We reconnected at the IHOP, since I needed to retrieve

my Jeep from where I'd left it near the Dumpster.

Over a round of hot coffee—not my favorite, but the caffeine couldn't hurt—I offered what I thought was the most logical suggestion: to storm the estate. Mother could alert her friends in the media, have them blind Petrenko with flashbulbs and cameras while we tore his mansion apart, looking for Malone.

Unfortunately, no one else was too keen on the idea.

In fact, Stephen shot it down ASAP, no more thrilled about that than he'd been when I explained why I'd set off the red dye packs, ruining several bundles of the borrowed counterfeit bills. ("Oh, Andy, you didn't have to do that, did you? I hope Dan doesn't kill us both." I figured Stephen's pal, the former Treasury agent, wanting to strangle me was the least of my worries.)

Stephen suggested going back to Mother's and getting some sleep first, as it was nearly midnight by then; but I wasn't willing to wait until morning.

My momentum was rolling forward, and I had no intention of putting a halt to the bulldozer within until we'd freed my boyfriend.

Oddly enough, Allie felt the same way, nixing rest until Brian was safe. And since she had more insight to Petrenko than anybody, I ventured to guess she was as afraid as I was that Oleksiy might dispose of Malone posthaste.

What we all could agree upon was the element of surprise, which would be on our side, as what alleged money launderer slash kidnapper slash killer would suspect the ding-dong of the front bell in the middle of the night?

Although I wasn't keen on what kind of schedule applied to criminal types; maybe they kept different hours than the rest of us, working at night like vampires rather than during the daylight.

I found myself wondering if Oleksiy could see his reflection. Or if he ate garlic, or slept in a coffin in his wine cellar, which Margie had told Cissy was temperature- and humidity-controlled and capable of housing upward of a thousand bottles.

Well, heck, there was stuff about blood for wine in the Bible, right? Who says it couldn't work in reverse?

Could be Oleksiy satisfied his blood thirst with a fragrant merlot or cabernet sauvignon.

I heard a buzz in my brain, like a bug fried in a zapper.

Holy cow.

Wait a minute.

Wait a dad-gummed minute.

Oleksiy's wine cellar.

Could that possibly be Malone's prison?

I thought back to Brian's phone call, the way his cell kept going in and out, like he was driving through a tunnel. The only time my phone did that was when I was in a concrete-reinforced building, driving beneath an underpass, or using underground parking.

Maybe my dude had been subterranean when he'd been forced to dial me up and act like we were finito.

Digging basements beneath existing houses was all the rage for the well-to-do in the Park Cities and Preston Hollow. I figured Petrenko's manse had to have a nice-sized hole in the ground if it housed such a spectacular room for wine storage.

I'd detected a faint noise, too, before Brian had cut me off. The clicking sound of an AC turning on, or so I'd assumed;

though I was beginning to wonder if it wasn't a unit that maintained temp and humidity so the air around the bottles of *vino* would be perfectly controlled.

"Andrea, are you listening to me?" Cissy poked my shin with her boot, and I shook off the brain fog, noting that Stephen and Allie also stared at me from across the blue vinyl booth. "I had an idea about how to distract this man, Paprika, so we can get into the house unnoticed."

"Paprika?" It took a second to register who she was talking about. "You mean Petrenko, don't you, Mother?"

She gave me one of her looks. "Yes, of course I do. Who else?"

Oh, I don't know. Mr. Paprika's good chums, Dr. Pepper and Mrs. Dash?

I wondered if either one was available for a midnight B&E.

Hmmm.

"We should call the police," my mother continued, which got my full attention.

Call the police? Was she out of her mind?

I saw Allie open her mouth, and I was sure she itched to comment as well; but Cissy waved a manicured hand, effectively cutting off any argument.

"Let me finish, please," she said, and I acquiesced, no matter how painful. "I could phone on my cell, pretending to be a neighbor, asking those rather unpleasant detectives who interrogated us to check on a domestic disturbance at the Petrenko place."

Ah, yes, the infamous Starsky and Hutch.

I'm sure they'd be a big help, particularly since they wanted to pin Trayla's murder on Brian. No doubt they'd be overjoyed to aid in his rescue so they could toss him in the slammer and throw away the key.

Cissy caught the roll of my eyes and frowned. "I'm not done yet, Andrea."

"Sorry," I mumbled.

"We could use the delivery entrance in back to slip onto the property," she went on, ignoring me. "Margie assures me the unmanned back gate isn't much more than a metal arm, like at any standard parking garage. Mr. Petrenko"— she emphasized his name—"hasn't yet upgraded."

"Well, that's great, except for one thing," I piped up, as Allie and Stephen both looked unwilling to contradict my mother. "Once we get onto the property, who's going to let us into the house? I'm sure Mr. Petrenko doesn't leave a door unlocked for strangers."

"I can let you in," Allie said in a quiet voice that sounded not at all like her, though she'd been unusually silent since we'd left the strip club. I figured she was upset that Stephen had kept her from joining me in exploding red dye packs on Lu and Cricket. "I can let you in," she repeated.

"And just how do you plan to do that?" I asked.

She leaned her forearms on the table, blond hair swaying over her shoulders, as she explained: "I think I should arrive first, before you call the police, Mrs. Kendricks. I could insist on talking to Oleksiy about the witness list and the problem of Brian going AWOL after interviewing the woman who turned up dead, Betsy Wren. I'll tell him I couldn't sleep, worrying about it, which is why I ended up on his doorstep when it's not exactly business hours."

"That could be dangerous, honey," Stephen said,

obviously taking her seriously. "But if we've got the police en route, maybe it's worth the risk."

Allie leaned forward, over the table, her eyes flickering with excitement. I could tell she enjoyed being in the middle of things, rather than playing second fiddle. "After I've been there a few minutes, I'll ask to use the ladies' room, only I'll slip into the back and unlock a door to let y'all in. I'll be there before he thinks twice, and he'll never know the difference. That'll give you a chance to scurry down to the basement and see if Brian's there. If he is, we'll have the cops showing up on the premises to take care of things, won't we?"

That's assuming Starsky and Hutch believed Mother's portrayal of a distressed neighbor and showed up at all, versus sending a patrol car; and, if they did, we'd have to hope they listened to our tale of Petrenko as kidnapper as opposed to arresting us for breaking into the millionaire businessman's abode.

"How many hired guns does Petrenko have watching his back, Allie?" I asked, since no one else had.

"So far as I'm aware, he has two bodyguards," she said.

"Are they really armed?"

"Oleksiy can't pack heat, or he'll have his bail revoked," she told me, which wasn't what I'd asked.

"But his goons can?" I squinted at her.

"They won't shoot me, Andy," she insisted, and flipped her blond tresses like a girl in a shampoo ad.

Yeah, but would they shoot moi?

"He goes on trial in a couple weeks, Kendricks, with enough charges against him to put him away for the rest of his life, if he's convicted. He's not gonna risk murdering people in his own backyard," Blondezilla assured me.

Though I wasn't entirely convinced. The dude had killed Trayla, hadn't he? (Or ordered a murder-to-go, at any rate.)

Still, I couldn't come up with anything better than Allie or Mother had suggested, so I caved.

"All right." I sighed. "Let's do it. And now. I don't want to sit around talking anymore. We're wasting precious time."

I was already hearing the music from *The Sting* in my head, imagining Robert Redford and Paul Newman setting Oleksiy up to take a big fall.

Until I turned to Stephen and read his sour expression.

For Pete's sake.

"What's wrong?" I asked him, almost afraid of what I'd hear.

"I'm not sure I like any of this," Cissy's beau remarked, looking as worried as I'd seen him. "But let me figure a few things out. I've got a map on my laptop, and I need to make a call or two before we leave. Can you give me ten minutes, Andy?" He stared straight at me; like he was afraid I'd take off without him and botch the whole thing up.

"Yeah, okay. Ten minutes." That was about all I could stand.

"Y'all stay here, and I'll be back in a few."

He picked up the bill and headed toward the cashier, before disappearing out the door; if I peered through the dark of the window, I could see him heading to his Volvo in the parking lot.

Mother, Allie, and I finished up our coffee, no one saying much of anything until Stephen returned, smiling tightly. He sat down and set a piece of paper on the table so everyone could get a gander.

Then, slowly and carefully, he laid out the plan for infiltrating Oleksiy Petrenko's mansion to search for Brian, with an emphasis on minimal muss and fuss. When he was done and all questions had been asked and answered, he took the page, folded it up, and stowed it in his jacket.

I realized as I looked around at my posse that we were all dressed in black, rather like a murder of crows, perching on bright blue vinyl benches.

I felt more than a little like James Bond as we synchronized watches, made sure cell phones were switched to vibrate and 911 was locked into speed dial.

After which, Stephen clapped his hands, something my father used to do, and said, "What say we get this show on the road?"

I don't think I could've hopped to my feet any faster had he yelled, "The griddle's on fire, the barrels of syrup have exploded, and the whole danged pancake house is set to blow!"

It was time to rock and roll.

Chapter 22

 The clock struck midnight as we dropped off the extra cars at Mother's house and began putting our plan in motion.

Allie would go first, driving her shiny red Roadster straight up to Petrenko's front security gate, while Stephen parked his black Volvo just beyond the delivery entrance in the back. We'd slip past the metal bar on foot; well, Stephen and I would, anyway.

Cissy had agreed to remain in the car, waiting at least fifteen minutes before she phoned the police pretending to be Petrenko's neighbor. Stephen would be my scout, making sure the coast was clear before I headed in; like a third base coach, he would signal me in when the time was right.

I was supposed to speed-dial Cissy on my cell and cry uncle should anything seem amiss. If that happened, Mother was to contact the cops immediately. Otherwise, once Allie unlocked the back door, I would immediately slip down to the cellar to see if my dude was being held captive.

If Malone wasn't there . . .

Well, I'd think about that later.

For now, I'd believe that we'd find Brian before Mother tipped off Detective Swiercynski (aka Starsky) and his partner to the "disturbance" at Petrenko's place; which meant we'd be ready for them when they arrived, so Malone could spill all. I had a feeling he'd have a lot to share with them about stolen art and murder.

I could hardly wait.

Seeing Brian alive and well and Petrenko and his goons in handcuffs would be the best birthday present ever, far better than a dinner party with a menu full of food I didn't want to eat.

Mother went over each step of the plan ad infinitum while Stephen guided the Volvo north of Highland Park, to the wide streets of Preston Hollow. Most of the large residences looked like hulking shadows, silhouetted against the faint glimmer of the moon and the dull glow of street lamps. I saw few windows lit up, attesting to the fact that all the good blue bloods and new bloods had long since gone to bed.

A handful of the mansions were set too far back to glimpse, particularly when hidden by tall brick or wooden fences. Nearly all had metal signs posted with various logos of security firms.

We didn't pass a single car en route to Petrenko's place, though Stephen's dark Volvo sedan blended well enough into the neighborhood so as not to arouse suspicion. If we'd been driving my Jeep Wrangler, on the other hand, someone might've dialed the cops, thinking an underage teen, out past curfew, was looking for a yard to trench.

As we rolled through a back alley, as per the printed-out map Stephen had located on an outdated Web page with the property listing, I glanced nervously around us, out the windows into the bleak of midnight, the dim shapes of trees and shrubbery standing sentry on our either side. I kept waiting for someone to jump out, one of Oleksiy's men armed with an AK-47, but we pulled up to the back gate without incident.

Stephen shut off the engine.

I dialed Allie's cell, waited for her to pick up, and announced, "We're in place."

"Ditto," she said. "I'm at the gate. Give me five minutes, and if you don't hear from me, I'm in. Oh, and Kendricks," she added. "Looks like you were right all along about Brian not being a dickhead. You're a better girlfriend to him than I ever was. So, um, good luck. I hope you get your man back in one piece."

"Um, thanks." *I think.*

I stared at my phone for a moment after, deciding that adversity made for strange bedfellows. In a matter of days, I'd gotten to know Malone's ex better than I'd ever imagined, and she wasn't all bad.

Damn her skinny blondness.

When five minutes had come and gone without a peep from Ms. Price, Stephen looked over his shoulder into the backseat and said, "You ready, Andrea?"

"Ready." I felt like the Energizer Bunny with my AA's full-charged.

Cissy got out of the car with us and all but spit-washed my face and tucked my shirt in before she'd let me go. She tried to foist some pepper spray on me—at least, I thought it was pepper spray—and then I realized it was the travel-sized canister of Febreze she kept in her purse to neutralize odors. Did she figure I could neutralize a bad guy if I ran into one?

I understood she was nervous. Not many socialites went on midnight raids to free their daughters' boyfriends. I'm sure a few had done 2:00 A.M. trips to the Highland Park police station to bail out drunken teens, however, so rescuing a kidnapped beau from the home of a Ukrainian mobster wasn't such a far stretch.

Stephen led the way through the dark, moving with such stealth that I nearly lost his black-clad form several times before we'd made it through the landscaped lawn, past the creek and waterfall, beyond the extensive outdoor patio, and to the back of the house where several sets of French doors loomed.

Thankfully, no barking rottweilers attacked, nor did any motion lights blink on, exposing us in floodlights.

Growing up in affluent Highland Park, I'd come to understand that the rich were different. Unlike the masses, relatively few were paranoid enough to douse their homes in nighttime illumination or let loose with attack dogs.

I had a theory that financial security made the wealthy feel secure in general, at least when it came to minding their castles.

My mother had grown up not even locking the doors, and I think some of that carried over, no matter how squirrelly the world had become. Though the house she lived in—the one on Beverly where I'd grown up—was equipped with a complex system of alarms, I knew she rarely set them. Neither did she have a front gate or privacy fence.

Cissy had told me once that living in fear was akin to giving in. "A home shouldn't be a prison," she'd remarked, or something to that effect.

Obviously, Oleksiy Petrenko didn't feel the same, not with his front and back gates, his armed goons, and his wine cellar that might well have doubled as a jail cell.

The jerk.

"Psssst."

I leaned around the tree I'd been using as camouflage to find Stephen gesticulating madly.

No time for my mind to be wandering.

I skedaddled, wanting to keep up with him, passing a six-car garage on my left. I didn't see any vehicles parked outside the closed doors. So I hoped that our buddy Oleksiy hadn't invited any mobster pals to stay overnight.

Stephen motioned that I follow him right up to Petrenko's rear doors, and I scurried forward and flattened myself against the rough wood of the wall, a splinter pricking at the soft flesh of my palm.

We crab-walked beneath the eaves of the house toward the door pegged on the real estate map as the kitchen, as that's the one Allie had been directed to unlock. There was a bathroom near the *cocina,* which gave her a great excuse should Petrenko or his goons catch her wandering.

I held my breath as my peripheral vision caught the flicker of lights going on inside the house, and I figured Allie had made it in.

Step one, accomplished.

What felt like a billion to go.

Stephen gestured for me to sink down, behind the low-cut shrubbery that ran beneath the windows, and I did as he asked, but not without discomfort. The danged bushes were holly, and the thorny leaves poked like tiny knives against the denim of my pants and the cotton of my jacket.

I did my best to keep my bare hands away from the stuff, as well as my chin and cheek as I squatted behind the prickly cover. Stephen had urged me to don gloves, but wearing them made me feel even clumsier than I already was. So I'd tucked them in my pockets.

I didn't care about fingerprints at this point. I could only think of reaching Brian.

Soon I understood the need for cover, as I spotted a square-shouldered man rounding the corner of the house, crossing the lawn; the faint sliver of moon doing little to erase the menacing hook of his angular features.

I listened to my own hastened breaths, as loud as cowbells in my ears. Every whiff of the breeze that ruffled my hair felt like an ominous hand, pointing out my hiding place.

Then I could see the man no more, and I sighed softly, figuring if one of Oleksiy's guards was outside, it meant only one indoors. I was hoping the dude inside would be sticking to his boss like glue.

I couldn't imagine time could move more slowly than it did in the minutes before I heard a rustle from beyond the door, as I crouched beside it like an alley cat hoping for a tuna handout.

My ears pricked up as the lock clicked, the sound clear as breaking glass.

I didn't even wait for Stephen to signal, but scrambled out of the holly and up the steps, grabbing hold of the door latch and pushing inside.

I saw Allie's backside disappearing through a doorway as I let myself in and quietly closed the door.

My eyes had already adjusted to the dim, so I was hypercognizant of my surroundings as I surveyed the enormous chef's kitchen, seeing the gleam of stainless steel appliances and glint of brass cookware dangling from overhead racks. There was even a shiny and rather large George Foreman Grill, perched alongside a fancy toaster-oven and a cappuccino machine, all of which seemed to glow in the dark.

I knew from viewing the realtor's layout of the house on Stephen's laptop that the door to my left led into a large butler's pantry, and the one to my right, beyond a breakfast nook, segued into a large enclosed sun porch.

That meant the door to the cellar lay in between, directly behind where I stood.

Doing the fastest tiptoe ever, my sneakers barely squeaking, I rushed toward it, grabbing for the knob, twisting, and finding resistance.

Well, hell's bells.

The thing was locked!

My brain sparked, wheels spinning as I tried to come up with a contingency plan. I could always go back outside for Stephen, and maybe he could pry the damned door open with a knife or a screwdriver.

Thinking that was my only shot, I turned and started back, only to spot a set of pegs hanging high beside the door I'd come through seconds earlier.

And what hung on those pegs?

Keys.

A good dozen of them.

I didn't know which one would open the portal to the wine dungeon, so I grabbed them all and set off a tinkling that I was sure could be heard from one end of the house to the other.

Quiet, Andy, quiet!

Oh, poo, was that footsteps?

The steady *thud-thud* seemed to grow ever closer, as I pondered where to hide, coming up with nothing better than the big chef's island in the middle of the room. I crawled beneath, into a hole through which I could see the legs of stools and the empty doorway to the hallway that Allie had vamoosed through.

I held my breath as a pair of legs came into view and then illumination filled every space that had been dark.

If I'd been less freaked out, I would've closed my eyes and prayed to be made invisible; only I had to watch the progression of the legs as they moved around me. I concentrated on the gray slacks with neat creases, polished black oxfords peeking out below the cuffs. Obviously, this was a thug who cared about his appearance.

I started, nearly hitting my head on the bottom of the island, as a throaty voice said, "Anybody here?"

Um, yeah, like I was going to answer?

Nuts.

I counted almost thirty Mississippis before the legs ceased their patrol around the king-sized kitchen and headed back toward the door. They paused there for a moment before the lights went off and a hard shade of gray settled around me again.

I exhaled deeply.

Yeesh.

I'd call that too close for comfort.

I exited my hiding place and rose on shaky legs, my stomach rolling like the giant wheel on a Zamboni as I hurried to the cellar door and, with trembling fingers, shoved each of the dozen keys into the lock until I found the one that turned it.

Bingo!

It was number eleven.

I carefully shut the door behind me and felt for a switch, my hands running over smooth plaster before I found it and flicked.

I blinked as the stairs turned bright, track lighting leading me down and down some more, where the air turned suddenly cool, enough to make me shiver.

As a certified claustrophobic, I felt a tingle of panic the deeper I went below ground level, though I kept reassuring myself that I was all right, that I'd be out of there in no time. When I finally hit bottom, there was plenty to distract me besides.

Dark-stained wood shelves went from floor to ceiling, all holding bottle after bottle of wine. I approached and ran my fingers over a half-dozen Italian cabernets.

I heard a click succeeded by a slow hum, and I glanced up to see something that looked very much like an air-conditioning unit, set into the far wall.

WhisperKOOL, its label read.

That was the whirring sound I'd picked up when Malone had called.

No question in my mind.

My heart smacked against my ribs, beating way too quickly.

"Brian?" I called out, louder this time, remembering what Lu had said about the soundproofing, trying not to dwell on the fact that I was surrounded by concrete walls a yard thick. "Malone?" I called a bit louder, wishing my knees weren't practically knocking together so I could move faster, exploring Oleksiy Petrenko's massive underground wine library.

I paused to poke my head down each row, and there were at least a dozen of them, sprouting off both to my left and my right. The only thing beyond was a heavy-looking wooden door, closed and bolted with an old-fashioned padlock. When I'd checked row after row, seeing nothing but bottles, I had few places left to look. Just the final aisle that cut off to the right of the massive door, which I walked up to, set a palm against, and pressed my mouth as close between door and jamb as I could, croaking out, "Malone, are you in there?"

I pushed my ear to the crack and listened.

Nothing.

Maybe that's where Oleksiy kept the really expensive stuff, I told myself. Maybe he had Brian upstairs in a nice, warm bedroom as opposed to this chilly, dusty place.

Sucking in a deep breath, I turned away and glanced down at my feet, my knees ready to buckle when I saw the stain of dark red on the blond oak floor.

Was it blood?

I grabbed the nearest wooden rack and braced myself as I slid down on my haunches, looking closely at the discoloration and feeling relief flood my system when I realized it had the purplish tint of red wine.

It had to be.

I stood again, steadying myself, before I turned and peered down the depths of that last aisle, between the towering shelves filled with glorified grape juice . . . which is when I did a double take.

Was that a body, curled against the far wall, wrapped in a tan blanket, nearly blending into the pale oak of the floor?

"Malone?" I called tentatively.

In response, I heard a faint but distinctive, *"Uuuuuhhh."*

Dear God.

My brain buzzed, and a wave of adrenaline propelled me forward. *I've found him,* I told myself, hardly believing, and I rushed as fast as I could on trembling legs toward the source of the pathetic sounds.

As I strode nearer, I could see a wrist shackled to a pipe along the base of the wall, a crown of tousled mousy hair, but little else except a lump undercover.

"Malone!"

His name flew from my lips as I dropped beside the immobile form swathed in tan wool and fumbled to see the familiar face.

The blanket dropped away, as I gently touched a soft cheek and turned the head toward me.

"Aaaack!" escaped my lips as dilated brown eyes blinked and looked at me blankly, as if drugged. The tiny nose and thin mouth with the parched lips didn't belong to Malone . . . didn't belong to any man.

This prisoner of Petrenko's was a *woman.*

One I didn't know from Eve.

I jerked my hand away, fell back on my heels.

"Who are you?" I asked, wondering if the resident mobster collected humans as well as wine, further creeping myself out.

Would I find Jimmy Hoffa next?

Geez, Louise!

"Lana," the woman breathed, a weary-sounding whisper. "Lana Petrenko."

"What?" *Had I heard her right?*

She wet cracked lips and said, "Oleksiy's wife."

I stared at her, dumbly, as more of Lu's words came back: *Trayla mentioned one time that he had a cellar . . . said he kept his wife down there for a week after he found out she'd been shagging his brother.*

Allie had thought Mrs. Petrenko had skipped town. *Who can blame her for seeking refuge once the shit hit the fan? We're gonna have to work like hell to get him off as it is, so it's better for our side if Mrs. Petrenko doesn't come back to testify.*

But Oleksiy's wife hadn't gone anywhere.

He'd had her all along, bound to a pipe in his basement. And I'd wager he didn't plan to let her go, at least not until after the trial was over. Maybe not even then.

My fear resurfaced, though it had never been fully submerged, as I wondered, *Where in the hell was Malone?*

Lana squinted at me, tried to lift her head.

I saw a bottle of water nearby and reached for it, but she grimaced as I held it to her lips. I noticed then how murky it appeared, and I figured my guess about her being drugged was correct. Which likely meant Petrenko had Malone doped up, too. If my boyfriend was behind that locked door, it was no wonder he couldn't answer. He was probably dead to the world . . . figuratively speaking, I meant. I hoped.

"Please"—tears fluttered from her lashes, splattering on dirty cheeks—"help me."

I checked the chain at her left wrist, binding her to the slim black pipe running the brief length of wall between the racks, and I saw the padlock caught between two links, holding her fast.

"Have you seen anyone else brought here, a young man with brown hair and glasses?" I started babbling, and Lana Petrenko wrinkled her forehead, eyes falling closed, so I hoped she was listening. "His name is Brian Malone, and he's been missing for several days. He's one of your husband's lawyers, but we think he might've seen something . . . might have witnessed the murder of a girl named Trayla Trash . . . um, Betsy Wren."

Her eyes fluttered open, pupils so dark and wide they nearly hid the brown of her iris. "He's here," she whispered, "in the vault."

"The padlocked door?" I asked.

She nodded weakly. "There was a fight . . . he hit them. . . ."

"With bottles of wine?"

She gave another slow jerk of her chin.

So Brian had tried to macho his way out by grabbing some fancy cabernet and swinging.

That explained the red stains on the floor.

"Who has the keys to the padlocks?"

"Bernard," Lana told me and tried to sit up. The blanket fell from her shoulders, and I saw bruising on her arms, besides the raw red circle from the chain around her wrist.

"By any chance, is Bernard the goon with the shiny shoes and creased pants?" I asked, all I saw of the dude who'd trapped me in the kitchen, not five minutes before.

"Yes." She shivered, and I helped cover her again, wondering how she'd endured being trapped in a basement for weeks and weeks.

Wasn't anyone looking for her? Wondering where she was? Or was Oleksiy all she had, and any curiosity about his wife's absence had been explained away with the excuse that she took off to avoid the heat of her affair and his court appearance?

I wondered if my mother had called the police yet, because I'd had a change of heart already, figuring the sooner the better.

Finding Petrenko's wife chained in the cellar was plenty of reason for them to search the premises, wasn't it? And they could get keys to the padlocks and pinpoint where Oleksiy had stashed Malone.

I no longer felt sure that my makeshift posse and I were up to this.

"Stay here," I told Lana, and, though she looked panicked, she nodded. "I'll be right back, and we'll get you out of here fast, I promise."

I left her there, much as I hated to do it, snatching my cell from my pocket and hitting speed dial to call Mother.

Only I couldn't even get a bar, not until I'd reached the stairs and started climbing.

Halfway up, I got two bars and tried again, hearing a muted ring.

"Hello? Andy?"

My mother spoke, but it sounded like she was in a tunnel. It was the same patchy connection I'd had with Malone when he'd phoned to tell me he needed space.

"Call the cops," I told her. "I found a woman chained to a pipe. I think Malone's locked in a vault. We have to get the keys."

"You dropped . . . your pipe . . . chains in a vault . . . what does that mean? It's been . . . ten minutes . . . should I wait a few minutes . . . need more time?"

Aw, hell.

She was only catching every other word, if that, and I was getting about the same back.

I had to get out of the basement, or she'd never understand.

So I shut off the light, felt for the knob of the door with my fingers, slowly turned and warily let myself into the still-dark kitchen.

"Andrea?" Mother was squawking. "Are you there?"

I could hear her now, clear as crystal.

"Yes, I'm here," I said, keeping my voice low, letting my eyes adjust to the dim again, closing the basement door and listening to the thud of my heartbeat as I told her, "You have to call—"

The police.

That's what I would've said, anyway, if I'd been allowed to finish.

Instead, something hard hit my wrist, knocked my cell from my hand, and I felt the sudden pressure of cool metal at my temple and the voice of a man, telling me, "Nobody's calling nobody, girlie."

My gaze fell on his shoes—so shiny they glowed in the dark—and moved up the sharp line of his pants, creased to perfection.

His face, too, was creased and hard as flint.

Bernard, I presumed, and my head felt suddenly woozy. Maybe the gun pointed at my brain had something to do with that.

All the while I kept thinking that I wouldn't be much help to either Lana or Brian if Bernard turned me into mince meat.

Chapter 23

"Move," Bernard ordered, nudging me with the butt of his gun, and I inched my way over toward the table, where he indicated I should sit down in a chair. "Don't even twitch," he told me in a voice that brooked no argument—as if his weapon wasn't threat enough—and then he went to the light switch and flipped the fixture on.

I squished my eyes shut against the brilliance, heard Oleksiy's goon roll open a drawer and rummage around.

"I thought I heard somebody in here before, and it was you, wasn't it? I should turn you over to the cops," he said, "for breaking and entering."

"Do that," I said, not wanting to make Bernard mad so much as kill some time with conversation. I glanced at my cell, lying dead on the floor, and I hoped like hell that Mother had dialed the Dallas P.D. once I'd been cut off. I tried to peer beyond the window glass into the backyard;

but all I could pick out was my own reflection, sitting at Petrenko's dinner table like a cooked goose.

Was Stephen out there still? Could he see me? Did he know I was in trouble?

Mr. Shoe Shine returned, brandishing his weapon and a roll of duct tape. "So you want to be tossed in jail for trespassing?"

I met his near-black eyes and fought the urge to pee in my pants. "What would be even more fun would be hearing you explain to the nice policemen why Mr. Petrenko has his wife drugged and chained to a wall in his cellar."

Something in his face shifted, turned even meaner, if that were possible. "What are you? A reporter? You sniffing around for a story, huh? Well, girlie, you came to the wrong place."

"I'm not a reporter."

He laughed, and it was a most unpleasant sound. "Yeah? That's what they all say. We even had one try to get into the house by pretending to be a meter reader. How dumb is that?"

"Not as dumb as kidnapping a lawyer from a strip club and stashing a dead hooker in his trunk," I got out.

Mr. Shoe Shine stopped smirking. "What'd you say?"

"You know what I said." I was trying to channel my mother, psychically urging her to speed-dial the Dallas P.D. before things got any dicier than they already were.

"I've had about enough yakking out of you, girlie. Now put your arms behind your back and sit still." He shoved his gun inside his waistband and pulled out a generous stretch of duct tape from the roll.

I didn't exactly cooperate, keeping my hands clasped

tightly in my lap. "You sure you want to do this, Bernard? I mean, what would your mother think about you tying up innocent girls?"

"That's it. You asked for it, remember that," he said and ripped off a piece of tape big enough to cover my mouth.

Crap.

I felt the adhesive stick to my lips and cheeks as Bernard patted it down. It pulled at my skin like an unwanted face-lift. I railed against it, desperate to bite or scream, but only producing ineffectual noises of protest as he situated my wrists, preparing to bind them.

Just wait until Starsky and Hutch show up.

I tried to comfort myself with the thought, not wanting to acknowledge the fact that they might never come; that Mother's ruse of disturbed neighbor might fall flat; that Oleksiy might end up tossing me in a trunk without a pulse, as he had Trayla Trash.

Where was Superman when you needed him, huh?

My head jerked up at the sound of rending, and I watched helplessly as Petrenko's goon tore off another length of duct tape, eager to seal me up like a package bound for UPS. "Keep your hands behind your back, right where I put 'em," Shoe Shine growled, and this time I did as I was told.

As he bent down to tape my wrists, the French doors flew open, and a black figure hurled itself directly at the squatting Bernard.

Stephen?

The chair I sat in nearly tipped over as Petrenko's goon grabbed at it, fighting the weight of Mother's beau on his back. Only one of my wrists had any tape on it, so I broke free easily and scooted away from the two men, who rolled around, duking it out on the kitchen floor.

"Run, Andy!" Stephen managed to shout at me, his slender form fighting hard to keep the far stockier Bernard pinned down.

But I wasn't about to leave a member of my posse in an obviously untenable position. There had to be something I could do, some way I could help; besides, I needed the keys to the padlocks, and according to Lana, Bernard was the one who had them.

The tape still on my mouth, I ran around to the well-stocked counters, thinking I'd grab a knife—but not exactly wanting to use one—when I spotted the George Foreman Grill.

Stephen had lost hold of Oleksiy's goon, and Bernard was scrabbling to pull his gun from his waistband, when I came up behind him and swung the grill as hard as I could. It landed with a resounding clunk against Shoe Shine's head.

He tottered for a moment, then shook it off, muttering, "Dumb move, girlie," before he turned to me and raised his weapon, and I closed my eyes, prepared for the bullet that would surely sink into my chest and take me out for real.

Instead, I heard a groan followed by a thud that made the earth move under my feet, and Stephen said breathlessly, "Good going, Andrea."

I opened my eyes and realized I was alive, and Bernard lay on the floor, a large egg-shaped welt turning purple at his left temple.

I stared at the grill in my hands for a moment and did

what any girl in my situation would do: I whispered thanks to the Big Guy.

George Foreman, I mean.

"You okay?" Mother's ex-Navy dude asked while he got to work, using the duct tape to bind Bernard's hands and feet. I saw Goon Boy's gun, now stuck in Stephen's belt, a much safer place than where it used to be.

I nodded, unable to speak until I'd peeled off the strip of adhesive Bernard had used to shut me up. "I'm fine," I said when I finally could. "Thanks for saving my tush."

Stephen didn't glance up from binding Bernard's ankles, merely replied with a perfunctory, "Any time."

As if stuff like this happened every day.

I reluctantly put the grill away, half expecting Petrenko himself to surge into the kitchen upon hearing the commotion. Then I reminded myself that his mansion covered ten thousand square feet. He'd need bat ears to have caught wind of this. Besides, he was a heterosexual male who'd murdered his mistress and chained his wife to a pipe, so he was doubtless ripe for female company. I'd wager his full attention was focused on the very pretty and very blond Ms. Allie Price and her tight sweater. . . .

The keys, I reminded myself.

I crouched beside Stephen, sharing what Lana had told me as I picked Bernard's pockets until I found a full key ring and palmed it.

"The police'll be here any minute," Stephen assured me. "Your mother got worried when your call was cut off. She came to find me . . . well, after she ran into the other guard and sprayed the fellow in the eyes with her Febreze.

But don't worry, she's okay, and I'm sure he's only temporarily blinded."

Ah, so it could be used to neutralize a bad guy.

"Where is she?"

"I told her to wait in the car."

"And you think that's where she is?"

Hello? When did Cissy Blevins Kendricks ever listen to anyone?

"If she knows what's good for her, she will be," he said, and he actually winked.

Bernard took that moment to groan, before Stephen slapped a strip of duct tape over his mouth, and I had a lovely sense of justice being served, in a small sense anyhow.

The rest would be taken care of once the cops showed up on Petrenko's doorstep.

But I couldn't wait for them.

Call me antsy.

I crossed the kitchen to the basement door and opened it, just as I detected the wail of sirens in the distance, drawing nearer.

If I'd needed an extra boost of courage, I felt it then, and I descended the well-lit steps into Oleksiy's wine dungeon, sure of where I was going this time and what I would see.

I went to Lana first, found the key that unlocked her chains and set her free, though she was too weak to do much more than stay put until help arrived. She wept as I told her that would be soon. I could only imagine how happy she'd be to crucify her jerk-off husband after this.

My fingers trembled as I shifted through the ring for the key to undo the padlock on the door in the cellar's rear.

When I pulled the latch off and pushed wide the heavy wood, my heart zigzagged as I smelled something very familiar: the scent of citrus-tinged cologne mixed with sweat.

Malone was there.

He was lying on a flimsy mattress, between racks of what I assumed were Petrenko's most priceless bottles of *vino*. Dusty old things that leant a musky odor to the cramped room.

"Malone, oh, God." His name slipped from my lips as I flew the few steps between us and knelt beside him, weeping with joy as I pressed my cheek against his, saying, "It's okay, it's okay," over and over again, as he breathed guttural breaths, like someone in a deep sleep.

I drew away and looked him over, making sure he was all in one piece, noting with dismay the torn state of his pink shirt, the bruises at his jaw, and his unshaven cheeks. One eye was puffy and purple. His glasses were missing.

His feet were bare and filthy.

My God, what had they done to him?

He had empty water bottles around him, as well as one still half full. It looked as cloudy as Lana's.

"Oh, Brian," I said, and I buried my head in his shoulder, feeling such relief that it made me dizzy. I ran a hand over his rumpled hair, and his eyes fluttered against my cheek.

"Andy?" he murmured.

"Yeah, baby?" I looked into his face, saw his dilated pupils try to focus on me.

"I had the strangest dream."

"I had it, too, but it's over now," I told him. "The

nightmare's ended." I pressed my lips against his fore-head, holding him close.

No more fake ransoms, no more strippers, no more worries about whether my heart had been broken to bits.

From this moment forth, life would be a piece of cake.

And I would savor every morsel of it.

Epilogue

 Thankfully, Brian and I had a few days to rest and recover before we had to face another gauntlet.

My birthday dinner at Cissy's.

Which meant no torn jeans, no ponytails, no whining about the birthday cake, even if it was some kind of frou-frou mousse soufflé.

Though I didn't feel much like complaining about anything these days, not after I'd had the fright of my life and realized how much I could have lost and how easily, before I'd even had the chance to grasp how much I cared about Malone.

I'd learned more about my beau in one night of living hell than I had in the four months before it.

It was way too easy to take someone for granted, wasn't it? I had vowed, after surviving such a scare, that I would never do that again.

And I wouldn't.

Which meant enjoying Mother's catered celebration to honor my turning thirty-one, even if it killed me. Cissy had invited twenty of my nearest and dearest, which translated mostly into *her* nearest and dearest, though I knew my old pal Janet Graham would be there. Janet had already phoned, after she'd caught wind of the "Petrenko Stinko," as the media had taken to calling it. Janet was dying to do a piece for the Society pages she edited for the *Park Cities Press* and wanted an exclusive. She already had a headline for it: NIGHT OF THE LIVING DEB.

As tight as we were, I'd declined.

Brian and I had been through enough already, and I honestly didn't want to relive the horror of it, not even for the length of an interview.

The Dallas police—namely Starsky and Hutch—had raked poor Malone over the coals as soon as he'd been fit enough to answer their grilling; though they'd ultimately let him off the hook. After Lana Petrenko started talking, no one doubted for a moment that Oleksiy was behind Trayla's death and Brian's kidnapping.

I could only imagine what Lana would say on the witness stand. If I were Petrenko, I'd start having my tailor whip up a few custom-made jumpsuits in jailhouse orange.

Call me vengeful, but the thought made me smirk.

"Andy, do I look all right?"

I turned to see Brian standing in the bedroom doorway, wearing the new pair of glasses that Lenscrafters had cranked out for him in an hour flat. He still had a shiner that ringed his right eye and made him look like he'd been

in a bar fight. Other than that, he appeared to be the same
Malone, and I was eternally grateful for that.

"You're gorgeous," I told him, and was about to say
something frighteningly mushy when my cell rang, playing that idiotic music until I made it stop.

"Hello?"

"Kendricks? Where the hell are y'all? You're late, you
know."

I sighed, met Brian's eyes and mouthed, *Allie.*

"Your mother's chomping at the bit, and my new
Manolos are kind of pinching. So could you hurry up and
get a move on?"

Cissy had invited the Blond Menace to my party, and I
had made not a single noise of protest. How could I, when
she'd been the one who'd done the most to get me through
the "missing Malone" mess? She'd smoothed things over
at Abramawitz, Reynolds, Goldberg & Hunt, so that Malone had kept his job; in fact, he'd been named "Associate
of the Week" after a number of pieces of stolen artwork
were found in Petrenko's possession, and after one of his
goons had 'fessed up to disposing of Trayla after the Boss
Man had killed her in a rage with Malone's Big Bertha.
Petrenko had a lot more on his plate now than money
laundering, seeing as how he'd been charged with kidnapping, art theft, and murder one.

Brian's firm was no longer representing the Ukrainian
bastard, thank God, as Malone would be testifying at his
trial. I planned to have a front row seat, as I didn't want to
miss a lick of the proceedings. If I had never been interested in Brian's work before, I was now.

But first, another type of trial: dinner at Chez Cissy.

"We'll be there in twenty," I told Allie, before I hung up on her, albeit with more affection than malice. Really, I'm sure she felt it, too.

"You ready?" I asked Brian, and he nodded.

"If I can handle being drugged and locked in a wine cellar for two days, I can sit through one of Cissy's dinner parties."

"That's the spirit."

At least he hadn't lost his sense of humor.

"But I do feel bad about something," he told me as I helped him shrug into his jacket. "I had a card all ready for you, but I couldn't find it. I nearly tossed my place looking, but it wasn't there."

"It doesn't matter," I said and smiled ear-to-ear, meaning every tooth of it. "I don't need a card when I have you here."

Hmmm, would lightning strike me, for lying by omission? Was it wrong not to admit that I'd dug up the Frankenstein greeting card with his scribbled "I love you" while I was pawing through his things, desperately seeking clues on where he'd disappeared to?

Naw.

What Malone didn't know wouldn't hurt him.

"But at least my birthday gift is intact," he said as he followed me out of the bedroom. "A whole four days away, in a cozy little cabin in Kennebunkport, Maine."

Ah, yes, the trip. The surprise penned in red on his calendar. We'd be gone at the same time Cissy went to Vegas with Stephen.

Talk about perfect timing. I wasn't going to protest my mother's trip with her beau, not after what Stephen had done to help me get Brian back. But I didn't want to have to think about it.

I sighed.

"C'mon, let's go," I prodded. "Allie reminded me we're late."

I wrapped a pink pashmina around my shoulders (a gift from Lu McCarthy, as it were, which had come with a note thanking me for not having her and Cricket arrested and forgiving me for covering her in red dye, which she was still scrubbing off days later).

I grabbed my purse off the hall table and was reaching for the door when a knock sounded on the other side. I peered through the peephole, seeing a pair of faces, distorted by the fish-eye lens and yet vaguely familiar.

Something told me they weren't reporters, which was a good thing, as I'd seen enough of them to last a lifetime.

So I pulled the door inward, uttering a civil "Yes?" to the couple standing on my welcome mat.

"Andrea Kendricks?" the woman said, and I realized her blue eyes were very much like Brian's.

Malone came from behind me. "Mom and Dad?"

Mom and Dad?

My brain went suddenly dead, throwing my pulse into "panic."

"Allison Price left a message with Pam at the office, said it was urgent, that you were in trouble, and to get down to Dallas ASAP." The gray-streaked brunette with my boyfriend's gaze cocked her head like a curious poodle. "She gave us this address for Andrea, so pleased to meet you, and what a pretty thing"—a smile flickered on her face—"though I'm told you don't have pets, eh? We'll have to fix that someday." Then back to Brian, "We came as soon as we could get away. Are you okay? What happened to your face? Allison's message said you'd vanished, or some such thing. Were you on a vacation?"

Malone's father scratched behind his ear but didn't speak.

Had he picked up bugs on their pet retreat?

I stood numbly as Brian briefly explained he'd had some trouble with a client but that he was fine and we were on our way to my mother's for a birthday celebration . . . and would they like to come along?

Oh, my, I thought, imagining what my mother would say when we arrived at the house on Beverly with Mr. and Mrs. Malone in tow. Heck, what would *I* say? Something along the lines of: "Hello, Mummy dearest, meet the parents. Only watch out for Brian's dad. He has fleas."

Oy vey.

Happy Birthday to me.